Hakuna
Moscato!
Jane E

POISON

PARCHEESI

and WINE

A Cardboard Cottage Mystery

JANE ELZEY

Scorpius Carta

Scorpius Carta Press
Arkansas

Scorpius Carta Press
83 Wall St, Suite P
Eureka Springs, AR 72632

First Scorpius Carta Press Hardcover edition: November 2022
ISBN 978-1-7346428-6-5

First Scorpius Carta Press Paperback edition: November 2022
ISBN 978-1-7346428-7-2

First Scorpius Carta Press Digital edition: November 2022
ISBN: 978-1-7346428-8-9

The interior of this book is typeset in Adobe Caslon Pro.

Cover design by Bailey McGinn.
www.baileydesignsbooks.com

For Daddy

"What heaven brought you and me
cannot be forgotten."

— *STEPHEN STILLS*

CHAPTER ONE

Amy watched as Genna dumped the signs on the table. *A Vote for Villiger is a Win for Arkansas* splashed across the glossy cardboard in bright blocks of blue and red. *Jerry Glen Villiger. U.S. Representative, District 4.*

Genna rubbed her arms where the posters had been cradled against her. "This is about as patriotic as you can get on a printing press. And if that's not a name destined for Congress, I don't know what is." Her southern Arkansas accent drew the words out with a lilt like a song. She tapped the signs with a red fingernail. "The Big European Tour of Arkansas has officially begun, my friends. We'll get that boy to Capitol Hill if it kills us."

Rian pushed the cardboard edges away from the pitcher of white sangria, sweating in the sun. "The big European what?"

Genna ignored the question and plopped down in the last seat at the table. "Did you know there are twenty-nine cities in the world named London? Imagine! Twenty-nine."

Amy grinned from beneath her hat. It was one of those floppy summer hats that kept the sun off her freckles and made a bit of shade on her shoulders under a mid-day sun. The outing had been Zelda's idea — a poolside brunch away from their shops in town. Amy felt like bacon crisping on a griddle.

"The Big European Tour of Arkansas," Genna repeated, her blue eyes twinkling. "Arkansas has a London." Her silver ponytail fell in a thin braid over her shoulder, and she now tugged at the brush-end.

She tapped the boards rhythmically with her fingertips. "*We* have a Dublin. And a Belfast, Havana, Hamburg, Moscow, Paris, Subiaco, Stuttgart, and Scotland." She ticked off the names with her fingers and manicured nails.

"I'm taking my candidate on a back-to-your-roots political stump tour. We'll stop at all the towns in his district named after European cities. Too bad we can't go by train. A stump speech from a red caboose would be the cherry on top."

"What a grand idea," Amy said, hoping to sound more enthusiastic than she felt. Politics were not her thing, but Genna didn't seem to notice her apathy. Genna's eyes had that inspired glassy glow, like a scientist who had just discovered the speed of light. Amy grinned again at the thought. Genna might actually be the Einstein of publicity. At least in Arkansas. She could make anyone look relevant, give them gravitas, and well-crafted press if they had the money to buy it.

Zelda reached for the plate of brownies that were getting gooey in the sun. "What's a stump speech, anyway?" she mumbled through the bite.

"It's a short little speech that candidates deliver at each tour on the stop. It's how you feed a message to the media without them having to put in too much effort. It's very effective in reaching the masses."

Zelda reached for a second brownie. "I think I'll pass."

"You don't want to miss out," Genna declared. "I mean, it's the Big European Tour. There's something uniquely European about each of these little towns. And if there's not, I'll make it up. Every town has a peculiarity I can embody."

"You mean exploit," Rian said, smiling with a wry crook to her lips.

"*Tomayto, tomahto,*" Genna drawled. "This brainstorm came to me when I was hobnobbing at the Gillett Coon Supper."

"Coon as in raccoon? And supper as in dinner?" Zelda's mouth dropped open with disapproval.

Genna nodded. "Surely, you've heard of the famous Gillett Coon Supper? It's one of the biggest political events in Arkansas."

"I don't believe you," Rian said.

"You're making this up," Zelda agreed.

Genna grabbed the pitcher and poured a slug of sangria and a slippery sliced peach. She poked at the sprig of fresh mint escaping her glass. "I am not making this up. Any candidate running for office anywhere in the state better show up and eat their fill of barbecued raccoon. And they better donate a wad of cash to the cause, too," she added. "It is a rite of passage for politicians, and it's been a tradition since the late 1940s. Unofficially, that is," Genna added.

"And they actually eat raccoon?" Amy asked.

Genna nodded again. "Two thousand pounds. People say it tastes like pork roast, but I opted for the ham and sweet potatoes, myself."

Zelda made a gagging noise in the back of her throat.

"Oh, don't be such a wuss," Genna said. "People have eaten worse. Do you know what's in a hot dog? Besides, it's the tradition that matters." Genna paused and drank deeply from her glass, then relaxed against the back of the chair.

"Clue me in," Amy said, adjusting the brim of her hat to shade the sun from her face. "How does this all tie in with your Big European Tour of Arkansas?"

Genna tidied the promotional boards in front of her. "District 4 is home to the wine country of Arkansas, and their European roots are why we have a wine country. They brought rootstock with them when they settled here, and these families are big and loyal. I'm hoping loyalty will vote Jerry Glen to Congress."

"I didn't know Arkansas had a wine country," Amy said.

"Well, we do. And Villiger is one of the oldest names on the books there. His great, great granddaddy was a leader in the old country and then came here to raise grapes. Or was it cattle?" Genna frowned. "I don't remember now. He raised something. Maybe he raised money for a church." Genna nodded and sipped her wine. "I think that's it…. A church. That's even better for the stump tour. Anyway," she continued, undeterred. "We're long overdue for a road trip."

Zelda perked. "We're taking a road trip to the wine country!"

"To the wine country!" Genna responded and raised her glass. "Ching, ching."

Rian eyed Genna. "Don't you mean Cin Cin?"

"Wait a minute." Amy peered over her glass at Zelda. "We can't close the Cardboard Cottage for a trip in the middle of May. It's one of our busiest months!"

"Oh, live a little," Zelda said. "You have Suzie to fill in for you. That worked out great when we were on the cruise. Rian and I had great success sharing Willow Birkenstocks."

"That is not her name," Rian said sternly.

"Oh, really? Then what is her name?"

Rian scrunched her nose. "Well, it is Willow something."

"Willow who wears Birkenstocks," Zelda shot back.

Rian raised her hands in defeat. The two had been lucky to find temporary help for their shops. It came down to the wire — days before Zelda's birthday cruise to the Galapagos Islands. The young woman who answered the help wanted ad was all dreadlocks and tie-dye, but she turned out to be more than competent. She ran the two tiny shops without incident during their time away. It sounded like Zsa Zsa Galore Decor and The Pot Shed would be in her care again.

Amy looked at Genna. "How long is this stump tour?"

"Three weeks."

Amy shook her head. "No way."

"You don't have to be there for all of it," Genna answered shortly. "Just one road trip through Arkansas wine country. You can drink wine right from the source. What's better than that?"

"Politics make my stomach hurt," Zelda complained and patted her belly.

"It's all those brownies you're stuffing down," Amy said. "You know those are Rian's special brownies, don't you?"

POISON PARCHEESI AND WINE · 5

Zelda's eyes widened. "Oh no! I'll be worthless all afternoon!"

Rian chuckled. "They're just plain Jane brownies." To make her point, Rian grabbed a brownie from the plate and shoved the entire square into her mouth.

Zelda sighed and brushed the crumbs from her bathing suit. The black polka dots helped disguise the chocolate smears. "I hate politics," she declared. "Somebody's always cleaning up somebody else's mess, and somebody else is always complaining about how they're doing it. If we put politicians in a room and locked the door, they'd never escape. It's futile madness."

"It would be entertaining to watch," Genna added.

"Not a bad idea; lock them in a room," Amy said, a beat behind. "Isn't that what we do in Washington? Lock them in a room and ask them to make good decisions?"

"That is the very reason why I am *not* going to make Villiger's campaign about politics," Genna urged. "People tend to vote blue or red, but I want people to vote for the person, not the color of their tie. I want them to be proud of how unique Arkansas is. I want them to be proud to have Jerry Glen Villiger represent us."

"You sound like a paid political announcement," Rian declared.

Genna beamed with wide lips. "A very well-paid political announcement, thank you."

Amy peered at Genna from behind her shades. Even though Genna claimed she was retired from the business, she wasn't. The three of them were used to her soapbox. Most of the time, the blather went in one ear and out the other.

"Did you know there are twenty-one different kinds of armadillos?" Genna asked now, breaking into Amy's thoughts. Genna sipped her sangria and then chomped the peach that slithered to the rim. "There exists a screaming hairy armadillo and also a pink fairy armadillo about the size of a toilet paper roll. And that is no lie."

The three of them laughed, and then Genna joined them, and when Genna snorted like a pig, they almost lost it.

"Are you sure those are just plain Jane brownies?" Zelda asked.

Rian wiggled her eyebrows. "Only time will tell."

"Not only do these creatures exist," Genna added "but they all gather in Hamburg, Arkansas, every year to be part of the World Famous Armadillo Festival." That set them off again.

"Please don't say they eat those, too!" Zelda squealed between giggles.

Genna snorted and shook her head. "No, they race them!"

"I wonder how the armadillos know which day to drive in?" Rian asked.

"Be serious," Genna warned. "They come by truck!"

Rian laughed and shifted her weight in the chair. "This synchronicity is not lost on me. Armadillos may be dimwitted and shortsighted, but they could take over the Americas someday — both North and South. Maybe we should vote *them* to Congress."

Amy pictured a room full of armadillos in suits and ties. "But not the hairy screaming ones. We have too many of those already."

Genna poked at the sprig of mint, now trying to grow up her nose. "Armadillos are not relevant to my Big European Tour anyway. Hamburg isn't even in Jerry Glen's voting district, but Paris is, and they have a road rally every year. This year we're participating."

Amy flinched. The last time she passed through Paris, she had a killer riding her tail. She didn't know it at the time, but the memory of what happened was not far enough in the past to feel good about racing to Paris any time soon.

"A road rally?" Rian asked. "Like a race?"

"Not a speed race," Genna said. "But it's still right up your grill." She motioned to Rian with two slim fingers, now holding a cigarette. "And that's my point about these big little towns. Jerry Glen will cross-promote all these events, and I can position him as the candidate who cares deeply about each one."

Rian raised a curious brow. "Does he care?"

"Of course, he cares. I've known him since he was still nicking his chin with a razor. He's all about the people. He's all about taking care of Arkansas in Congress."

Rian rolled her eyes.

Zelda rose quickly, her dive into the pool well timed, if not as elegant as she intended. The splash was large enough to make it to the table, splashing Genna's precious signs. Not that the water mattered much. The political signs would be outside in the elements, anyway.

"My foot slipped," Zelda sputtered as she swam back to the pool's edge. "Are you sure those are just brownies?"

Rian jumped up and cannonballed over the top of Zelda's head, this time drenching Genna completely.

"You rat!" Genna roared, flinging her wrap to the chair and then herself into the deep end.

Amy followed with a dive. Kicking her way to the surface, she remembered how cold the Pacific Ocean felt, even with their colorful wetsuits. Zelda's backyard pool wasn't as cold and it didn't have sharks in it, either. The water was almost as blue as the Pacific, though. The heated saltwater pool had been added to Zelda's backyard shortly after they returned from her birthday cruise. It had taken months to construct, with winter weather creating delays. It was early spring before they had their first buoyant dip in the best decision Zelda had ever made.

Zelda dragged the floats from the surround and pushed them to the center of the pool. "This is paradise," she said, climbing aboard a vinyl raft that resembled a mermaid. "I don't know why we didn't do this sooner. No more hotel pool-hopping. No more hoping we don't get caught and humiliated in the light of day. Why didn't we do this sooner?"

"Money," Amy answered.

"Oh, yeah, there is *that*," Zelda said. "It was money well spent."

"I'm guessing the pool boy doesn't enter into the *money well-spent* equation in any way," Amy teased.

Zelda shoved at Amy's float with her foot. The vinyl dolphin skipped across the water's surface, taking Amy with it. "He's cute. He's built. And he's about 18. No, thanks," Zelda said.

Rian floated by on a seahorse, her eyes closed to the bright sun above. "So, where and when is the launch of this Big European Tour of Arkansas?" Her voice sounded a million miles away.

Genna paddled over on a flamingo. "It's already started, but it escalates at the state conference on tourism right here in Bluff Springs. I booked a room just so we would have a place to gather between sessions. Amy, I'll help you get ready for your panel discussion. You know, a prep talk before you hit the stage."

Amy eyed Genna over the top of her shades. A prep talk or a pep talk? Neither sounded like much fun. Warranted, maybe, if she was honest with herself. The thought of facing an audience was terrifying. She had known about the conference before they left for the cruise, so she had ample time to prepare. Genna gave her the full-on client treatment — at no charge — offering detailed pointers for making the most of her time in the spotlight. She appreciated the help. She glanced at Genna now and wondered if she would bring up Merriweather Hopkins. *Again.* Merriweather was the person who asked Amy to speak on the conference panel. Her name had dredged up something old and dark from Genna's past and it had followed them all the way to the Galapagos Islands.

"We're not going to eat wild vermin on this tour, are we?" Zelda asked. "You're not setting us up for a grilled armadillo-fest, are you?"

Rian laughed, and Amy pictured Zelda at the table, fork in hand. That wasn't going to happen. Not in a million years. Not in a trillion.

"If everything goes as planned, I'll get a picture of the governor with Jerry Glen Villiger, and maybe we can finagle one with you, too. If everything goes as planned, that is. And why wouldn't it?"

Amy raised an eyebrow at Genna. Did anything go as planned when the four of them were together? Not much chance of that. Maybe not even a fifty-fifty chance. Amy turned over and slid through the water like a dolphin slipping through the waves. The water felt good on her sun-baked shoulders. Swimming to the ladder, she pulled herself to the deck, snatched a beach towel, and wrapped herself like a burrito.

The conference was a big deal in her schedule, and once it was over, she wanted her easy life back, with busy days at the shop, evenings on the deck playing games with her friends, and a lazy cat in her bed at night. As she wrung the salt water from her copper-red curls, she smiled at her best friends floating in the pool like a zoo-filled Macy's parade. What could possibly go wrong? She reached out and knocked on wood. Never tempt the Fates.

CHAPTER TWO

The elevator door opened, and cool, damp air greeted her as she stepped through the sliding door. The doors closed behind her with a heavy whoosh, and she looked down the steep stairs.

It was not pitch dark at the bottom of the staircase. A dull amber glow illuminated the steps. Amy glanced back toward the elevator, but it was gone.

With nowhere to go but down, she descended the stairs, silently counting the steps. Two, three…she let one hand run across the smooth, cold stones of the wall.

Four, five … a row of pendant lights appeared from where they hung from the ceiling. The long, twisted cords and metal shades were covered in cobwebs and dust. Cigar smoke hung like an eerie blue haze rising toward her. It was pungent but not unpleasant.

Six, seven… the racks of wine bottles climbed the walls like a honeycomb. The neck and foil of the bottles poked out from each cell as if they were bees in a hive.

Eight, nine… she stopped mid-step, uncertain of what lay ahead. A chorus of laughter echoed from below — a clattering, chattering laughter that sounded like something from another world.

Ten… she reached the landing and turned. And then giggled. And then opened her mouth, threw back her head, and howled with laughter.

Before her, perched on bar stools around a table, four pairs of coal-dark eyes in bandit-black masks blinked back at her, the stub of a cigar clenched in their sharp little teeth. Four fat raccoons stared back. She stared at them in disbelief.

Another raccoon sat belly up on the floor beneath the table, with his plumed tail splayed. He clutched a bottle of wine in his nimble little hands. His eyes were open, but he saw nothing. This raccoon was dead.

"Don't mind him," one of the other raccoons said in a high-pitched falsetto. "He's corked."

"Crocked," another one wheezed.

"Hammered," said the third.

"Had it coming," the fourth one growled. "Filthy thieving trash panda."

They laughed, a clattering, chattering sound, cigars bobbing. Amy laughed with them.

She woke herself up laughing.

Amy sat up and threw off the spread, displacing Victor from his spot against her thigh. "Sorry," she said and patted the cat's head. Victor blinked, yawned, and then settled back into the crease of the coverlet.

She laughed at the image of the raccoons as she ambled to the bathroom, then looked in the mirror at the mess of copper curls now sprung in all directions. *Sparkplug*, they called her when she was a kid. She hated that, and yet she did look a bit wired. She swiped at the smudge of mascara and stared into her own hazel brown eyes. The eyes of her grandmother looked back.

This will come to pass.

The voice in her head was as familiar as her own. Her chest tightened as the water circled the sink, then gurgled down the drain, taking her mirth with it.

Better to ignore it, dear, she heard her grandmother whisper in her mind. *Nothing good will come of it.*

She shook her head and glared at herself in the mirror. The pale complexion with faded freckles scattered across her nose and cheeks reflected back. Just a silly dream about raccoons. It wasn't a snippet. It was not another premonition of something to come. It was an ordinary old dream spun by their silly talk around the pool.

She reached for the peridot charm at her neck, and her hand brushed the moldavite earrings hanging from her ears. A jolt of energy rushed through her. Was it just a dream? How could she tell?

She called them snippets. Genna had called them nonsense. Magic malarky. Fatuous dreams. But Genna was violently angry then, wounded by pride. And yet, the words cut like slivers of glass. When it was all over, Genna had teased her even as she presented the gift.

"The stone is called moldavite," Genna had said as Amy opened the tiny gift box. "It's supposed to aid in channeling information. You know, like voices from the beyond and all that hocus-pocus hoodoo."

She said the gift was an apology for how badly she behaved onboard the Darwinian during Zelda's birthday cruise. Inside the box were two drop earrings with a moss-green crystal paired with her birthstone. She admired how the alexandrite looked like an emerald during the day and more like a ruby at night. Two pairs of earrings in one. A day look and a night look. She had barely worn anything else since.

The stones of the earrings were similar to the peridot she always wore at her neck. The silver filigree setting in the earrings paired with the Celtic knot in the necklace as if the two made a set. The earrings were unexpected – as unexpected as the apology – but when Genna said that moldavite was one-of-kind just like Amy, the rift between them closed. With this simple gift, Genna not only offered her apology, but also appeared to accept Amy's nighttime visions.

"Moldavite comes from only one place on Earth," Genna had explained. "It's mined in the Czech Republic where an alien meteorite struck the silica sand about a gazillion years ago."

Amy had slid the earrings into her ears and instantly felt a warm rush.

"Now you can add aliens to your clairvoyant visions," Genna

kidded. "But, if you start speaking in strange tongues, we may have a problem."

She sighed now into the mirror. She still felt like a tele*pathetic*. Not telepathic. She wasn't clairvoyant nor clairaudient. She was tele*pathetic*. She didn't speak to spirits or move things with her mind. And yet, her snippets always seemed to hold a trace of truth. Sometimes a little more than a trace. If only she knew how to interpret them before... well before it was too late.

"No," she said to her reflection, stuffing the dread down deep into her belly. "That was a silly dream."

Nothing good will come of it.

Amy sighed and shook her head. Grandmother Ollie was always right.

CHAPTER THREE

"Why don't you tell us a little about yourself," the emcee urged.

Amy gulped and scanned the audience in the conference room. There were only a few empty seats, and the sea of faces were all looking at her expectantly. Genna had said, 'whatever you do, don't picture them naked. That's the worst thing you can imagine.' She was inclined to believe it.

She scanned the room for her friends and found Genna at the back of the room. Their eyes met. She squared her shoulders and inhaled deeply.

"Welcome to Bluff Springs, everybody! My name is Amy Sparks," she said to the room. "I own the Tiddlywinks Players Club and the Cardboard Cottage & Company at the corner of Bluff and Main. Just follow your nose to find us. Our Irish bakery makes the best cinnamon buns you've ever tasted." She paused and smiled. "The Cardboard Cottage is a cooperative of four retail partners, whose shops are housed under one roof…" she glanced at Genna and smiled. "… along with a fifth, somewhat silent partner — our public relations consultant, who operates out of the hall *broom* closet."

The audience laughed.

"I'm sure y'all know Genna Gregory." Amy motioned to her

friend at the back of the room. Genna nodded and gave a queen's wave as eyes gravitated in her direction.

"Tiddlywinks is hosting the social hour in the hotel tonight, so please come partake of wine and Parcheesi." She glanced at Genna again. "Oh! And Jerry Glen Villiger is our special guest! Remember: *A Vote for Villiger is a Win for Arkansas!*"

Relieved she had made it through the most challenging part, Amy glanced at the moderator, who nodded, and Amy fell silent. The woman asked the same question of the other panelists seated beside her. Amy strained to hear over the whine in her ears as her heart raced. She ran through Genna's polished talking points in her mind, and the whining ceased. She could do this! She was doing this! She had every right to be here, the same as these other women seated beside her. She felt proud of what she had accomplished and honored to share the story of the Cardboard Cottage. She could do this!

And just like that, forty minutes flew by. She barely remembered answering the questions from the audience or the comments from the other panelists.

All except one. The last one.

"Why don't you tell us more about your psychic visions," a woman spoke from the front row. "I heard you can see killers in your dreams."

"I, well, I," Amy stuttered into silence, her cheeks suddenly aflame with embarrassment. She glanced at Genna who quickly averted her gaze. She could hear the shuffling from the audience and her blush deepened. "I'm afraid you are mistaken," she said evenly.

"Can't you give us details?"

Amy stared at the woman. Was she trying to create trouble? Or was she genuinely interested? Who could tell?

"I can't," she answered with shake of her head. "It's all under investigation, and I've been sworn to silence."

That was a stretch. Both ordeals were already a thing of her past, and no one had sworn Amy to any such thing. But this was not the place to disclose her foreshadowing snippets or the crimes that followed. She looked at the moderator for help, feeling beyond embarrassed.

"Well, that's all we have time for," the emcee erupted with a noisy shuffle of papers at the mic. "Thank you, ladies, for your engagement here today and for your contributions to the Natural State. We're proud to hear from the women-owned businesses thriving in Arkansas." She frowned briefly at the woman, and Amy knew she wasn't the only one who had been blind-sided by her questions. The emcee tilted her head toward the audience and began to applaud. On cue the audience followed her lead.

Amy rose, shook hands with the other panelists, and hurried out the door, her cheeks still flushed and burning.

Glancing at her watch, she felt her shoulders drop with relief. There was just enough time to regroup before the social hour. She could hunt down Rian and Zelda for comfort, except she hadn't noticed them in the audience. She didn't want to speak to Genna. And now that she was alone, she was glad to have some time to herself.

She exited the building for fresh air and the sunlight of a warm May afternoon. She stepped into a pungent cloud of smoke.

"Well, hello, darling," a deep baritone voice said from the corner of the building. He waived with a cigar between his fingers. "A man can't smoke anywhere but his castle anymore. I can't even do that now. Doesn't seem right."

Amy nodded and lifted a hand in greeting. She didn't want to be rude, but she needed a break from the hello and hullaballoo of the conference. Right now, she felt as beat as if she had run a marathon.

She glanced at the man out of the corner of her eye. He puffed his cigar, blowing the plume out with a slow whistle. Leaning against the wall, he had one cowboy-booted foot against the wall, the sharp toe pointed toward the ground. The hat made him look even taller than he was. He glanced at her, noticed her looking at him, and before she could turn away, he dropped his foot from the wall and swaggered over.

Well, the conference was all about meeting people, wasn't it? Might as well meet one more. She forced a smile.

"Duke," he said, extending his hand. It felt more like a warm pork chop. She tried to pull her hand free. He gripped it tighter. "First name's Donald, but I like it when friends call me The Duke. Now that was a man to look up to."

Amy bit the smile from her lips. That and a 10-gallon cowboy hat was something to look up to, quite literally.

"Amy Sparks," she offered, finally pulling her hand from his. "I like it when people call me Amy."

He laughed. The little pearl snap buttons on his shirt flashed in the sunlight as his belly quaked. There was ample overhang at his belt, which had the most enormous belt buckle she had ever seen. She pulled her eyes away and looked up. He towered over her, his face broad and smooth-shaven, but clean-cut didn't quite describe him. His eyes were mud brown, and dark circles beneath them said something was keeping him awake at night.

"You're here for the conference." It was a question with no ask.

She nodded. "I have a shop here in Bluff Springs."

She felt his eyes scan her head to toe. It wasn't as if he ogled her like a Playboy bunny in a centerfold, but the wolfish gleam in his gaze made her feel exposed.

"Your other half here at the conference?"

Amy shook her head. "I'm not married."

He nodded slowly. "I'm going to be single soon myself. Not that I care. The wife had too many ideas about how things ought to be." He stepped forward. She stepped back. He dropped the stogie on the sidewalk and smashed it with his boot, glancing down at her.

His comment felt like an accusation. Looking at the parking lot, she hoped for a rescue, but the only person visible was several yards away. Dressed in a casual business suit and slicked-down hair, that person was too far away to save her; his attention was on a collection of cars with a Diamond Auto Group placard on the windshield. She watched as he flicked something from one of the hoods with a handkerchief.

"This could be your lucky day," Donald Duke said abruptly, regaining her attention. "I'm unveiling a new appellation tonight." He glanced at his watch. "Doesn't start for another few minutes. I can't check into my room at the hotel until five. You want to grab a drink at the bar?"

"No, thanks. Wait… are you the sponsor for this event?"

"Sponsor? Nothing as formal as all that. Don't need to put out money when you bring the wine to the party. I'm Alpha Wine and Spirits, the biggest wine and spirits distributor in the state. Bar none. Pun intended. We deliver everywhere." His chest pushed at the snaps. "Diamond Auto won't mind if I borrow his spotlight."

She knew Diamond Auto Group was the sponsor for the event, and now it seemed Donald Duke had wormed his way into the gig. She couldn't call the kettle black. Genna finagled a politician into the mix and then managed to have Tiddlywinks assigned to the decorations committee. She started to share this when he spoke first.

"I'm here to showcase a best seller tonight. When this shindig is over, I will have more orders sold than I can fill in a year. Who doesn't like a thrifty Pinot Noir?" He hiked at his jeans, and she noticed they had the kind of crease only a dry cleaner can press into denim. "I know my wine. I know wine better than the back of my own hand, and everybody likes a Pinot. Let me tell you how I discovered this gem…"

She glanced again at the parking lot. There was no escape.

"…I was lost on a dusty road, standing eye to eye with a man as old as Moses. Maybe he was older." In his tale of two corks, he paused, hands moving as if playing a game of charades, his gesture part of the story. "We drank a glass … and then the bottle… and I swear I was drinking the best Pinot I've had since 1999. It has a glorious bouquet. Ripe plum. Just the essence of flint and wild herb."

He gestured with a swing of his arms that barely missed her. "I'm going to put this vineyard on the map." He took a breath, then hooked his thumbs over his buckle. "Now, it's not a *Bonnes-Mares grand cru*, mind you. I'm not saying that. But it won't cost you three hundred bucks, either."

It was not a question, but Amy shook her head anyway.

"This is your lucky day, and you can thank me later." He grinned then, and chills ran up her back. She didn't know why, but if a shark wore a big cowboy hat and an oversized belt buckle, he might look like Donald Duke grinning at her now. His lips flattened against his teeth. He ran his eyes over her again as she ran through a mental list of escape clauses. None seemed to fit.

"You don't want to miss out on the best thing you ever had," he cooed. He pulled out a business card and pressed it into her palm, his sweaty flesh lingering. "The Duke is always eager to put a fine pair of lips to a fine wine."

She felt herself stiffen.

His phone rang from his pocket. "That's money calling me. Gotta grab it," he said, fumbling with the passcode, pressing the number pad several times. "Stupid phone," he muttered. "I only have one password I use everywhere. You'd think this phone would know it was me.

Duke," he barked at the phone. "I know. I'm not a slow as you think I am." He hung up and jammed the phone back in his pocket.

Amy had stepped away to give him privacy, but he was close enough that she heard him whistle under his breath. She followed his gaze. Zelda was pulling packages from the trunk of her car, her rear end bobbing in a pair of jeans. She turned to face them and waved with an arm laden with packages.

"Hey, Sparks!" Zelda called. She motioned with the packages. "Big sale on shoes." Joining them on the sidewalk, Zelda glanced at the man beside Amy.

"Zelda Carlisle, this is Donald Duke," Amy said flatly.

He reached out the same pork chop, pulling Zelda's hand to his lips, almost pulling her off her feet.

"Whoa, big guy," Zelda pulled her hand away and gained her balance.

"Call me the Duke," he crooned. "I was just trying to buy your friend a drink at the bar. She declined, but maybe I could twist your arm to join me for a quickie?" He lowered his gaze to Zelda's chest.

Zelda looked at Amy, and Amy widened her eyes. The look in her eye said Zelda had a zinger ready to fly. "You're just flirting with disaster," Zelda said with a cold smile. "Besides, we have a thousand things to do before this evening's event. No time for a quickie anything."

"Ah, honey, what could be more important than having a drink with the Duke?"

Zelda juggled the bags and flashed another smile. "A thousand things, if I can be honest."

His face fell for a brief moment, and she caught the slight jerk as his jaw clenched and his eyes narrowed. He flung his fist to his chest. "Darlin', you break my heart," he said, looking like a scolded puppy. "You enjoy breaking hearts, don't you?"

Amy wanted to kick him with his own pointy-toe boots, but just then, the door opened, and a handful of people stepped out into the sun to warm up from the cold conference rooms inside.

The door opened again, and Genna stepped out, eyes blinking at Amy. "Where have you been? I've been looking everywhere for you!"

"You found me," Amy said. "I had to take a break. Especially after…"

"After that woman grilled you in front of all of Arkansas," Genna interrupted.

"Not in front of all of Arkansas," Amy muttered, "just half of them. Genna Gregory," Amy said reluctantly as silence filled the space between them, "this is Donald Duke. I gather he's in charge of the wine for tonight's event."

"Oh, yes!" Genna gushed. "Donald Duke! Well, of course, I've heard of you." She reached out and pumped his hand. "I didn't realize you were the other sponsor tonight. We appreciate your support in Jerry Glen Villiger's election campaign."

The Duke's brow knitted as he raised the tip of his hat. "I don't give a rat's behind about Villiger's *election* campaign. I'm here to promote my wine, and he better stay out of my way. Better stay away from my wife, too."

"Oh?" Genna said, eyebrows drawn.

"Our paths cross now and again, but we'll never be on the same side of the fence." He put his thumbs on either side of his buckle.

"How can that be?" Genna asked, forcing a wide smile. She put her hand on his arm. "You're a successful man. You know a vote for Villiger is a win for Arkansas."

Amy winced.

Donald Duke's eyes narrowed, and his mouth tightened. "It will be a cold day in Hades before he gets a vote from me or anyone I do business with, and that's every wet county in the state. Elected to Congress? Over my dead body," he grumbled. "I promise you that."

Somebody snickered behind them. Genna's eyes widened and then narrowed. Amy sucked in her breath. She could hear Zelda do the same.

"Oh, come now, Mr. Duke," Genna said with a hard, tight smile. "You can't mean that. You wouldn't want to make a promise you aren't willing to keep. Jerry Glen Villiger is going to be elected to Congress. Even if I have to send ice to Hades myself."

Donald Duke threw back his head and laughed. "I've made plenty of promises I didn't keep." He wiped the spit from the corners of his mouth and rubbed his fingers on the cuff of his sleeve. He eyed Genna now from under the brim of his hat. She didn't have to look up to meet his eyes. "You must be how he hijacked this conference. He's always got women doing his dirty work." He grinned, pulled another cigar from his pocket, and stuck the butt in his teeth.

Amy felt her shoulders tighten. His expression changed again abruptly, and she followed his gaze once again.

"Oh, shoot," he muttered under his breath.

A woman with a bounce of silver-white hair strode across the parking lot toward them. She was tall and slender, with a long blue duster whipping from her legs. Her gait and gaze said he was her intended target.

"Is that someone you know?" Zelda asked.

"My almost-ex-wife," he muttered and stalked off to meet her halfway.

"Good riddance," Genna muttered under her breath.

"Good timing," Zelda said.

Their banter was more than a few yards away. Still, it went from a low rumble to an angry pitch in seconds.

Zelda grabbed her elbow and pulled her toward the door. "Time to hustle," she said, glancing behind her. "We don't want to get in the middle of that. I don't even want to eavesdrop!"

Zelda punched the elevator call button in the hall. "Only fools and full-time jerks flirt while wearing a wedding band. Although that wasn't flirting, that was gross."

"He did say he would be single soon. He must be practicing for what lies ahead."

"Dark days and lonely nights lie ahead," Zelda quipped. "He needs a better playbook of pick-up lines if he's looking for wife number next."

Amy grinned at her friend. Zelda knew all about acquiring spouse number next. She had sworn off marriage after husband number four, but it was unlikely Zelda could wait more than a couple of years before she would be on the hunt again. Women like Zelda needed a man in their lives. She didn't, although it would be okay if one found his way to her heart. She had come close on the cruise. Almost too close.

"Did he pull that same line on you?" Zelda asked. "Did he really ask you for a quickie?"

"Well, he wasn't panting like Rin Tin Tin until you showed up."

Zelda stepped into the empty lift, shifting the packages to make room. "I don't think men ever grow out of puberty."

Amy laughed as the doors closed and the ancient elevator rose to the top floor.

Genna put her hands on her hips akimbo. "Over his dead body. We will see about that. Villager is going to win!"

CHAPTER FOUR

They dropped Zelda off on the third floor with the key to the room and her mission to match her outfit with her new pair of shoes. As the elevator doors opened again with a ping, she and Genna stepped into the hallway. The noisy chatter of the attendees in the room greeted them. Hooking Genna's arm in hers, they made their way to the reception area for the evening social hour.

Amy drew a breath. "Wow!"

"Yes, wow," Genna said, grinning. "This is just as I imagined it would look."

The decorations had turned out better than she thought they would. They had taken photos of vintage game boards from the shop and blown them up to poster size, adding *Tiddlywinks Players Clubs • Bluff Springs* to the bottom in bold black print. Genna had pitched that idea.

The bistro tables lined the walls with the posters hung behind them. With a glance, the colorful display said playful times were ahead. Pictures of *Monopoly, Twister, Scrabble, Clue, Operation,* and *Parcheesi* games were big and glossy. Bright colors and childhood memories beckoned from the walls.

Cradling her glass of wine from the bar —having noticed the bottle of Pinot Noir prominently displayed — she and Genna walked the room. Each table held a stack of postcards that matched the posters on the wall. The names of the four Cardboard Cottage & Company businesses were printed on the back, along with a 10% discount offer when you brought in the card. That had been Zelda's idea.

In the center of the table, next to a flickering flameless candle, a small bowl held a jumble of playing pieces, charms, and trinkets you would find in any I Spy game. A small tent card announced that *A Vote for Villiger is a Win for Arkansas*. A balloon floated the diamond symbol of the Arkansas flag high above the tables. The blue diamond with stars was Arkansas' proud heritage as the nation's only diamond-producing state.

"If you are going to do big, do BIG," Genna declared when they brainstormed their plans.

The double doors to the reception opened with a *clang*. A stream of women dressed to impress and men in business casual flooded in, headed to the bar and buffet with its chaffing dishes of hotel hors d'oeuvres. Genna marched off toward a crowd she recognized, leaving Amy feeling dumped on the doorstep. She eyed the tiers of petit fours, selected one with the Arkansas diamond drawn in blue icing and popped it into her mouth. Licking the raspberry jam from her lips, she contemplated a second and then turned away to resist temptation.

"Amy Sparks!" a woman exclaimed cheerfully. It was Merriweather Hopkins. "I want to introduce you around," Merriweather said, taking Amy's elbow in her hand. "There are so many people here who want to meet you." She grinned and her eyes circled the room like a scope on a rifle.

"Your game posters have created a marvelous setting," Merriweather continued. "They make this room cozy and colorful, just like your shop. I feel like I could be ten again." She laughed briefly, showing a polished smile framed with deep rose red lips. She reminded Amy of the character Julia Dreyfus played on the show *Seinfeld*, except Merriweather was taller and a lot more southern. If Genna was right, the woman didn't have the same what-you-see-is-what-you-get kind of simplicity as the character, Elaine, on TV. Amy wondered, when she introduced herself early in the day, why Genna's defenses were on such high alert. She warned her to watch her back for a sharp knife if Merriweather was behind her. There had to be more to this story because the woman seemed nothing but encouraging and inclusive. What she saw in the broad smile was an unpretentious humility that invited her to be part of whatever she was doing. She didn't believe Merriweather asked her to be on the panel just to get back at Genna.

"Now, who shall we approach first?"

"Do you know everyone here?" Amy asked.

"Oh, not *personally*. From a professional perspective, I make a point of knowing who's who. It's my job to help set up the speakers for these events. That's why you were on my radar. Genna has done a wonderful job promoting your business. She always does a good job, doesn't she?" Merriweather smiled and Amy raised a brow. The smile looked genuine enough and Amy didn't see the forked tongue or feel a knife in the back. But then, Genna could be engaging, too, when she wanted something.

"Oh! There's Pamela Duke. Now that is certainly someone you need to know." Merriweather's attention landed on the table in front of the *Parcheesi* poster. Amy recognized the Duke's soon-to-be ex-wife.

"The other two sitting with her are her best buddies," Merriweather added. "You'll like them, and they will like you. Come on." She tugged at Amy's elbow, and Amy followed.

"Pamela Duke, this is Amy Sparks. Why don't you share the latest wine country gossip while I mingle?" The words were barely out of her mouth before Merriweather drifted off in another direction.

Pamela stuck out her hand and pumped Amy's. "We almost met in the parking lot. You escaped before I could say *hello*, but I recognized you from that magazine article. I'm the one who called last month about setting up a game night at Tiddlywinks." The woman nodded with enthusiasm, her mop of fluffy silver-white hair bouncing softly. She was much calmer now than in the parking lot. The dark cloud that had been in her face then was gone.

Her green eyes flashed. "We all love an excuse to come to Bluff Springs, and I thought a night at your club would be fun while we're here for the conference. We come every year to pay homage to our little agri-wine tourism mecca, but sometimes it can be a bit ho-hum."

"There's no ho-hum allowed at Tiddlywinks! This game night is a fantastic idea," Amy said, smiling. "I wish I had thought of it myself. I love that you want to play dominoes."

Amy glanced at her watch. "I'm going to have to hustle to get from here to the shop in time, but we'll be ready by the time you get there tonight."

"You're expecting us before seven, right? We will have just enough time to freshen up before we drive over to your Cardboard Cottage."

"We are really looking forward to it," one of the other women added. She was a tiny bird of a woman. Her brown eyes were two large orbs in a face no bigger than a child's. Framed by a helmet-like bob, every salon-blonde hair was precisely cut, arranged, and sprayed firmly into place. Nothing dared move.

The bird woman smiled. "Where are our manners? My name is Tilly. And this is Gloria. Or as we like to call her, Mrs. Doctor Chad Barling."

Mrs. Doctor Chad Barling tilted her head toward Amy. "My husband is a cosmetic surgeon," she whispered as the color rose to her cheeks. She smiled, showing off laugh lines around her mouth and blue eyes. They were Goldilocks laugh lines. Not too many, not too few, just the right amount. Her soft linen suit was accented with a large silver cross full of diamonds and a single ruby at the heart. Amy reached for the simple Celtic knot at her neck, pressing the tiny diamond with her fingers.

"As for wine country gossip, there's no better place to fill up than with us. You give us Bluff Springs gossip, and we'll trade you wine country dirt. We're twenty-eight square miles of some of the best sacramental wine on the planet," Gloria Goldilocks said.

"I can't bear the stuff," Pamela muttered. "It's too sweet."

Tilly's thin-drawn eyebrows rose into her bangs. "That's because you're a wine snob."

"Donald is the wine snob," Pamela countered. "No doubt he has somebody cornered out in the hall right now blabbering on and on about '*glorious bouquet! Ripe plum! Essence of flint and wild herb!*'" She flung her free hand expressively. "And then he'll launch into one of his wine origin stories. Probably the one about the little old man who makes wine from the sweat of his ancestral brow somewhere off a dusty road."

Amy grinned into her glass. The words did sound familiar. She could hear the tension in Pamela's voice.

"So, how do you three know each other?" Amy asked, hoping to move the topic on.

Gloria giggled. "Lordy, we've known each other all our lives, and most of us are related by blood or marriage."

Tilly nodded with enthusiasm while her hair stayed in place. "Folks called us the Six-Pack because there were six of us who ran together. It's been that way all of our lives, give or take a lousy spat. We still meet at the same hair salon every third Thursday."

"There's only one salon in our town," Gloria added. "That's why."

Amy nodded. She knew all about small towns and close knit communities. In big cities, you might not even know your neighbor's name unless you received their mail by mistake. In little towns, neighbors knew a lot more than your name.

Tilly motioned to a tall, athletic-looking woman a few tables over and she looked up as she felt their eyes on her. She smiled briefly. "That's Doc Dot. She's been married three times," Tilly added in a not-very-hushed whisper. "Two of them were Gloria's cousins. But she's not married to either of them now."

"She's a doctor, too?" Amy asked.

"She's a vet. She's the best equine veterinarian in a hundred miles.

Rodeo and farm horses, mostly. Of course, she also sees all the run-of-the-mill house pets, but horses are her passion."

"And men," Tilly added.

"Well, there is *that*," Gloria said. "See the person next to her?"

Amy nodded.

"That's Bonnie."

She was petite compared to the vet and so loaded with bling it made Amy's eyes blur. Prada on her feet, judging by the bright red sole.

"Bonnie is all shopper and no taste," Tilly said under her breath.

"That's not fair, and that's not nice," Gloria spat. "Bonnie has great taste, just too much of it all at once."

Tilly whispered to Amy. "Take a look at those earrings!"

Amy looked. From this distance, the earrings resembled sapphire-encrusted jellyfish. "Are Bonnie and Doc Dot part of the six?"

"They are," Tilly agreed. "And the two of them are thicker than mud. They've been riding together since they were knee-high. Although they are always arguing about which horse is the best. Bonnie is hardcore about Missouri Fox Trotters. Dot thinks the sun rises and sets on a Quarter horse. I happen to agree with Dot."

Gloria snuffed. "Well, you would. You think the sun rises and sets on Dot."

"I think I know a better rider when I see one. Just because you dress like a cowgirl doesn't make you one."

"Just because you dress like a tennis pro doesn't make you one of those, either."

Tilly angled her head sharply, opened her mouth, then snapped it shut.

Gloria turned to Amy. "Tilly is dating the handsome new tennis pro at the club."

Tilly's hand flew to her head and smoothed the sculpted bob. "We're not dating. I'm taking lessons."

"*Ohhhh*," Gloria said and smiled. "If you say so, Tilly."

Tilly blushed.

"You two are the Rolls and Royce of Arkansas," Pamela said, interrupting their banter. "Rolls and Royce were always arguing about something petty. Just like Donald and Kirk."

"That's not true," Tilly declared. "Gloria and I are best friends." She smiled at Gloria, who nodded and smiled back.

"And the other one? Is she here?" Amy asked.

"The other who?" Gloria asked.

"The other member of the Six-Pack."

"She's passed on," Gloria answered, touching the cross at her bosom. "May the Lord keep her close. She's been gone a long time."

Tilly nodded solemnly. "We aren't a six pack anymore, but we like to think she's still a part of us."

Amy glanced at Bonnie and her sparkle, Doc Dot and her square jaw, Gloria the Goldilocks with her plump lips and fine lines, and Tilly the bird, blonde plume and all. They reminded Amy of her best friends and the contentious camaraderie that seemed to get them into trouble.

Gloria looked up as a man with salt and pepper hair strode to a table where Dot and Bonnie were sitting. Amy followed her eyes.

"That's Bonnie's husband, Kirk," Gloria said, motioning with a nod. "Kirk Waters."

"He's the Duke's business partner. I don't know whether he's the Rolls or the Royce." Gloria glanced quickly at Pamela. "The Duke handles the sales end and Kirk runs the office. Or as Bonnie says, he cooks the books."

"You mean he's crooked?" Amy asked.

"Oh, no," Tilly answered with a grin. "He's a laity elder at our church. That's just Bonnie's way of saying she gets whatever she wants."

Amy glanced at the earrings and smiled.

"He sure looks different without his beard," Gloria commented.

"I don't think I've ever seen him without it," Tilly agreed. "He looks a little like Duke."

She glanced at Pamela, who was looking at Kirk, a strange

expression on her face. The man's jawline was a shade lighter than the rest of his face. He carried a pair of envelopes, the kind hotel room keys come in, which he stuffed into his coat pocket as he approached the table. Kirk grabbed the drink sitting in front of his wife with the earrings and drained it. He set it back in front of her. Empty, Amy noticed. He turned and scanned the room as if hunting for someone he knew.

"Speak of your devil." Gloria nodded toward the door. "Look who just waltzed in."

Amy saw the two men come through the door. Both wore cowboy hats, boots, and giant belt buckles. They stretched the doorway to its limits as they entered side by side.

"Twiddle Dee and Twiddle Dumb," Pamela muttered as the men entered the room.

"Her husband is the one *without* the red bolo," Tilly whispered to Amy. "He likes to be called Duke. The Duke. Like John Wayne."

Pamela raised her wine glass to the light as if admiring the color. "Wine snob. Well, he thinks he's so important, but he's just a glorified salesman who day drinks with clients and sommeliers. And anybody else who will listen," she added, looking over the top of her glass.

Amy noted Pamela's mocking tone. "What's a sommelier?"

"Pamela says it's a fancy word for *wine snob*," Gloria said, her Goldilocks grin stretching plump lips. "But actually, it's a person who is in charge of the wine."

"And usually, one with boobs and a pert little bun on top of her head," Pamela added.

"*Hmph,*" Tilly said through pinched lips. "He's not cheating anyone but himself."

Amy recognized the man without the red string tie. It was the man she and Zelda and Genna encountered outside. "Who is the other guy?"

"Double Diamond Auto," Tilly answered. "Well, it's not called that now. Now it's something fancy like Diamond Group. Hank

Summerfield. He was a jock in high school, now he's all corporate and too big for his britches." Tilly giggled. "We called him Stanky Hanky."

Amy laughed, even though she knew she shouldn't. Nicknames left scars.

Pamela followed the men with her eyes, the corners of her mouth tense.

"Divorces are so ugly," Gloria said. "Don't worry," she whispered and put a hand on Pamela's arm. "It will be over soon enough. He'll get his and you'll get yours."

"I need another glass of wine," Pamela said abruptly, and pushed away from the table. Amy watched as she walked to the bar at the far end of the room, the one furthest from the door and her wanna-be-ex. Her gait was brisk and determined, her blue duster kicking out with each step.

"And here comes Jerry Glen," Gloria added. "Right on cue. I heard he was going to be here."

The guests applauded as the man entered the room. Amy didn't know Jerry Glen Villiger by sight, but she knew he was running for U.S. Representative, District 4. That had been drummed into her like a meditation mantra by Genna.

He looked more mature than she thought he would. His dark hair was cut short, with springs of grey showing at his temples. He looked *political*. He grinned with what appeared to be genuine pleasure as the room greeted him with warmth. He made his way through the crowd, one hand in a handshake and the other on a shoulder. Genna was behind him. Although pretending to mingle, Genna was watching his every move.

A rumble of laughter caught Amy's ear. Donald Duke, commanding the attention of a small group gathered around him, was animatedly recounting a tale. There was a woman standing close to him. She looked to be in her mid-thirties, perhaps, with dark blonde hair piled in a bun on top of her head, a bit disheveled, as if she had been running to catch up. She straightened her skirt and her bangs and looked at Duke with a smile. Kirk Waters crossed the room again, this time handing something to his partner with a manly pat on the back. It looked like the same envelope he had stuffed into his jacket pocket just moments before.

"Howdy, ladies!"

Amy turned her attention again as the politician approached the table. He took Gloria by the shoulders and gave her a gentle squeeze. "What a pleasant surprise to see you, cousin."

"Likewise," Gloria answered and let him peck her cheek.

"Tilly, Pamela," he said and nodded with a bright smile. He touched Pamela's hand briefly, then reached for Amy's.

"Jerry Glen Villiger," he said as he shook her hand in a tenacious grip. "District 4, U.S. Representative. I hope you are voting age!"

Amy chuckled. "I'm Amy Sparks," she said, smiling at his handsome face. "I'm Genna Gregory's friend."

His grin widened, and his grip tightened. "Amy Sparks! Well, of course, you are. You're just as she described you! You're Genna's psycho-detective. She told me all about how you caught those bad guys single-handed. We need more citizen activists like you in Arkansas."

His words were buzzing in her ears. She had stopped listening at *psycho-detective*. He did say that, didn't he? Not psychic detective. *Psycho*.

Was that what Genna was calling her now? Hadn't Genna humiliated her enough? Amy's cheeks burned. Genna's harsh and haunting words echoed in her head. Tele*pathetic*. That was true enough. But *psycho*?

She touched the earrings — Genna's peace and amends. She wanted to slip them from her earlobes and drop them into her purse. Or maybe her empty glass of wine. Enough was enough. An apology wasn't genuine if she kept making the same offense.

"Yes, more activists," Villiger echoed, as Amy stared blankly at the knot in his red, white, and blue tie. "I hope you'll vote in November!"

Pamela waited until the politician left to greet the adjacent table. "I heard about that, too," she said. "But I didn't know you were a detective. A real physic detective? Is that like a medium or a mind reader?"

"He said *psycho*," Tilly corrected. "But I don't think he meant to say that."

Gloria frowned at Tilly. "Of course, he didn't," she blurted. "He may be running for Congress, but he's still a few watts short of bright." She patted Amy's hand. "Honestly, men are like wine," Gloria added, now raising her glass. "They start out like grapes on the vine. It's a woman's job to stomp on them long and hard and then keep them in the dark until they mature into something we want to have dinner with. Sometimes that wine is fine. Sometimes it's better left corked." Gloria raised a perfect brow as if to punctuate her belief.

Men *were* a lot like wine. There were good ones and there were bad ones. Sometimes it was hard to tell until it was too late. And sometimes you were pleasantly surprised. She remembered how good it felt to have the weight of Piero's chest against hers on the dark stair on the *Darwinian*, his lips pressed to hers in a clove and anise kiss. And yes, there were others who were better left corked.

"To women," Pamela said, raising her glass in a toast. "If we don't stand together, we don't stand a chance."

CHAPTER FIVE

Amy looked out at the cacophony that was her shop. The women were slightly tipsy, overly excited, and all talking at once. Tiddlywinks Players Club had been taken over in the after-hours by Pamela Duke and her group who came to Bluff Springs for the conference. It had been a rush, but she managed to leave the social hour and be back at Tiddlywinks in time for the event. Had the choice been hers, she would have chosen another evening for this after hours gig and give herself a break. But Pamela had been persuasive when she made the call prior. The money she offered for the opportunity made the hustle seem well worth her time. Amy had been thinking about ways to add extra revenue at Tiddlywinks. When Pamela Duke suggested the outing, it felt like fate.

In the time they had been in the Cardboard Cottage & Company, the women had shopped, devoured a charcuterie of food, and sipped a round of Champagne cocktails. Sammie next door at Crumpet's and Cones had laid out a delicious spread.

"I was unavoidably detained," Genna offered Amy as explanation when she burst through the doors and headed straight for the champagne flutes. Genna arrived just moments before Pamela Duke, who was the last of her group to arrive.

Amy wanted to raise her hands to her ears to block the pleasant — but deafening — chatter of women. Instead, she cupped her hands to her mouth. "Ladies!" she bellowed. The pitch descended by a mere decibel. "Ladies!" she called again.

Amy jumped when a loud, shrill whistle cut through the din. Silence erupted, and all eyes turned to Rian O'Deis, whistle-fingers still pressed to her lips. Rian shrugged. Amy grinned at her friend.

The women turned their attention to Amy. "I'm glad you're having such a good time," she said while she could. "Let's play dominoes!"

She resisted the impulse to put her hands on her hips. "You've met Zelda Carlisle — she owns Zsa Zsa Galore Decor." Amy motioned to her friend amid a round of polite clapping. "And Rian O'Deis, who owns The Pot Shed." Several women giggled. Rian lifted her glass in salute. "And this is Genna Gregory, finally.

"Here's how this is going to work. The four of us will host a table. That makes four players for each table. Your host will share the rules of the game and keep score. The highest score wins their very own Cardboard Cottage domino set!"

A loud phone alert interrupted them. Pamela pulled her cell phone from her purse, glanced at the text, and frowned. "Sorry," she muttered, shoving the phone back into her purse.

"Is everything okay?" Amy asked, noticing the frown lines deepening on her forehead. Pamela nodded.

"Then choose your host and choose your competition." Amy smiled with encouragement as the women migrated to seats, chair legs scraping across the old wood floors. She exhaled loudly. So far, so good, although she felt she was herding cats that had rolled around in catnip.

Amy glanced at Pamela, happy to see she had gravitated to her table. She took her seat and smiled at the other players at her table. Pamela was seated to her right. Gloria and Tilly rounded out the foursome. "Long time no see," she said and grinned.

Gloria giggled and waved her jangle of bracelets. "I'm so excited! I've always wanted to learn how to play dominoes."

"I brought you a bottle of wine as a present," Pamela interjected, handing a bottle to Amy. "It's one of my favorites. I snagged an entire case from the cellar for this weekend, and I am not a bit sorry. Especially after he lied about Claret."

Amy nodded noncommittally and dumped the tiles on the table. "Claret? Who's that?"

"She's my fur baby. Duke agreed to take care of her while I am here this week. She doesn't like being boarded."

"So, where is your dog now?"

"At Duke's hotel. That's why I was so mad when I saw him earlier. He left her in his truck in the parking lot with the windows down. She could have jumped out and run off!"

"Or worse," Tilly added. "Someone could have stolen her right out of the cab. At least she's safe now."

Gloria touched her necklace. "He's just trying to get under your skin. Don't you dare let him succeed."

Pamela nodded. "I would have brought Claret with me, but our lodging doesn't allow pets." Pamela frowned and glanced at her watch. "He usually takes really great care of her. He didn't think things through this time, that's all. It will be okay. It's only for one night."

"Are you ready to learn how to play dominoes?" Her teammates nodded enthusiastically.

They each dragged their tiles from the pile as Amy launched into the rules of the game, how to make points to score, about the spinner, and the doubles that followed. She shared tips on blocking other players and left the boneyard to the last.

"Pips are the dots on the dominoes, which are called tiles. We call them bones. And this," Amy said, tapping the pile of leftover tiles, "is called the boneyard, where you must draw from if you can't make a play. You don't want to visit there too often, but your opponents want you there at every hand."

"Why is that?" Tilly asked. "Doesn't it give you more options to play?"

"Yes, and usually an opportunity to block," Amy answered. "But every pip left in your hand when a player goes out – meaning plays her last tile – is added to her score. Rounded up or down by fives," she added.

"Ah," Pamela said and nodded. "Blocking forces your opponent to the boneyard for pips."

"For tiles," Amy corrected. "The pips are what score the points."

Amy glanced at the other tables with Dot Doc the Vet and Bonnie Bling, Duke's partner's wife. The other women in attendance, Amy didn't know. She recognized a few faces from the conference, and had enjoyed talking with some of them earlier, although she had felt rushed to get everything in place on time. The faces she remembered. The names, not so much.

The room was full of chatter, laughter, and the clank of dominoes on the tables. They played an open hand, revisited the rules, and then reshuffled the tiles to begin a new round. Amy let her attention drift to the other tables, hoping to eavesdrop on how things were going. Every now and again, she recognized a familiar voice.

"You can't just pass," Rian said in her matter-of-fact tone. "Even if you can't score, you must play a tile. If you don't have a tile that matches any in play, you have to draw from the boneyard until you do."

"Twenty-five," Genna called. Amy frowned. She had warned Genna against taking advantage of these newbie players. She wanted the guests to score and win.

"Well, I looked fat in that article."

Amy knew that giggle anywhere. It was as Zelda as her signature perfume and noisy designer shoes.

"The photographer caught me at the wrong angle," Zelda said. "Genna said he needed a wide angle lens to shoot my little shop, but he didn't have to use it on me. He should have photographed me with a thin-angle lens. And that's all there is to that."

Amy grinned and returned her attention to the game in front of her. She intentionally missed a chance to score and played a tile that opened the game to more options for the other players. She could see them counting pips, lips moving while searching for the golden five, ten, or fifteen-point score hidden in their hands. Like Zelda, Tilly counted on freshly manicured nails.

Her Tiddlywinks' first domino-for-hire game was going as smoothly as she could hope. Her guests were having fun. And since Bluff Springs was no stranger to ladies' getaways, if she could tap into that more often, she could turn after-hours at Tiddlywinks into extra income. The idea had appeal. She could rebuild savings drained from the down payment, renovations, and stock for the shop. She did okay by selling her vintage games and toys, and the rent income from the other shops in the building went a long way toward the mortgage. Everything seemed to cost more than she budgeted, including her new part-time help.

They had plenty of business. Bluff Springs was a popular destination with tourists. Crumpet and Cones, the fourth shop housed in the historic old building, drew the tourists in like a magic trick, blowing the scent of baked cinnamon right out of the ovens into the street. Much like a finger curling seductively to beckon its prey, the bakery drew customers with a sweet tooth to its door. The bakery was closed in the evenings, but Sammie would be up before the sun getting the dough ready to rise.

She was grateful Sammie had chosen to reopen her pastry shop after their hiatus for repairs last year. The break-in and burglary had put Sammie on edge. It was understandable, since Sammie was the one who discovered the broken glass. Amy knew why it was so upsetting. Raised in Northern Ireland, Sammie had seen enough violence and shattered lives to last a lifetime.

Although also part of their business cooperative, Sammie kept to herself and her baked goods. Amy didn't ask her about her social life. Sammie didn't join in theirs. It would be hard to break into their foursome; they were already thicker than thieves. They had built their friendship over dominoes and road trips. They had weathered big storms, rough patches, two crimes, and hundreds of game nights that called for banter, goading, and even a little cheating on Genna's part.

Amy smiled. She might consider them a bit like thieves from time to time, although they were innocent thieves, really — only out to steal a good time in the throes of middle age. Make that post-middle age — none of them would live to be a hundred.

Amy was startled when the cell phone ringing with a chirpy little melody interrupted her thoughts. Pamela reached for her purse hanging on the back of her chair. And then pressed the phone to her ear.

"Hello, Kirk," she said as if annoyed by the interruption. "What is it? We're busy." Silence followed, her body stiffened, her jaw dropped, and her free hand flew to her chest.

"What is it?" Tilly asked. "Is everything okay?"

Pamela lowered her gaze to her lap and then closed her eyes. The phone slipped from her fingers and clattered to the floor, spinning like a flat-bottomed top on the wooden planks. Amy moved to retrieve it, but the phone spun out of reach, stopping against a chair leg at one of the other tables. Bonnie Waters reached down and plunked the phone from the floor. The male voice blared from the other end.

Bonnie barked into the phone. "Kirk? What do you want?" She paused to listen. "Oh, no," she whispered. Her brow creased as she rose from her seat and crossed the few feet to the other table. She pressed the phone into Pamela's limp fingers. "You need to take this," she whispered.

"No," Pamela said, pulling away from her touch.

"What's the matter?" Gloria whispered. "What happened?"

Pamela looked up from her lap, her green eyes wide. "It's Donald," she whispered. "He's dead."

"What!" Gloria's hands flew to her face.

"The Duke is dead," Pamela whispered. "Suicide."

CHAPTER SIX

"That was a big bust," Genna said as she gathered dominoes and stacked them into their cases. Zelda and Rian dumped dirty dishes into a bin borrowed from next door. Victor came out from his hiding place once the cacophony had left the building. Amy sat in the front window in one of the two armchairs, absently stroking his soft fur.

She couldn't wrap her head around it. She should have been helping her friends clean up, but her head felt like a bomb had exploded between her ears. The bomb being Pamela's words.

The Duke is dead.

She pictured the man standing outside the building at the conference with his big hat and even bigger attitude. He wasn't someone she'd ever want to be alone with, but he didn't seem like someone who would do something like that. The stuff that lies under the skin that no one sees is what makes people who they are. She didn't see it, but there had to be more to Donald Duke than arrogant hot air, questionable morals, and a wife who wanted him out of her life.

The police had shown up not long after the call and asked if Mrs. Duke was in attendance. The pair of local policemen had tenderly but efficiently escorted her aside, offering her one of the armchairs in the Tiddlywinks window. The same chair Amy was sitting in now.

The entire room watched as one of the policemen bent toward

Pamela to give her the news. It was news Pamela already knew.

"What a nightmare," Genna said. "I knew he was trouble from the first time I laid eyes on him."

Amy didn't feel comforted. She had worked so hard on the evening's plans. Even figuring out how to teach a dozen women how to play dominoes had taken considerable thought. It felt selfish but having the evening end with disastrous news didn't sit well. Not well at all. Dread simmered deep within her. *This shall come to pass.*

"What a horrible weight to bear," Amy said. "I can't imagine being the one left behind in a circumstance like that. Even if you were getting a divorce. How would you cope?"

"I don't know," Zelda answered in a hushed tone. "Having your husband run down in a parking garage is one thing but doing himself in… that's a load of grief I wouldn't wish on an enemy."

Amy glanced at her best friend. Zelda was affected by Zack's mishap more than they realized, even as she played the heroic widow. They had had a problematic marriage. Zack had been a complicated man. He didn't fit anybody's description of marriage material, but it was hard to justify what happened to him. He didn't deserve Zelda, but he didn't deserve death, either.

"You never know how someone will react to news like that," Amy said. "Pamela seemed almost frozen. She seemed so calm and quiet. Do you think she was in shock?"

By contrast, Zelda was sobbing gibberish when she heard the news about Zack. Pamela Duke was none of that. Her friends had rushed to her side when the police left. They gathered around her in a swarm, and then in a flash, they were gone. Every trace of their presence had gone out the door with them, including the shopping bags and the laughter.

Rian dumped the dish bin on a table and wiped her hands on her blue jeans. "Twelve women sure make a lot of noise, don't they?" She plopped into the chair opposite Amy. Victor opened his eyes and glanced at Rian, stretched a paw as if contemplating a move, then snuggled his nose back into the crook of Amy's arm.

"Twelve women can spend a lot of money, too," Rian added. "I sold a bunch of heirloom seeds and several items to ship. I didn't think they would be interested in my shop, but they were. Several of them belong to a garden club."

"All wealthy women belong to a garden club," Genna retorted. "It's just something you do."

"You don't," Rian returned. "You wouldn't know a crocus from a crocodile."

"I'm more avaricious than altruistic," Genna admitted with the flip of her long silver ponytail. "Garden clubs like to raise money for charities. And politics."

"Who was at your table, Genna?" Amy asked.

"A crafty lot. They're used to playing games together. That Bonnie blocked me at every turn. She would have won if she hadn't been interrupted mid-game. Especially since I was not allowed to win." Genna glanced briefly at Amy. "Believe it or not, I was following your rules. No win for Genna."

"Bonnie Waters," Amy said quietly. Bonnie Bling in her mind. "She's married to Donald's business partner, Kirk."

"Was," Zelda added. "*Was* his business partner."

Wasbund. Another husband that was.

"I had a veterinarian at my table," Zelda added. "She's the one that looked a little like a Great Dane – all lanky and legs. Square jaw, long nose. She was hilarious. One of the players was a fretful player; always shifting her bones around. The other one was shy at first, but then she warmed up when I told them all about that horrible picture of me in the magazine. She said it was the reason they were here. That article was. Not the picture of me."

"I had a mayor at my table," Rian said. "She's been the mayor of her town for twenty years running. Nothing gets past her without notice. I'm pretty sure she counted dominoes the way Genna counts cards at a casino."

"I don't count cards," Genna replied. "I watch people's body language. Everybody has a poker tell. You taught me that."

"Oh, look, they left a bottle wine," Zelda said, motioning to the bottle on a table. "Do you think they will come back for it?"

"They'll find an empty bottle if they do," Genna said, looking around for a clean glass. "If it's open, it's fair game."

"It's not open," Zelda warned, settling in a chair near the front window. "We should keep it for them just in case they return."

"This was a gift to us from Pamela. She said she took a case from her husband's wine cellar." Pamela had mocked him as a wine snob. She implied he was greedy with his collection but generous with himself. And now he was gone. She could take all the wine she wanted without asking. She would never again need his permission for anything.

"We'll drink it another day," Amy decided. "On a happier occasion."

"I'll keep it safe," Genna offered, tucking the bottle under her arm.

Rian laughed. "Yeah, that's like asking a bear to guard the honeycomb."

"At least I don't smell like a bear," Genna sassed in reply.

Rian sniffed her armpits. "Are you saying I do?"

"No, I'm saying I don't smell like a bear. There's no need to read between the lines."

The room got quiet then. The streets were empty at this hour of the night, except for a pair of tourists window-shopping hand in hand. She turned off the overhead lights, leaving the room in the glow from the streetlamps across the street. They could see well enough to see each other, and the cover of darkness was a relief from the harsh reality of the evening's outcome.

Amy turned to her friends. "What do you think we should do?"

"You mean, do we send flowers and a pot roast?" Zelda asked.

Rian snickered. "I could eat a pot roast. I'm still hungry."

"You're always hungry," Zelda chided. "I don't understand why you don't gain weight. I eat, and it goes right to my chunky parts."

"It's all about hormones and DNA," Rian answered.

Genna crossed her long legs and swung a sandal from her toes. "You wouldn't have chunky parts if you exercised. Calories in. Calories out."

"Don't you dare fat shame me," Zelda said. "Just because you're thin doesn't mean you're healthy. You're as allergic to burpees as I am. And you smoke a pack a day."

"Point taken," Genna said. "Besides, they don't make Prada tennis shoes."

Zelda put a hand on her hip. "Oh yes, they do. I have three pairs."

"Let me guess," Rian said. "At least one of them is pink."

Zelda grinned at Rian in the dark.

CHAPTER SEVEN

Relief flooded her shoulders to see that it was almost closing time at Tiddlywinks. The week since the conference and her first-ever Tiddlywinks after-hours fiasco had been quiet. It wasn't her fault the evening ended sadly. She knew that at heart, but it didn't ease the sting. No one could have predicted the turn of events. That didn't change the way she felt. She leaned against the doorframe in the hallway, looking out the front door. Rays of afternoon sunlight pushed the dust motes around the floor like an invisible broom. She should get after that. No one else would bother.

Next door at Crumpets & Cones, the crowd gathering for their daily bread and fancy sweets was thinning out. She hadn't seen Zelda for hours. The UPS hunk in shorts had delivered a pile of boxes to Zsa Zsa Galore Décor first thing. Zelda disappeared inside her cubbyhole shop to unpack, price, and stage the items that made her shop so lucrative. She had an eye for what people wanted as they feathered their home nests. Across the hall, the *Blooming Open!* sign hung on the outside door of The Pot Shed. A colorful, earthy, pungent green world grew in pots inside. Rian was somewhere in there puttering, no doubt. If she was catching the tune right, riffs of Vivaldi drifted out into the hall. The musical score arrived at a decrescendo, and it was just then that she heard the front door of the Cottage jangle open.

Genna Gregory, dressed in a blue and white pinstripe jumpsuit, rushed through the door. Amy followed her into Tiddlywinks as Genna tossed a pile of newspapers to the table.

"Take a look at that!"

"And hello to you, too," Amy said with a twinge of sarcasm. She glanced at the color photo at the top of the page, just below the newspaper banner. "That's impressive."

"No, it's not! Well, yes, it is, but look again!" Genna demanded.

Reluctantly, as if a current events pop quiz was looming in her future, Amy picked up the newspaper and studied the photo. In his red, white, and blue striped tie and dapper gray streak to his hair, candidate Jerry Glen Villiger shook hands in a crowd, a big, toothy political grin on his face. The photo caption touted his candidacy, and the article that ran underneath it went all the way to the newspaper fold. She looked up to see Rian and Zelda walking through the door of Tiddlywinks. At least she wouldn't have to take Genna's pop quiz alone.

"Genna's Big European Tour of Arkansas is working," Amy said brightly, hoping she wouldn't be required to read the article to satisfy Genna. "It's getting great press. Isn't that what you wanted to accomplish? Front page exposure?"

"Above the fold, too," Genna said as Zelda dumped her heavy bag on the table. "But take a look at who is also in the photo."

The three of them crowded around the newspaper.

"Oh! That's Pamela Duke standing behind him," Amy said.

"Precisely." Genna pulled another newspaper to the top of the pile. The photo was similar in composition, although taken from a different angle and the newspaper banner at the top was from another town. Genna poked a fingernail at Pamela Duke, also in the photo. She pulled yet another newspaper to the top with a similar shot.

The last paper Genna pulled to the pile showed a photo of Pamela and Donald Duke and a long ribbon of news copy.

"What does that story say?" Zelda asked, poking the picture of Donald Duke.

"It says…" Genna pulled the paper closer. "That Donald J. Duke was found deceased in a hotel room in Bluff Springs, Arkansas, by his business partner, Kirk Waters. They don't say how he did it — you know — died — but Waters is quoted as saying that he 'should have recognized all the signs.'"

Amy peered over Genna's shoulder.

Genna read from the page: "*I was concerned about the Duke's state of mind, but I was under the impression he was seeing someone. In fact, he mentioned it once or twice. I didn't realize how troubled he was. And of course, I am devastated. He was the best friend and business partner I've ever had, and it will not be the same without him.*"

"Seeing someone," Amy repeated. "I got the impression that if Donald Duke was seeing someone, it had to be a girlfriend on the side, not a mental health professional. I remember Pamela commented about a sommelier with pert boobs and a little bun. Or maybe she said it was a pert bun and little boobs. I think the woman she was talking about was at the conference. Did the article mention the divorce?"

Genna scanned the page and shook her head. "No, nothing about their divorce."

"I wonder if there will be an investigation," Zelda asked.

"I think all unattended deaths require an autopsy. And probably an investigation of sorts," Amy answered.

"I read that same news story this morning," Rian added, and stuck her thumbs in her pockets. "Donald Duke was a big deal in the wine world. He was considered a pioneer in the industry. He was part of the initial push to sell native wines in local stores, and that was quite an accomplishment. There were forty dry counties on the battlefront at the time. Arkansas had to repeal a twenty-year-old ban on the sales of native wines to make that happen, and now, Arkansas wine is a two hundred million dollar a year industry."

Zelda whistled under her breath. "That's a lot of wine."

"That's a lot of money," Rian added.

"Well, there was not the usual *in lieu of flowers* statement," Genna added, "so the local florist must be delighted. She'll be deluged with orders."

"Did you read the other story?" Rian asked, tapping the page with a fingertip. "The writer went pretty deep on the *message of hope* angle. How mental health tragedies like this need never happen."

Genna nodded. "Yeah, but it buried my story about the Big European Tour of Arkansas."

"That's sad," Zelda said.

"I know," Genna answered. "Now, I'll have to re-release all the information about the Big Tour dates."

"I didn't mean *that* was sad," Zelda snapped.

"How was I to know what you were talking about?"

"Empathy is kind of like *gaydar*," Zelda said. "You either have it, or you don't."

"That's not politically correct," Amy said. "Better to say *emotional radar*."

"Gator?" Rian asked, pulling out one of the chairs and dropping into it. "What do alligators have to do with it?"

"See?" Genna said a little too loudly. "Rian, you're going deaf."

"I'm not going anywhere," Rian answered. "And besides, alligators are a fascinating subject matter."

Genna grunted. "All I know is that I've worked my buns off to launch this tour, and if Pamela Duke thinks she can ruin it with her cameos, she has another thing coming! You just watch me... I'll feed *her* to alligators!"

Amy shuffled the papers on the table into a neat stack. "Do you think she's having an affair with Jerry Glen? Maybe that's why Donald Duke ..." she let her words trail away. It was hard to say certain things and not sound disrespectful of the deceased. The four of them had done something disrespectful onboard the *Darwinian*, but that wasn't their intention at the time. They were only trying to derail the inevitable and they got carried away in the moment. It was a moment of regrettable madness, but it was part of their history, nonetheless.

"Has someone said something about her being in the pictures?"

"No, but they're bound to. That whole place down there is a grapevine. Quite literally…. a grapevine. It's wine country." Genna slammed the table with a fist. "I knew he couldn't keep his eye on the prize. I knew it. What is it about politicians?"

"Politicians like power. They like attention. And they like women. Maybe not always in that order," Rian answered.

"I don't know whether to ask him point blank or to needle it out of him on the sly," Genna said. "I'd like to think this is an innocent happenstance, but some little bug in my ear is telling me it's not."

Zelda shuffled the bracelets on her arm and smoothed her dark hair. "What will you do if they *are* having an affair?"

Genna sighed and dropped into a chair. "I don't have a single answer at the moment," she drawled in a plaintive southern whine. "Trying to triage this triangle has me in a pickle."

Amy stole a glance at Genna. A *wasbund*, a widow, and a politician. Triage. Triangle. A tricky state of affairs. When Amy met Jerry Glen at the social hour at the conference, he hugged Gloria in a light embrace and called her cousin. He put his hand on Pamela's before shaking hers. The gesture had gone by without meaning -- at least at the time. Was there more to that gesture than she realized?

"Hank Summerfield of Diamond Auto Group is friends with Jerry Glen," Amy said, thinking out loud.

Genna turned her chin in her hand to look directly at Amy.

"Hank knows Duke. Hank knows Jerry Glen. Maybe he knows what's going on," Amy offered.

"I'm listening," Genna said, her blue eyes focused.

"Diamond Auto Group is the biggest dealership in that region. They sponsored that event. Maybe it's about following the money. The car dealership has money. So does the wine industry. Politicians follow the money."

"You mean he's a puppet?" Zelda asked. "A political puppet?"

Amy shrugged. "Who knows. Power, money, and politics."

"Everything needs money, power, and politics," Rian interjected.

"But how does this relate to Pamela Duke?" Zelda asked.

Amy shrugged again and shook her head. She had piled her copper curls on top of her head this morning, frustrated with the mass after washing it and letting it air dry before bed. A couple of chopsticks stuck in the knot held it in place, but now, chunky ringlets were springing down around her neck. She brushed them with her fingertips.

"We know Donald Duke wasn't a Jerry Glen fan," she said.

Genna nodded. "That's putting it politely."

"Didn't he say it would be a cold day in Hades before he voted for— "

"He said, *over my dead body*," Genna interrupted. "And what do you know... now he's dead. But he wasn't dead when I talked to him last. He was perfectly alive and loathsome."

"Wait! When was this?"

Genna looked sideways at Amy. "Right after the social hour. He left a case of wine and an invoice for it. The invoice was made out to Villiger's Campaign HQ, in care of Genna Gregory. He even had the audacity to draw a little smiley face on the bottom. Well, I marched it back to him and said, *'thanks but no thanks.'* Not unless he wanted to make the case of wine a tax-deductible donation to Villiger's campaign. And that I'd be happy to send a recording receipt — in care of Donald Duke!"

"You went to his hotel room? How did you know where he was staying?"

"That was no magic trick. I think Duke told every woman in the room where he was staying."

"Was someone there with him?" Amy asked.

"He had a dog with him."

"That's not nice," Zelda said. "First, you fat shame me, and now you're calling a sister ugly."

Genna huffed. "No, it was a real dog. The kind that barks at strangers."

"One of those little yapper breeds?"

"No, a big one. A big dog with curly hair. Kind of like yours, Amy."

"Oh, thanks a lot."

"It was a very nice looking dog," Genna added. "It had very nice hair."

Amy shook her head. "Like that makes so much difference."

"Did you go inside the room?" Rian asked.

Genna exhaled. "I didn't intend to."

The three of them dropped their jaws and gaped at their friend.

"Well, that wasn't my plan. I was just going to return the wine and the invoice and then ask if there was anything Jerry Glen could do to win his vote."

"And?" Amy asked.

"I told him we could better appreciate him as an ally than an enemy if he was so inclined. And then he invited me in to discuss the particulars."

"So, you went in the room."

Genna frowned.

"You carried a case of wine all by yourself," Zelda asked, blinking in disbelief.

"Oh, for crying out loud. That's what dollies are for. I borrowed one from the conference hall kitchen."

"And then you went inside his hotel room," Rian repeated.

"Not for very long," Genna admitted. "It was obvious what kind of *particulars* he had on his mind. He said he had a price if I was willing to pay it." Genna shuddered. "I couldn't get out of there fast enough."

"And that's it?" Amy asked.

Genna grinned. "Well… I tacked a campaign poster to his door when I slammed it behind me. With my wad of chewing gum."

"As in chewed from your mouth. So now they have your DNA, too." Amy grinned. She had seen enough of the political poster and slogan to last her a lifetime. Everywhere they went during the conference, there was evidence that Genna had already been there, done that, and plastered a poster to mark the spot. She was surprised Genna's propaganda hadn't broken all the rules at the conference, but if he did, no one seemed brave enough to bring it to her attention. Tacking one to the enemy's door was beyond brazen. Genna must have really been angry.

"Did he look like someone ready to … you know… do himself in?" Zelda asked.

"How would I know what that looks like?" Genna replied.

Rian whistled under her breath. "You may have been the last person to see him alive."

"Maybe this Pamela-Villiger-Duke triangle is more complicated than it looks," Amy added. "Something pushed Donald Duke over the edge."

"It wasn't me. But you know what they say, if the tree is in the way, chop it down."

"What does that mean?" Zelda asked pointedly.

"I'm just saying that maybe someone knew he was already at the cliff and deliberately pushed him over. It wasn't me. If Jerry Glen is implicated in any sort of impropriety in this mishap, his campaign could run downhill faster than a rock in a flash flood. I may need your help to bail this boy out. We may need you to do some snooping. Get some gossip. Uncover the goods. I need to know what's been going on between Pamela, Jerry Glen, and Donald Duke."

Genna frowned. "I'm thinking I shouldn't have stuck that poster to his door, with hindsight being twenty-twenty. I left the borrowed hand truck behind in my hindsight, too."

Amy narrowed her eyes at Genna. "When you say — 'we may need to do some snooping'— are you asking me to do some *psycho*-detecting?"

Genna winced. "I didn't mean it *that* way. I meant *psychic*-detective, but it came out the other way, and everybody laughed. I was trying to play up your mystique so people would come purchase your Ouija boards. I promise I won't say that again."

"I want you to promise you won't talk about me at all. Don't say I single-handedly did anything heroic, and don't talk about my snippets!"

Genna raised a brow and her lips twisted into a smile. "You know it makes a good story, don't you?"

"Promise me," Amy urged. "Promise me, or I will do no snooping. Zilch. Nada. Promise."

Genna sighed. "I promise."

"I want to snoop, too," Zelda said. "Does this mean we're going on a snoop trip? That sounds like a road trip with extra baggage and booze."

"What right do we have to stick our noses where they don't belong?" Rian asked, jamming three fingers into her pocket.

"Couldn't we ask Officer Handsome to help us?" Amy wondered.

"Where is Officer Handsome, anyway," Zelda piped in. "We haven't seen him in ages. Not since you got back from Peru."

Rian grinned. "I wore him out. The terrain is indescribably beautiful and unbelievably exhausting. Even for a person in good shape, the climb was strenuous. I was grateful we took the advice of the natives."

"What kind of advice?" Amy asked.

"We chewed coca leaves and drank coca tea to ward off the altitude sickness."

"And it helped?"

Rian nodded. "That and our porters. We wouldn't have made it without their hospitality and help. Such happy people."

"Must be the coca."

"Must be." Rian grinned.

"So, tell us. What has Officer Ben been up to these days?" Amy asked.

Rian eyed Amy with a scandalous grin. "He's still recuperating."

Amy grinned back. Ben was a handsome guy with a great personality and an even better physique. Even a hard day's hike wouldn't tame the chemistry between he and Rian. "Must be the coca," Amy added.

"Must be," Rian agreed.

"The Big European Tour of Arkansas — Cardboard Cottage style," Zelda said, grinning. "Look out, wine country, here we come!"

Amy laughed at her friend's wholehearted enthusiasm and the raccoons suddenly flashed into her thoughts, their laughter sounding like something from another world.

"*Nach a Mool*," Amy said under her breath.

"There you are with that funny expression, again," Zelda said. "And so and so on."

"Hail Mary," Rian agreed.

CHAPTER EIGHT

Amy recognized the voice on the phone with the first, *hello*.

"This is Pamela. Pamela Duke. Do you remember me?"

How could she forget? She remembered most recently Genna's front page news and her picture. That was only yesterday. But the memory that seared into her thoughts — maybe forever — was the call and the clatter of Pamela's cell phone hitting the floor and spinning out of reach.

"Yes, of course," she said. "Again… I – I am so sorry."

Pamela breathed "*thank you*" heavily into the phone. The fatigue behind the words was almost palatable. How many times had this woman responded to that same condolence? Given his circle of influence and the small town they lived in, this widow cum ex-wife had probably heard it a thousand times already. Here she was adding to the tally.

"I know this sounds like an off the wall call, but I have – well, I have a strange request to make."

"Please," Amy responded. Her heart thumped. "What do you need?"

Hearing Amy's voice, Victor bounced into the room, butted her shin, and chirped his sultry meow. His purr said he wanted her attention, and he wanted it now. She reached down and stroked his soft fur from the top of his head to the tip of his tail in one smooth stroke. He lifted his head for more. Victor leaned his well-fed flank against her leg and then plopped down on her bare feet. He chirped again — *pyrrt pyrrt* – and looked up at her expectantly.

"Now that I need to say it aloud, I realize how strange it will sound."

"Please," Amy soothed. "Tell me what I can do to help."

Victor jumped into her lap and nudged her chin with his nose as if to answer her. She pushed him off, and he stalked off in a huff, his long tail whipping the air with feline disdain. He settled himself on his favorite windowsill two stories above the creek. There, leaning against the glass pane, he hiked his leg like a ballet dancer and began his bathing ritual with undeniable proof of his indifference.

"Donald's death..." Pamela paused, then continued haltingly, "his death was not...well, it may not have happened as we thought at first. Everything about the scene in the hotel said it was self-inflicted. That he had taken an overdose of pills. Even Kirk Waters said so. But now, the police are suggesting this was intentional. That someone intentionally made it look like an overdose. The police are suggesting it was premeditated. A homicide."

Amy regretted her involuntary gasp.

"Yes," Pamela continued. "I had a similar reaction. Because they suspect I had something to do with it."

She sat tensely on the edge of the sofa. The morning sun reached through the kitchen window, a narrowly focused ray making its way through the doorway of her living room, traveling the floor like a search beam. The shaft of light stopped abruptly at the coffee table in front of the couch. It was as if the beam had found what it was seeking. Ordinarily, the room in the sunshine would feel lazy and luxurious. She felt chilled to the bone.

This will come to pass.

Pamela exhaled into the phone. "You helped your friend when everybody thought she killed her husband. I heard about it. You took it upon yourself to find ..." she paused again... "to find the truth. I didn't do this. I can't prove it. Everyone seems to be looking at me with guilty suspicion. You know how word travels in little towns, even when it's not true. You can't say anything you don't want to be repeated."

No kidding. Just like in Bluff Springs. She was aware of how quickly news spread through the grapevine, that tangled, sprawling network of gossip and half-truths. The rumors that Tiddlywinks was somehow involved in the recent death were already making rounds among the other shopkeepers. Someone had noticed the police outside the shop door and the gossip grapevine put two and two together.

"I know you have no reason to help me. I'm not much more than a stranger to you. I breezed into your shop with a horde of friends and left just as quickly. I led chaos to your doorstep, and now I'm back. I need your help…" Pamela paused, "and before it's too late."

"Too late?"

"Don't they always think the wife is guilty? Duke and I said things about each other we shouldn't have. But now…" her voice trailed away.

There was another long silence. Amy could hear Victor smacking his tongue against his fur.

"But you were here at Tiddlywinks."

"Oh, yes, I have an alibi. I was playing dominoes with my best friends at your shop. But that's not going to satisfy them." Her voice dropped. "I went to Duke's hotel room to take Claret for a walk. That's why I was so late getting to Tiddlywinks. We argued." She let out a sigh. "We're always fighting. He said everything was my fault. Everything *he did* was always *my* fault."

Amy could imagine the cold-white rage below the surface. That feeling of being blamed and shamed.

"I told the police I was there. I didn't try to hide it from them. Of course, they knew that already because they saw me on the camera. They saw me leave with Claret. They saw me bring her back to his room. He was sound asleep already, TV blaring as usual. And this all happened right before I went to Tiddlywinks. And I wasn't anywhere else." She paused for moment. "You must know everybody in Bluff Springs. Ask questions. They'll trust you."

"Aren't the police doing that?"

"I don't trust them. The police know I wanted Duke out of my life, and I made no bones about it."

Vamoose! Zelda had said almost the same thing.

"Will you help me? You could start with his business partner. Kirk can tell you what he knows. He's the one who found the bod…" she stumbled over her words again… "He's the one who found him. He's the one who called the paramedics. He tried CPR, but it wasn't —" She dropped her voice again, and Amy pressed the phone closer to her ear. "It wasn't helpful."

She paused again, and Amy wondered what was going through her head. Sorrow. Guilt. Confusion. All of the above. Tick any box.

"Kirk was as surprised by this news. He was convinced it was an overdose. But he can give you details the police won't. He wants to help. If Duke had an enemy, Kirk would know. Let me give you the number."

Amy grabbed a pen and scorecard from the table and jotted down the number. She drew a box around the name.

"I'm sorry to ask, but how did he die? The newspaper never said."

"He was poisoned. There was poison in the wine."

Her thoughts cleared like a cold winter sky, bringing a chill to her skin. Poison in the wine. *I know my wine*, he had said.

She didn't know much about poison except the throat-grabbing gasps she saw portrayed on TV. Poisoning seemed more like an arm's length murder. One that took some planning, some time to think it through; premeditated think-it-through. This crime was not the act of revenge, and it was not the act of impulse. This act was steeped in something darker; the way wine steeps in a barrel in a cellar in the dark. This was someone dangerous and deadly. Amy pictured the woman on the other end of the phone. If she needed an alibi, being with a carload of women would be a pretty good one.

"What changed their opinion about the manner of death?" Amy

asked quietly.

Pamela's pause seemed to go on forever.

"Why would he drug the whole bottle for just one glass?"

* * *

Amy dialed the number the minute the call with Pamela ended.
Kirk Waters' voice message was short and to the point. She left her
message and hung up. If Kirk Waters didn't return her call, maybe
she wouldn't have to get involved. A crime had been committed in
the quiet little town of Bluff Springs and there wasn't much she could
do about that; except trust it wouldn't happen again. She didn't want
to chase after someone devious enough to poison a bottle of wine and
stage the scene like theatre. That might include wives who wanted
their husbands gone and then they were. She felt as if she had been
singled out in the crowd. Not as someone to admire. More like
something separated from the herd. She grabbed Victor and swooped
him to her chest, his fur warm from the sunny window.

"You're always there for me, Victor," she said, kissing his brow.

"Jerp." He butted her chin.

"Time to go to work. Are you coming?"

"Jerp."

Amy slipped down the stairs of her apartment with Victor on her
heels, and out the door that separated her private world from the
other. There were twenty-nine steps that led from her apartment
above the shop to the sidewalk under the curlicue Cardboard Cottage
sign. Today she didn't feel like skipping over the hopscotch grid
painted on the sidewalk at the front door. Nothing seemed to dampen
Victor's spirits. Like a dark Cheshire Cat, he appeared at the shop
door eager to be let inside. She turned the key in the lock, and he
rushed inside with a melodramatic meow that echoed down the hall.

CHAPTER NINE

Amy watched from the front window of Tiddlywinks as an unfamiliar car pulled into the loading zone at the curb. Surprised to see Rian get out of the driver's seat, she looked at the car, then at Rian, and then back at the car. She walked out onto the shaded sidewalk.

"What is that?"

"That is a 1972 AMC Gremlin X. Mint condition. And yes, that is a factory color," Rian answered as if anticipating the question.

"Looks more like a moldy loaf of bread."

"It's called chartreuse. And the Gremlin was the first 'American-built' import. A 'pal to its friends and an ogre to its enemies.' That was long before we knew about Shrek." Rian grinned, making air quotes around the slogan. "I think she should be called Fiona."

Amy grinned. "Obviously, this is for one of your vintage car collectors."

"Not exactly. But it is for a customer of mine." Rian shot Amy a knowing look. Amy suspected the name was in Rian's little black book in that weird code of hers. She had tried to decipher the codes when she went trailing in Zack's footsteps. It was a long shot that had ricocheted. Although Rian claimed she burned the little black book of evidence, that didn't mean she didn't have a backup, nor that she had abandoned her best customers entirely.

"She told me if I found a chartreuse Gremlin in mint condition, she would sell me five acres of Cynthiana grape vine at a rock bottom price."

"A vineyard? What are you up to now?"

Rian folded her arms across her chest, nearly blocking out the letters on her tee-shirt that said, *& don't call me Shirley* on a background that matched the color of the car. Knowing Rian, it was not a coincidence.

"I think Arkansas is ready for cannabis wine," Rian said.

The inside of Amy's mouth puckered. "That doesn't sound very good to me."

"It isn't. Not yet it isn't. So far, it tastes like Kool-Aid-flavored bong water. We're calling it Skunk Wine, but that's just a working title."

"We?"

"Me and Ben."

"Ben? You have a cop making cannabis wine?"

"He's going to tend the vineyard. Already scoping out all the gear and machinery."

"Isn't that a bit far for him to travel to mow the grass?"

Rian stuck her fingers in her pants pocket and leaned against the car. "He bought a hunting cabin outside Ozark. It's a couple of acres and a shack on the Arkansas River. The vineyard is not far from there. He says he's about ready to give up the police force. Too many rules and red tape. He's still getting heat about the helicopter search." Rian grinned. "And all that time you were off hunting Easter bunnies in La La Land."

"Is that what you call it?"

Rian squelched a laugh. "You were pretty loopy on hospital meds."

"I see. When were you going to tell your best friends about this venture?" She was a bit surprised Rian had shared that much. Tight-lipped and private about her affairs of any nature, Rian was not prone to details, solicited or not.

"When it happens. I don't own a vineyard yet and I haven't perfected my wine recipe. But I do have a Gremlin. And I need your help."

Amy walked around the front of the car, peered into the window at the pristine-looking bucket seats, and then walked back to where Rian was standing. "It's in excellent shape."

"She's in amazing shape. Mint condition. The old guy bought it when he got engaged. He had it forty-one years, but now his wife is gone." Rian patted the snub-nosed tail-end. "He claimed he paid a little over two grand when it came off the assembly line. I paid almost twenty. The only problem is that the horn honks when you put on your right-hand turn signal. Not in sync with the blinker, thank goodness, just one short beep. She will have to get used to waving out the window at friends and pretending the honk was intentional."

Amy laughed. "Why a green Gremlin?"

"How did you feel about your first car?" Rian asked. "I know most people think of cars as a piece of metal with an engine and four wheels. But it's so much more than that. Your first car is your first real grasp of freedom."

Amy leaned against the black racing stripes. "I had a gold Oldsmobile Toronado. It was a bat-mobile with flip-up lights, power everything, and an eight-track stereo."

Rian laughed. "Slick. I can see you driving that. It probably weighed five tons and got ten miles to the gallon."

"Probably. And you're right; it was freedom. I remember how it felt when I slid into the driver's seat and cranked up Elton John." She glanced at Rian and smiled. "I bet you listened to Willie Nelson."

"Oh, come on," Rian said. "I was a die-hard Doobie Brothers fan."

"So why do you need my help?"

"I need you to meet me at a rendezvous spot down south and then bring me back here. Ben can't get free, and I'm eager to get this baby delivered and my little vineyard deal settled."

"When do you want to go? I don't want to leave the shop during the day."

"Then how about a midnight drive? It's a full moon on Thursday."

"I'll check my calendar."

"Yeah, you do that." Rian snickered. "You got a hot date or something?"

Amy grinned. "What if I do?"

"A date with a hot fudge sundae, maybe?"

"With sprinkles." Amy laughed. "Okay. We'll do it Thursday. I'll pencil you in."

A city cop car drove by, and Rian reached for the keys in her pocket. The loading zones in Bluff Springs were patrolled like enemy borders. The beat cops seemed to get satisfaction slipping parking tickets onto windshields like landmines. The tickets weren't much – ten bucks – but it was a costly nuisance if you forgot to pay on time.

"I'll be a bit late opening today," Rian called to Amy as she walked to the driver's side door.

"You are already late opening," Amy called back.

"Then I'm going to be even later," Rian said through the open window as she drove off behind the taillights of the squad car. Amy watched until Rian turned in the opposite direction of the police before she went back inside Tiddlywinks. No telling how many people she would wave to on her way home. There were a slew of right hand turns between here and her home.

The phone was ringing when she returned to Tiddlywinks.

"Is this Amy Sparks?" a male voice asked.

"It is."

"This is Kirk Waters," he said in a deep, gravel voice. "CFO. Alpha Wine and Spirits. You called me. Pamela Duke mentioned you. Said you're some kind of psychic eye. I think she meant private eye. Can't imagine how that's going to help her now."

"I'm not either one. And I …"

"I told the police this, and I'll tell you the same," he said, interrupting her. "I run a very tight ship. There's no monkey business at my firm. If Duke had something going on that got him killed, I wasn't part of it.

"Now, if I was the wife, I would want to shimmy out of this, too, but she wouldn't be the first one to get rid of her husband to get even. I can't imagine she liked all the dirt the lawyers dug up. I don't know what she expects to find by hiring you, but my goal is to get the facts in order and wrap this up. I owe the Duke that. He deserves a grand slam funeral and flashy farewell. I plan on making sure he gets it."

He paused, and Amy flipped the laptop lid on the counter and searched images until she found his name and the face she recognized. She studied the picture of him on the Internet. Kirk Waters looked younger in the photo than the man at the conference. In the image, she saw the trim gray beard Gloria mentioned was missing at the conference. It wasn't a Fu Manchu or a goatee, and it was both, yet it was neither. A barber would know the name of the style, but she didn't. He was past middle age, but he was obviously a man who paid attention to his appearance. She remembered him striding across the floor at the conference. She hadn't seen him up close, but he resembled the photo on the screen, other than a few extra pounds around his middle and a clean shave.

"The Duke was my friend aside from being my partner. He could sell the wool off of a sheep in the winter, and he knew more about selling wine than anyone else in Arkansas. He didn't shy away from letting you know that, either. He was never shy. I know we didn't always see eye to eye, but he was willing to admit when he was wrong."

Amy shut the computer lid. She glanced at the only two customers in the shop, studiously bent over a puzzle on the library table. The puzzle was a replica of a Thomas Kinkaid landscape with muted florals they'd been working on for more than an hour. They were still engrossed in the puzzle and Victor was sound asleep in the front window.

"Could you tell me what happened when you got to the scene?

Could you tell me what you saw?"

"He was crumpled over like a heap of sheets. That's what I saw. Propped up in bed as if he was watching TV. The sound was up so loud I couldn't think!"

He cleared his throat, which sounded like a grunt of impatience. "That's when I called 911. I saw him on the bed, and I called for help. I was still doing CPR when the EMTs arrived, but he never gained consciousness. He was already gone."

Kirk paused again. Was this memory making him emotional? She wished she could see his face.

He cleared his throat again and went on.

"When I finally got my senses about me, I saw that pill bottle on the nightstand, and that's when I knew. I knew the Duke had finally done it. The only thing he didn't do was leave a note. But that wasn't his style. Duke didn't write much more than his name to cash a check."

"What was the prescription?"

"Xanax. The bottle was empty."

"You touched it?"

"I touched everything!" He boomed. "Why wouldn't I? I was trying to save him!"

She tried to see the scene in her mind. Did he start CPR and then discover the pills? Or did he call for help and then start CPR? He couldn't do them all at the same time.

"Ms. Sparks!"

"I'm here. I'm listening. I'm trying to imagine what you went through. I know how difficult this must be, but if I am going to help, I need to understand what happened from the very start."

"Haven't you been listening? My best friend died. I am devastated. Just devastated. I can't even keep my thoughts straight. I tried everything to revive him, but the Duke was already gone.

"I told the police it was self-inflicted because that's what it looked like. When I saw the pills, I knew. He'd never be able to live knowing he wasn't the king of the hill people thought he was.

"And that text," he added. "That text said it all. I told the police I knew something wasn't right. I called, but he didn't answer. And that's not like him, either. He always answered his phone. That's why I went to his room. To see what was wrong with him."

"Do you remember what time you received the text?"

Amy pictured him scrolling through his phone. It wouldn't take much scrolling. The text was probably the last one Donald Duke had ever sent.

"It was seven twenty-four on the dot. I got it right here. *'A man's got to do what a man's got to do.'*"

"Isn't that a John Wayne quote?"

"Well, of course, it's a quote. Duke was always pretending to be John Wayne, the cowboy hero. That's what I told 911. I said, 'the Duke has done it. He's taken his own life. He just couldn't take the truth.'"

"Did you dial 911 from your cell phone?"

"I didn't have my cell phone with me. I picked up his phone because it was right there, by the pills, but I don't know his passcode, so I had to call from the room phone. And then I started CPR. I was just too late to save him."

Amy frowned. *Too late. This shall come to pass.*

Not my circus. Not my monkey.

Not my raccoon.

Kirk made a sound that Amy couldn't recognize over the phone, something that sounded a lot like wheezing.

"Now they've got some crazy notion it was homicide! The police won't say why they think such a thing. Won't give me a single solid reason. It's under investigation, they said. Can't divulge information that might be relevant, they said. It sure didn't stop them from asking *me* five thousand questions. You'd think a man of my standing could get more respect than that."

The wheezing was getting louder.

"It was an overdose… and if they think it was something else, they should look to his next of kin." He paused briefly, as if to catch his breath. "You call me if you find out anything important. You call Bethany if you need something else."

Bethany? Who was Bethany? The phone beeped, and the line disconnected before she could ask.

CHAPTER TEN

"Poison in the wine?" Genna bellowed. All eyes within earshot turned to look. The breakfast dishes were piled at the edge of the table, waiting for the waitress to haul them away. They were on their third cup of coffee and second shared cinnamon bun.

"*Ssshh*," Amy whispered. "No one is supposed to know."

"And why do you know?"

"Because Pamela Duke wants my help. She thinks she's going to be arrested."

"Arrested! Why am I just hearing about this now?" Genna set her coffee cup down so hard it splashed the table.

"Because no one can get a word in when you're on your soapbox," Rian grumbled. "You haven't stopped talking politics since we sat down."

"You already knew?" Genna demanded.

"I didn't know," Zelda chimed in. "If that makes you feel any better."

"But that's not what the papers reported," Genna said.

"Pamela claimed the police discovered poison in the wine. Kirk said it was Xanax. He saw the pill bottle. So, whoever did this wanted it look like something other than a homicide, and the most likely suspect is his wife. The authorities already know she went into his hotel room."

Genna looked sideways at Amy. "How do they know that?"

Amy glanced at Rian. "The hotel has security cameras."

"Oh, not again!" Zelda wailed.

Amy agreed with a nod. The foursome's escapade onboard the *Darwinian* was caught on camera, too. They'd almost faced a murder wrap for that cameo appearance.

"Oh, sweet Mary," Genna breathed. "I'm on that footage, too, then. And I'm dragging a blessed case of wine to his door! Room 132 Valley View Lodge!"

"Eww," Zelda said and pushed out her bottom lip. "That's a sticky wicket."

"Sticky and sticking right up my—" Genna stopped as the waitress returned with a pot of coffee. "Okay, this doubles down on our need to know," she continued when the waitress moved off to pour for another table. "Did my candidate get mentioned?"

"Not in my phone call with Pamela Duke," Amy said. "Or my phone call with Kirk Waters."

Genna nodded and poured the cream into her coffee.

"What is it with us and security cameras?" Zelda asked. "Do you think we're being watched right now?"

Rian glanced around the restaurant, then nodded to the corner. A ray-gun-looking thing hung from the ceiling. A little red light said it was doing its job.

"Is there anything else y'all are keeping from me? If you have a secret, now is the time to fess up. I'm not interested in playing twenty questions." The table was quiet for a moment, and Genna looked from face to face, her eyebrows raised in a thin line of expectation. "If you have a secret? Spill it."

Zelda sighed loudly. "I'm the one who took your favorite lipstick. I didn't mean to, but I dropped it on the floor after I accidentally on purpose got it out of your purse the last time we went out for dinner. I would have told you, but I didn't want to give it back broken, and I haven't had time to replace it."

"I am not talking about lipstick. I'm talking about Jerry Glen,

Pamela Duke, the Dead Duke, and anybody else who might have their dirty little noses in our business."

"I think it's the other way around."

Genna glared at Rian.

"I think we have *our* noses in *their* business," Rian said. "We should stay away from Duke and his demise."

Genna shook her head. "Well, we can't."

"Why not?"

"Because I told Jerry Glen about the case of wine and the invoice Duke tried to ram down our throats. You wouldn't believe the price on that invoice! Fifty-thousand dollars! For one case of wine!" Genna's eyes were wide with disbelief. "I asked him what would patch things up enough to turn Duke to friend from a foe. I think I might have told him about the *over my dead body* part."

"Oh, no," Amy said. "What did Villiger say?"

Genna frowned. "He said it would be better for everyone if the Duke was out of the picture altogether."

"And so he is," Zelda said. "This has a familiar ring to it, doesn't it?"

Amy blew out the breath she was holding. "All too familiar."

"I have something to confess," Rian said. "Something Ben told me. He wanted to give us the heads up."

The three friends looked at Rian expectantly.

"The decedent in the hotel room was found clutching a postcard. It was a picture of a *Parcheesi* board."

Amy and Genna exchanged glances. They had dozens of those postcards printed for the conference, and all of them had the Tiddlywinks name in bold print on the front. Poison wine with a *Parcheesi* board. It wouldn't take long for the authorities to come asking questions about how the Cardboard Cottage & Company was involved in the death of Donald Duke.

CHAPTER ELEVEN

Amy drove to the Valley View Lodge and parked in the only shade she could find. She tapped the wheel absently. It was as if she had driven here on autopilot. What was she after? Answers. She knew that much. But to what questions? That was the tricky part. And even more tricky was how she would get them.

As she approached the lobby, she was happy to see a face she knew behind the counter. The two of them didn't know each other all that well, but they had liked each other from the start. It had been over a year since they conversed about cats and causes. In particular, they talked about fostering kittens. They were at a chamber ribbon cutting for the new cat shelter, and Amy wanted to help.

As she petted the cats in the new cat lounge at the chamber event, she realized she'd never be able to give up kittens once they purred their way into her heart. She would have a dozen if she fostered any and Victor was all she could handle. In the end she made a generous donation.

"Hey, Doris, how's it going?" Amy said, greeting the women behind the desk.

"Amy Sparks!" The woman smiled over the rims of her butterscotch-colored glasses.

"How's your menagerie doing?" Doris had cats, dogs, *and* chickens.

"Furry and underfoot," Doris said and laughed. "All except for the kids. They're at a summer camp for two weeks. This must be what a staycation feels like. What are you doing?"

"I've been thinking about creating a ladies getaway game night at Tiddlywinks and I wanted to talk to you about how I could incorporate your hotel." It wasn't a complete lie. She had been thinking along those lines lately.

"What a fun idea. And you want your guests to stay here?"

"I'm not ready to book or anything. I'm looking at my options at this point. Would it be possible to take a tour?"

"We'd love to accommodate your guests!" Doris smiled, and Amy remembered first meeting this generous and warm-hearted person. Amy ignored the pang of guilt. She wasn't just looking for Tiddlywinks ideas; she was snooping.

"What would you like to see first? The suites? The recreation rooms, the pool and hot tub, the...?"

"I know many women travel with their dogs these days. Maybe I should start with the rooms that are pet friendly."

Doris nodded. "I'll show you those first." She turned to the woman working the desk with her. "It's in your hands," she said with an encouraging smile. "I'll be back shortly." The other woman nodded, returning her attention to the family with two kids already dressed for the pool.

Amy followed as they walked through the long hallway, counting the numbers on the door. *Room 132*, Genna had said. She looked behind her for the camera in the corner. It was there and it was blinking.

"Is there only one section that allows pets?"

"Just the one," Doris replied. "This wing has an enclosed grass courtyard behind each room. It was part of the original building back when it was an old roadside motel. We've gone through several upgrades since then, of course."

The room numbers in this section started at 130. There were six rooms, and they were now outside room number 140. Doris opened the door with a key card hanging from a lanyard at her neck.

The suite was hotel perfect. White everything, with a heavy blackout curtain at the courtyard door. The bed was centered in the room, with a night table on either side. A pair of white bathrobes were folded neatly and stacked near the foot of the bed, along with a pair of swim towels with blue stripes.

She smiled at Doris. Nice touch.

A beige push-button phone sat on the nightstand closest to the bathroom, which was to the left of the bed. The TV stood on the dresser, just to the right of the door as they entered.

A table and two gray chairs were placed near the glass door to the courtyard. Amy pulled the curtain aside and peeked outside. A painted concrete block wall about chest high bordered an enclosed grassy spot. The grass was spring green with a few tell-tale yellow-brown patches. A sanitary station stood in one corner and a tiny table with outdoor seating for two sat in the other.

"This is more than other pet-friendly hotels can offer," Doris said. "It's not Taj Mahal, but it's comfy, and we pride ourselves on clean."

Amy nodded. She turned and looked again at the bed and the bedside table.

"Are all the rooms in this wing laid out in the same way?"

As Doris nodded, Amy realized why she had come. She wanted to see the scene for herself. To put an image in her head. She wasn't at the crime scene, but she was seeing its twin. She pictured what Kirk Waters saw when he entered the room that night.

Donald Duke was tumbled over on the bed like a heap of sheets. That's what Kirk said. Did that mean he was on top of the bed covers or under them? Was he dressed in one of the bathrobes or still in his street clothes? She hadn't elicited those details from Kirk Waters. Hadn't thought to.

She looked at the phone on the nightstand where Kirk called for help. She couldn't remember if he said he dialed first or started CPR first. That part of his story was confusing. He saw Duke, he said. He saw the pills. Everything was there, except the note. That wasn't a given in every case, and Kirk had said writing wasn't Duke's style. The text had said all he needed to say.

Glancing around the room one last time, she wondered what evidence the police had uncovered that made them change their perspective. She wished she knew. Was Duke alone or did he have a guest that night? How many glasses were on the table or the nightstand? And had they been used? Had Kirk pulled Duke to the floor to begin CPR? Or was he propped up in bed until the EMTs arrived? Did Duke have luggage? Was he wearing his ten-gallon cowboy hat? And where was Claret while Kirk was rushing around to save his friend and business partner?

Her mind raced. She hadn't thought to ask any of these questions when she had Kirk Waters on the phone. Amy looked at Doris and smiled. She was glad Doris wasn't inside her head. Doris' mind was on booking a suite of rooms for a getaway, not on solving an unfortunate crime.

"What happened to room one thirty-two? I didn't see the number when we passed. It skipped over it in sequence."

Doris looked at her funny, eyeing her over the top of her glasses. "We don't have a room one thirty-two."

"Is it because of the incident?"

"I shouldn't discuss it," Doris said after a nervous pause. "It's against policy." Doris leaned toward Amy. "We'll change the room number when the room is ready," she whispered. "That's a common industry thing — changing the room number. All the hotels do it when they have an unattended death."

"You mean the room is still a crime scene?" Doris shook her head. "No, it's been released by the authorities, but we have to wait on the biohazard cleaning company. They're running behind on their schedule. None of the maids will go near it."

"Is it just sitting empty? Like it was when it happened?"

Doris shook her head. "Now it's filthy with that graphite fingerprint dust. You can't imagine how many fingerprints there are in a hotel room. Even a clean one." She zipped her lips with her fingers. "I never said that. Management has made it clear: keep our mouths shut and our opinions to ourselves."

Amy grinned and Doris pulled the door closed behind them. They were back in the corridor. Amy could hear a dog barking somewhere outside in one of the courtyards.

"They'll find who did this," Doris said with confidence. "They know everybody who went in and out of that room. Even the woman who forgot her key."

Amy stopped walking. "What woman?"

Doris took Amy by the elbow and ushered her to a nearby vending room. "I sat in on a police interview with one of my maids. Her English isn't as good as it could be, and she was worried she'd be blamed for letting the woman in the room. The woman claimed she forgot her key."

"What woman?" Amy repeated.

"*La mujer de cabello plateado.* The woman with the silver hair."

CHAPTER TWELVE

The Miata hugged the curves of the mountain highway beneath a sagging sun. The full moon was already rising behind her. The canopy of trees in the fullness of May broke the light like a strobe, brilliant colors flashing through the dark shapes as she leisurely maneuvered the curves. There was no hurry. Not like the journey she made a little more than a year ago. She *had* been in a hurry then, careless with her speed, daring anything to stop her from reaching Zelda. But it had been too late then. The snippet that had come to her that time was something that already happened. And now even that was a year in the past.

Yanking her wool cap down over her ears, she felt the warmth shield her against the brisk wind and late spring chill. With the convertible's top down, she beheld the vista of the Ozarks Mountains she traveled, cradled by the rocky bluffs on either side. A canopy of trees towered overhead, with the sun setting in one direction and a moon rising in the opposite.

At the stroke of five, she had tallied the day's profits, batched the credit cards, grabbed Victor like a sack of potatoes, and locked the door behind her. In her apartment above the shop, she fed him his evening meal, grabbed her jacket and an apple, and headed out the door. Now, nearly an hour into the drive, she wished she had grabbed more than an apple. Her belly grumbled. The first cafe she saw with a

parking lot full of trucks, she'd swoop in to find some dinner. Mashed
potatoes. Definitely. Maybe some fried chicken. Or pinto beans and
fried potatoes, an Ozark wonder that was so good you could swallow
your tongue to get at the last bean and potato bite. Oh, and a piece of
chocolate cream pie. Or maybe coconut cream. Her belly rumbled
again. Rian could wait.

Rian's directions sounded like a scavenger hunt full of cryptic
clues and old landmarks. She knew her destination was near the wine
capital of Arkansas. That much of the journey was straightforward.
Beyond that, she would follow Rian's directions as well as possible
and hope for the best. Rian said she would be waiting with a bottle of
red and the keys to her new vineyard. Amy wondered what kind of
keys went with a vineyard, but she hadn't asked.

Cannabis wine? Skunk wine, Rian had called it. She laughed out
loud. Rian's dedication to cannabis was lifelong. She wasn't a doper;
she was an elitist. Rian believed in the healing power of cannabis and
its place in medicine. For more than a decade, she had grown some of
the best bud in Arkansas and her clientele were big names with big
pockets and an interest in discretion. Buying and selling vintage cars
was the cover gig. Want a superb high? Want a pristine '65 Chevy?
Rian delivered on both counts. She had a knack.

Amy thought of Rian as an enigma, as cliche as that sounded. She
wasn't so much an introvert as she was cautious about what was said
and to whom. Not like her own chatty mouth that tended to
overshare. Or Genna's high horse and big words, or Zelda's penchant
for glamor and sultry men.

She wondered which came first, Rian's cautious nature or her
clandestine choice of career? Maybe it was as impossible to separate as
a pair of Siamese twins, always connected at the soul. Rian had a
hierarchy to trust: bees, birds, dogs, and coyotes. She knew the people
Rian trusted, really trusted, could be named on the one hand. She was
one of them and proud of it. Genna, Zelda, and Ben counted, too.

But cannabis wine? It seemed way off the track. Was Rian finally
selling out for the yuppie-hippie dollar? The new millennial buzz?

She hoped not. Her allegiance to right and wrong was a beacon in a sea of corruption. Amy depended on that anchor in her life, a steady blink and lodestar that reminded her that some things, like true friendship, were even more substantial than Noah's Ark.

Amy smiled. Rian would scoff at that. "Noah's Ark was a figment of someone's imagination," Rian would say. And then she would cross herself just in case that wasn't true.

The road began to flatten as she came through the last curve around the peak, and she saw the gravel turnoff into a parking lot already full of cars. Sighing with relief, she pulled in and parked beside an old Dodge Ram. The truck had been as shiny as her Miata once, but now it was dingy and covered with road soot. The truck towered over her car like the Jolly Green Giant. *Ho! Ho! Ho!* Dinner was only a waitress away.

Bette Jo's Cafe promised the best-fried chicken you ever ate and to be open every day until eight. The sign was hand lettered and hung a little crooked but read like gospel to Amy. She opened the door and maneuvered to the counter amidst the roar of people talking, the clink of silverware, and the hum of people enjoying good food.

"Hey Hun," the waitress offered as a welcome. Amy settled onto the bar stool at the counter. "Tonight's special is lasagna. Comes with salad and garlic bread. Seven ninety-nine." She smiled. Amy grinned. She had pronounced it *la-zag-nuh.*

"Save room for dessert," the waitress added. "We got five kinds of pie today. Berry, cherry, black apple, chocolate cream, and pecan."

Amy's stomach rumbled. "I'll take the special." She didn't want to be patronizing and say *lasagna*, and she didn't want to say *lazagnuh*, either.

"Ranch or Italian?" *EYE-tal-yun.*

"*Eye-tal-yun*," Amy repeated.

"Good choice," the waitress said and was gone.

Amy spun slightly on the counter stool and inconspicuously, she hoped, looked around the diner. It was full of country folk, families with their kids, working people, some a bit dustier looking than others, but all mannerly and content. She didn't recognize anyone, and there was no reason for her to, so she let the rumble roll over her like a wave. She turned her back to the room just as her dinner arrived.

She was fork-deep into her salad when a name spoken caught her attention.

"I heard Donald Duke was naked as a jaybird," a craggy voice intoned. "Only one reason a man gets naked."

"When he's gonna take a shower," another voice answered with assurance.

"Okay, two reasons," the craggy voice replied with a throaty chuckle. "I guess one will follow the other if you get my meaning."

"He thought he was the cock of the walk, didn't he? Always did. Thought his was somebody special. Took after his daddy in that regard."

"My boy's a rookie on the police force now. Joined right after the first of the year. He's wanted to be in uniform since he was a tike roping cow."

"What is he now? Twenty-five?"

"Thereabouts."

"Is that where you got inside dirt on this thing?"

"Can't say he said much. I heard Duke was selling wine from his cellar before his wife can get to it. That's just mean spirited."

"I wish I had a wine cellar and a pretty wife." The guy chuckled.

"I'm glad I don't," the other one said. "None is more than I can handle. Waters told the police Bonnie was trying to kill him, too. He said they had it all planned out. Drugged the wine. Women are awfully crafty."

"They're dangerous."

"I heard that. Waters is just an angry old bird. I've known Bonnie all my life. She'd enjoy every minute of taking him to the divorce cleaners if she was so inclined."

He called it *dee-vorce*. Amy wanted to match faces with the voices but kept her eyes on her plate and her ears on the exchange between these two gents.

"Naked as a jaybird. One heck of a way to meet your Maker."

They both laughed, sounding a lot like a pair of old crows.

Amy's brow wrinkled. What was Kirk Waters talking about? Had someone tried to poison him too?

"Your mare drop her foal yet?" The crow asked.

"Nope, but she's getting close. The signs are all there. Doc wants to be there, seeing as she's a maiden mare. Foal's gonna be a beauty."

Amy scraped the last of the sauce with the crust of her bread. If she was going to help Genna disentangle Pamela Duke from Jerry Glen, she had to find out more about all the players involved. She needed to find someone with facts willing to part with them. Rian might pump Ben for information if he was in a position to snag a few details from his peers, but he took flak for the last time he shared details he shouldn't have. She didn't want to get Ben into any more trouble.

She paid her bill, over-tipped, and made a quick stop to the restroom before powering up the Miata. Night had fallen while she was in the cafe, and the warm cocoon of the car's cockpit, top up and locked in place, felt as close to home as possible.

Now, glancing at the scribbles on the scrap of paper with only the dashboard lights to illuminate the words, Amy frowned at the improbability. Although the landscape was bathed in moonlight, it didn't help much. The only thing she could see clearly through the windshield was whatever her headlights spotlighted. The rest seemed formless.

Follow the highway until you see the grain silo covered with kudzu, and then turn left on the road just past that, follow it for a mile, and then take the right fork through the cattle grate. Those were Rian's instructions. She had just passed the *Welcome* sign, so she was at least in the right neighborhood. She had not noticed a silo, kudzu vine-covered or not since the sun sank behind the horizon. She dialed Rian's cell and got her voice message.

Now what? If she couldn't follow Rian's directions, and she

couldn't reach Rian by phone, how would she reach Rian at all?

A shape ahead caught her attention. A tall, shadowy cylinder rose from the landscape. She squinted at it. It had to be the silo Rian mentioned. The road veered to the left, and she bounced off the tarmac onto the gravel. She drove. And drove, the car crunching over the grit at a snail's pace. She saw no fork in the road, no cattle grate. No sign of Rian. She drove on. Maybe around this bend ...

Floodlights flashed, illuminating the entire road and beyond. Instinctively shading her eyes from the bright lights, Amy turned into the driveway and stopped. The gate was closed. The arched sign read DD Horse Ranch and Veterinary Hospital, in some tragic cowboy font burned into the wood.

Amy stepped out of the Miata into what seemed like daylight under the floodlights. She pulled at the gate, but it was secured.

Squawk! She heard the radio frequency before she noticed the box on the post.

"This is Doc." *Squawk!* "Who's at the gate?"

"Umm… Amy Sparks. Who is this?"

Squawk! "Who?"

She almost recognized the voice.

"Amy Sparks."

Squawk! "From Bluff Springs?"

"Yes. Is this Doc Dot?" She felt incredulous about her luck.

Squawk! "What in blazing saddles are you doing out here?"

"I think I'm lost."

The gate creaked and swung open. *Squawk!* "You're more than lost. Come up to the house. Follow the road past the barn."

Amy maneuvered her Miata through the gate, the motor whining as it closed behind her. As she followed the road, the floodlights followed her, turning on as the motion caught the sensors. By the time she reached the house, the entire campus was lighted. And then, just as suddenly, the lights went off. Amy stood under the portico of a log cabin, outside a tall double door, with a pair of heavy horse heads for knockers. The door opened just as she reached for the ring.

She recognized the woman immediately. A handsome square jaw and long legs in a pair of flannel PJs with horses galloping head to toe. As Zelda described her, Doc Dot was tall and lanky like a Great Dane.

"Blazing saddles…" She repeated. "You do look lost. Come on in. Are you alone?" She peeked around Amy's shoulder.

Amy nodded and followed her into the great room. Despite the enormous size of the room and the heavy round timbers that framed it, the room felt cozy. The leather furniture and woven rugs looked inviting. A low fire burned in the grate of the fireplace surrounded by flat fieldstone. The TV in the corner was on, with Dr. McDreamy frozen on the screen.

"I'm really sorry," Amy muttered. "But I'm so happy it's you. I can't believe I've stumbled onto your porch steps at night."

"What *are* you doing out here?"

Amy shared her plans to meet Rian and drive her back to Bluff Springs. "She's purchased a vineyard from someone down here. Sold her a Gremlin, too. I don't even know the woman's name. In fact, I don't even know your name. Just Doc Dot."

Dot laughed. "Who needs a last name? I've had so many I can't keep up. I go by Doc Dot well enough, regardless of my marital status. But it was Daniels to start. I was Dottie Daniels, born and raised here in wine country, Arkansas."

Amy smiled. She liked this Dot Daniels with her Horse Ranch and Veterinary Hospital.

"Have you tried to reach your friend by phone?"

"It's not connecting," Amy answered. "She's probably foot-stomping mad by now." She fished her phone from her pocket and dialed Rian's number. It went to voicemail.

"Well, there's not much cell service out here. Maybe I know where your friend is. Give me the directions she gave you."

Amy shared the cryptic clues.

"Oh, yeah. Your friend must be out at Katrina's lower forty. I had heard she was selling off some of that old vineyard she inherited.

There's an old barn out there we used as a clubhouse back when we ran wild as kids. This sounds like the place."

Amy nodded. "Can you tell me how to get there from here?"

"No."

Amy frowned.

Dot smiled as she grabbed a set of keys hanging on a hook made of horseshoes, pulled on a pair of boots standing at the door, stuffing her pajama bottoms into the neck of her boots. "I can't tell you, but I can show you. You follow me in your car, and I'll take you to her."

"That's even better than directions. But are you sure? I'm really taking you out of your way."

"We don't have much choice. You're not going to find this place on your own, even if I give you more directions. It's dark out there even under a full moon."

Amy followed Dot back through the front door. She waited while Dot retrieved her Suburban from the garage stall and followed the taillights down the driveway and out the gate. They backtracked on the blacktop, then turned off onto another dirt road. Amy saw the silo then, the right silo, the one covered in vines. In a matter of minutes, Amy's headlights shone onto Rian, sitting on a bale of hay just inside the open barn door.

Dot hollered out her window, "You think you can find your way out of here?"

Amy nodded. "I can't thank you enough," she called.

"Don't mention it," Dot said, smiling. "You would do the same for me. Us women, we got to stick together no matter what."

No matter what. That statement had baggage. There were a lot of memories she wouldn't have if she didn't have friends who stuck together no matter what. It was baggage worth carrying. Sisterhood was a profound sense of belonging. She wouldn't trade anything for what she had with Rian, Zelda, and Genna.

"Took a wrong turn, did you?" Rian asked, shuffling toward the car. "I was beginning to think I'd have to bunk in the hay in the barn. That wouldn't be so bad, really." Rian tossed the stalk of grass she was chewing to the ground. "Who was that?"

"The Vet from the Six-Pack."

"Who?"

"Pamela Duke's veterinarian friend. She was at Tiddlywinks that night, too."

Rian shook her head. "Small world. You found her and you couldn't find me? Needle in a haystack."

"Actually, I accidentally found her when I couldn't find you. The rest is easy to fill in."

"How come you didn't call me?"

"How come you didn't answer your phone?"

Rian pulled her cell from her jeans jacket pocket. "Oops. I had the ringer turned off. I see you've called me four times. Sorry."

"Jeez, Rian. It's a good thing I found you."

At least Rian couldn't be angry since she was as much at fault for Amy's delay. Amy spread her arms at the landscape in the moonlight.

"This is your new vineyard, huh?"

"And my new barn. That was an unexpected part of the bargain, but the building sits on my acreage, so it's part of the deal. I know it's run down, but hey, a few repairs and whatnot, and I'll have a cannabis wine tasting room out here in the wild. That's a good idea, don't you think?"

"I think people will find their way in and not find their way out." She imagined a carload of yippies having imbibed skunk wine and were now driving so slowly they never would reach the blacktop. "Cannabis wine being part of that picture."

Rian scratched her head. "You know, that is a snag. Maybe I'll add some overnight accommodations. We could build a teepee or a yurt."

Amy laughed. "Who are you, and what have you done with Rian? Are alien abductions commonplace down here?"

Rian chuckled. "Get a new horizon, you get a new vista. It's funny how when your routine gets sidetracked, all kinds of new opportunities tend to show up. I kind of like this new me. I like the new Ben, too."

"The new Ben? What are you talking about?"

"Well, he's broadening his horizons, too."

"Like how?"

"Like maybe he's done being a cop. He says he done filling out forms and following rules."

"Birds of a feather," Amy added.

Rian grinned. "You ready for a moonlit drive home?"

Amy jingled the keys in her hand. "I'm ready to be home, and driving is the only way we're going to get there."

After locking up the barn, which Amy thought ironically funny because of all the holes in the siding, they wound their way back to the blacktop. She followed it for several miles when she heard a thump under the wheel.

"Oh, no! I hope I didn't hit a critter!"

She braked, and the car swerved to the right, the wheel vibrating in her hands. And then came the loud, flapping noise of rubber slapping the road.

CHAPTER THIRTEEN

"A flat tire!" Amy screeched. They stood on the side of the road, knee-high in weeds, and glared at the front right tire. It was more than flat. The tire was emaciated from lack of air.

"I can't believe you don't have a spare!" Rian bellowed. "What woman doesn't have a spare tire in her trunk?"

"You sold me this car, Rian! You should know what's in the trunk, which, as you know, is not much bigger than a breadbox." Amy kicked the tire. It didn't make a difference to the tire, but the aggression made her feel better. "What are we going to do?"

"Walk to town," Rian muttered.

"I have roadside assistance. I can call a tow truck."

"Yeah, and they'll be along about next Tuesday."

"Right."

"Lock her up and let's get to it," Rian said. "You got a flashlight at least?"

Amy nodded, pulled the flashlight from the pocket behind the passenger seat, and flicked it on. Thank goodness it had power left to it. "Here," she said, handing it over. "You lead the way."

Rian grabbed the flashlight and plowed off down the road. Amy grabbed her purse, locked the car, and caught up.

She pulled the cap over her ears and hiked. Be a good sport, she told herself with every footstep. Even though they would not be in this mess otherwise. She would be at home in bed with Victor purring her to sleep after a noisy bath. She would try not to begrudge Rian any of this because Rian had come to her aid and never grumbled, no matter how difficult, dirty, or dangerous the effort.

They walked in silence. The fresh air felt invigorating if she ignored the inconveniences — like a flat tire with no spare and being stranded out of town in the middle of nowhere. The moonlight stroll was pleasant if you took all of that in stride. They had walked a few minutes when a pickup truck pulled in front of them.

"Saw your rig down the road," he said. Amy ventured closer, the smell of stale booze drifting out of the open window. Rian stepped in front of her.

"Would you give us a lift to town?" Rian asked.

He nodded with a toothy grin. "Get in."

"We'll ride in the back," Rian added. "More room."

"Suit yourself."

Amy couldn't tell if he was disappointed or noncommittal. It didn't really matter. She and Rian only hoped for a short, safe ride to get help. If he had other ideas, he gave them up quickly.

They clamored into the cargo bed and settled against the rigid, rusty walls, amidst a flurry of things Amy didn't want to identify. The truck bed smelled like car oil, wood chips, and rain trapped and simmered in the sun. Within minutes on a bumpy, windy ride, the lights of the town square came into view. The driver stopped outside the local watering hole, the only building with OPEN lights still on. *Budweiser. Ultra.* The neon lights flashed in the window.

"Thanks," Rian hollered as she and Amy clamored from the back.

He nodded, tipped the bill of his ball cap, and drove away.

CHAPTER FOURTEEN

"I'm hungry and thirsty," Rian said as she swung open the door and entered. "A beer, a burger, and a bed to sleep in sounds good to me. Your tire won't get fixed until tomorrow when we can hunt down a mechanic. We'll find a motel *after* we get something to eat and drink. At least I have money." She patted a bulging pocket. "She paid for the Gremlin in cash."

"You mean you're walking around with twenty-thousand dollars in your pocket?"

Rian grinned. "Nah, she gave me a thousand for good faith. She'll wire the rest to the bank tomorrow." Rian liked to live dangerously but that much cash would be over the top. Amy sighed and hugged her beer once the mug appeared in front of her.

"Ahhhh," Rian said with a foamy lip. "That's so much better. And things could be worse. They could be better, but at least we won't die of thirst, for thirst is a terrible thing."

Amy grinned and lifted her mug. "Winston Churchill said that."

"Indeed, he did."

"I hope we aren't in the Arkansas version of *Looking for Mr. Goodbar*," Amy said as she glanced around the neon-lit bar. "I feel like I'm in a place that hasn't changed since the 1970s. And neither Diane Keaton nor Tuesday Weld's characters fared very well in that movie. They were both… " Amy drew her finger across her neck.

Rian tipped her head back and laughed. "Honestly, the way your mind works boggles my understanding."

"We studied dark classics in a class in college. I think the professor was trying to tell us something. We're not going anywhere with anyone we don't know. Got it?"

"Oh yeah," Rian agreed with a nod. "Got it."

Amy pulled her phone from her purse and, with her cell battery fading, made the call she'd been dreading.

"Hey, Suzie, it's Amy. I'm sorry I'm calling so late."

"Are you okay? Is anything wrong? "

Amy pressed the phone to her cheek. "I had a flat tire and can't get it fixed until tomorrow. Rian is here, too. I know you're already scheduled to work this weekend, but I need you to handle tomorrow. Are you okay with that?"

"Of course."

"Can you check on Victor, too? He'll wonder where I am and why his dinner wasn't on time. There's a spare key in the cash register."

"Do you want me to feed him tonight? I don't mind going back out."

"Tomorrow morning will be soon enough. I left him with a bowl of crunchy bits. He won't starve; he'll just pout and complain. Keep an eye on him if he goes to the shop with you tomorrow. He gets rebellious when he thinks he's being ignored."

Suzie laughed softly in her ear. "I'll take good care of Victor. Let me know if you need anything else."

"When you see Zelda tomorrow morning, will you let her know what happened? I don't want to call and worry her now, but she likes to panic if she's left out of the loop."

"Count on it. Us girls, we got to stick together."

Amy hung up, satisfied that she had done her duty as a shopkeeper and a pet parent stranded out of town. It wasn't the first time she'd found herself dependent on the kindness of others. She was a believer in the rule of cause and effect. If you put good out in the world, you receive good luck in return. Knock wood, just in case.

She rapped the bar now with her knuckles. There was always room for an accident, a mishap, or a misunderstanding, but most of the time, people were ready to help those willing to help others. It was like the headlight flashing thing when a Miata driver met another Miata on the road. Or the way bikers signed to each other when they passed. Peace. Stay safe. Keep two wheels on the ground. Solidarity in action.

She didn't know why that old movie had popped into her head. She realized there was little resemblance between where they were now and the smoky, drug-drenched bars of the 1980s. They weren't men-crazed women, either. Everybody was looking for something back then; thankfully they had gotten smarter.

She scanned the room again, looking for DNA. Her favorite game of looking for signs of who-is-related-to-who made people-watching enjoyable, no matter where she was. So far, she hadn't seen faces related by the shape of their chin or arch of their brow. Even gestures could be inherited, but she hadn't noticed shared mannerisms among the bar crowd, either.

Her gaze landed on a woman sitting alone at a high-top table. She was probably close to mid-thirty. The woman's hair was piled into a bun on top of her head, with a long hank of hair pulled free on either side of her face to soften the style. She wore a business suit — a white collared shirt open at the neck, and the black jacket was thrown over the back of the chair beside her. The everyday businesswoman's purse — big enough to hold whatever needed to be stuffed into it — sat on the chair seat beside her.

The woman twirled the wine glass with her fingers on the pedestal. She didn't appear to be conjuring the legs of the wine or adding air to the bloom. Instead, she was moving the glass absently, as though she had a lot clouding her mind. Amy recognized the look. And for that moment, the woman looked very familiar, but she couldn't place her. Although her face was partly in shadow, she could see dark shadows beneath her eyes. Maybe she liked using heavy eyeliner.

Dining alone in a bar was lonely business. She might start chatting with this woman if Rian wasn't there and she was alone, too. She might accept a glass of wine if the woman offered, and they might talk about where they were from and what they were doing in this bar in this little town in Arkansas. She loved how southern etiquette allowed for such hospitality.

The woman looked up and smiled at the waitress when her food arrived. The waitress put the plate in front of her, spoke, and then moved away. It was then that Amy recognized her from the conference. When Donald Duke had gathered his pride of hens around him at the social hour, she was one of them. She had looked directly at Pamela and Pamela had suppressed her discomfort with a look of nonchalance.

It will all be over soon enough; Gloria had whispered to Pamela.

The woman poured more wine from the bottle, sipped, unwrapped the silverware, and began to eat. Amy turned back to her beer.

A skinny dude with yesterday's whiskers and what looked like last week's jeans sidled to the bar beside them. "Where you fillies from?" he asked, his voice smooth and southern. "I can tell you're not from here."

Rian swiveled on the stool. "This looked like the place to be to me."

"It's the only place to be. Bet you didn't know you're sitting right where Paris Hilton and her sidekick sat." He grinned. "You remember that TV show, don't cha? It wasn't much of a simple life when they were around. That was funny stuff." He turned and pointed to the table in the back, where two guys were playing pool. "You see that table? That's Alligator Ray's favorite pool table. One of them girls poured bleach all over it just because she got mad. Ray wanted to skin her alive and put her on the wall." He motioned with the bill of his hat to the brick wall where one giant bass, several snake skins, and a set of alligator jaws stretched on the brick wall among the din and dust.

He grinned again. "Those were the days, my friend. Jägermeister and Gator Bite shots. Right here at this bar. Say, you want a Gator Bite?"

"Thanks, but no thanks," Rian said firmly. Amy noticed Rian didn't ask what a Gator Bite was.

"Hey!" The bartender called. "Jimmy, you leave the ladies alone."

"I'm doing nothing but showing them courtesy."

"Move along anyway," the bartender ordered.

He hung his head and shuffled away like an obedient dog.

Amy and Rian exchanged glances. What?! Paris Hilton drank Jägermeister in this bar!

Rian beckoned to the bartender. "Is the kitchen open?"

He shook his head slowly. "Sorry, closed about ten minutes ago."

"We had a flat tire down the road, and have to leave it until morning," Rian added.

"I'll see what I can wrangle," he said, plopping a fresh mug of beer in front of her. "We've got our shift meals coming and it wouldn't hurt to ask the cook to add two more. She won't know the difference. What do you want?"

"Anything your cook wants to feed us," Rian answered. "But a burger would be great."

Amy nodded. "Same for me. And I'll be back in a minute," she whispered to Rian.

On her way to the restroom, she passed the woman and smiled. The woman smiled back. Any kindness was good kindness. Even a smile from a stranger. She paused, wondering if the woman would recognize her from the conference. Should she invite her to join them? The notion passed quickly when the woman returned her focus to the meal in front of her.

At the bathroom sink, Amy dipped wet fingers into her hair, which had gone static under the wool cap. She fluffed her curls with her fingers and wiped a smudge from her cheek. She hoped her Miata would make it through the night without being vandalized. She regretted not calling roadside assistance and staying until they arrived, but Rian put the kibosh on the tow truck idea, and now they were miles away from the scene. A call to roadside service wouldn't solve their dilemma now. She smiled mournfully at the thought of Victor, snug in her lavender-scented bed, hogging the pillow to himself.

As she exited the restroom, she noticed the woman now had a guest at her table. She recognized him, too. It was Kirk Waters. She glanced at Rian — sitting at the bar — and then back at Kirk, but he didn't recognize her. They had never met in person.

She turned to the wall next to their table so she could listen. Looking at the photos hanging on the old bricks, a layer of greasy dust covering the glass frames, she noticed that the photos were bar pics of the Arkansas famous. A big, bearded guy, Alligator Ray she assumed, smiled in the frame with Bill Clinton, another with an aging Glen Campbell. She recognized a young Mary Steenburgen but didn't recognize the others. Judging by their bulk, they had to be pro athletics with names she didn't know. They were probably all from Arkansas.

Out of the corner of her eye, she saw Kirk lean forward slightly, his eyes intent on the target of his attention. His face looked clouded with emotion, and she recognized his deep, clipped tone. This was not a lover's meet up. This was something else. She strained to hear as she studied the photos of Alligator Ray and friends.

"It's not going to happen that way," he said sharply. "I own this business and I call the shots. Villiger doesn't have any power over me. Never has. Never will. The Duke is out of the picture, and you're on your own. You better watch your step, or you may find yourself out of a job, too."

"You can't do that," the woman argued. "He already gave him the money. In cash. We agreed. He said you were all for it."

"I don't know what you're talking about." Kirk leaned back and scratched absently at the stubble on his cheeks and chin. He twirled a highball glass in front of him. It was something dark, like bourbon on ice. "I never agreed to anything, and I never saw any money. You know what I think? I think the Duke pulled a fast one over on you.

So, good luck with that."

Were they talking about Jerry Glen Villiger?

Kirk looked at his watch. "It's pool night and you're cutting into my game time." Glancing at the pool table in the back, his eyes moved and landed briefly on Amy and her heart thumped. He wouldn't recognize her, but he might notice she was listening. Instead, he pulled a leather case from the seat, drained the glass in front of him and stood up. It was definitely Kirk Waters, the beard style she saw from his Internet picture was filling back in. They were so close now she could smell his cologne. He acknowledged her politely with a nod, passing by on his way to the game, the cue stick case swinging at his side.

When she returned to her space at the bar, her burger in a basket was waiting. She could still see the woman reflected in the mirror behind the bartender. Amy watched as she lifted the wine glass and took a sip, and Amy wondered if that was anger in her eyes or fear. It sure wasn't love.

"What's this?" Amy asked as the amber shot appeared in front of her.

Rian grinned. "When in Rome…" She tossed the shot down her throat. "Here's to Paris Hilton!"

Amy laughed. "To Paris." She raised the glass. "Genna should make this a stop on her Big European Tour. Just for a little fun." Jägermeister was thick like syrup, icy cold on the back of her throat, and a hot burn all the way down. She licked her lips and bit into her hamburger, wiping at the catsup ooze.

"*Nach a Mool*," she mumbled around the bite. "Best. Burger. Ever." Rian picked at the French fry bits; her burger eaten in a few bites. Another shot glass appeared, and Jimmy the gossip, now at the end of the bar, waved and grinned, raising a shot of his own.

"Down the hatch!" He called and tossed it back.

"Cheers!" They chimed in unison. The second one went down even easier.

Amy leaned toward Rian and whispered, "Donald Duke's

business partner is here. He's playing pool. We could eavesdrop on his game and see if he says anything interesting."

Rian arched an eyebrow and spun on her stool. "I would be up for a game of pool."

"I want to find out who that woman is, too. I saw her at the conference." Amy glanced in the mirror and motioned with a nod. Rian spun in that direction. "Don't be so obvious. I don't want them to know we're on to them."

"We're on to them?" Rian asked. "What are we on to them for?"

"He mentioned Jerry Glen. And he mentioned something about money. That's all I got."

"Since when?"

"Since when I stood by their table to look at the photos on the wall. They were talking loud enough for me to hear, and Genna's going to want to know about this."

Rian nodded and drained her beer. "I'm on it," she said, and sauntered to the back of the bar to the pool table, garishly lit by a row of pendant lights that hung low from the ceiling. Amy watched as Rian put a bill on the rail of the pool table and smiled at the two players. She couldn't see it from where she sat, but it was probably a hundred dollar bill. Rian couldn't be carrying very many twenties in that wad in her pocket. Not if the Gremlin lady had paid her that grand in cash.

When she glanced in the mirror again, she noticed the woman had yet another visitor at her table. She hadn't seen her enter the bar, but there was Bonnie Waters in a white cowboy hat and a tight pair of jeans. Her hair was loose, falling around her shoulders in bouncy blonde locks. Amy looked for the jellyfish earrings, but round gold hoops had taken their place. Bonnie Waters sat beside the other woman, one arm lightly around her shoulder, as if consoling her in some way. She spoke quietly with her head bowed close. It was a tender advance, and Amy wondered what was being said. Even more curious, who was she?

Grand Central Station on a Thursday night in the wine country.

It must really be the only place in town open. Amy glanced at Rian who was now racking the balls for a game. It was time to make a move.

There were several men at the back of the bar. They were big and burly and loud with laughter. If they weren't waiting on a turn at the table, they were watching those who were. They hummed appreciatively as Rian made a solid shot and the blue striped number twelve slammed into the pocket like magic. She joined the crowd at the pool table, standing beside Jimmy the gossip, who seemed the most innocuous of the bunch.

"Don't let her hustle you," Amy said with a grin at Kirk.

Kirk looked up from his shot and grinned. "That's not going to happen. I haven't lost a game in years. Even beat Ray once. Nobody beats Alligator Ray."

"You play pool?" Jimmy asked Amy.

"I play a better game of badminton."

Jimmy grinned. "Paris Hilton couldn't play either. But that other one — her sidekick? She hustled everybody who put a twenty on the rail for a game. I think the guys played just so they could see her boobs when she leaned over the table." He grinned. "I didn't do that."

Amy rolled her eyes.

Kirk looked up at her and Amy felt her cheeks flush. He didn't seem to welcome chat from the gallery. She wanted to ask him all the questions that popped into her head after she and Doris looked at the hotel room back in Bluff Springs. She wanted to ask why the old crows at the diner had said Duke was naked, when no one else had mentioned that fact. She wanted to know why he didn't think it was something like a heart attack. She wanted to ask what made him think Pamela was guilty, and why he would choose to help her if she was. And what had happened that made him think his wife was in cahoots. Had she tried to poison him, too? She wanted to know what he was talking about with the younger woman with the dark, sad eyes, and how Jerry Glen Villiger fit into this puzzle. She started to speak when she noticed heads turning.

Bonnie Waters walked to the pool table, her hips swinging in her jeans. She heard Jimmy the gossip take a sharp breath of appreciation. Bonnie walked up to her husband, plopped her hat on his head, and cradled his face in her hands. When she kissed him on the lips, the burly boys behind her whistled under their breath. She handed Kirk the cocktail glass, now refilled. He took it in hand, sniffed it, and then set it down on the table without taking a sip. Bonnie eyed one of the men, who jumped up and offered his seat. It was then that Bonnie's eyes landed on Amy. She took a quick breath.

"Amy? Amy Sparks? From Bluff Springs?"

Amy nodded. Kirk's head jerked up from the table. He glared at Amy through the veil of light created by the lamps overhead.

Bonnie slid off the stool. "Dot said you got lost out by the ranch. I figured you'd already be on your way home."

"You know these two?" Kirk looked at Amy and then at Rian and back at Amy.

Bonnie shrugged and her gold hoops jangled against her shoulder. "I can't say I *know* them, but I know who they are."

"What are you doing here?" Kirk's tone was brusque. "Who sent you down here to hound me?"

Before Amy could answer, Rian stepped forward, pool cue in hand. "We came to see Katrina," Rian answered.

"Katrina? What business do you have with *her*."

Amy noticed the vocal slur and so did Rian, who raised a brow. There was a slight hesitation as if Rian was juggling the odds.

"I bought a piece of land from *her*," Rian answered, uncharacteristically. "We're all going to be neighbors."

Kirk narrowed his eyes slightly. Bonnie touched his sleeve. "Won't that be nice?" Bonnie smiled, but there was something not so sweet behind it.

"I'll be coming down here to wine country quite a bit from now on," Rian said, again uncharacteristically. "I'm working on my new label."

Kirk furrowed his brow. "What kind of a label?"

Rian shrugged and focused her aim on the ball, then made a clean shot. "I can't say."

"You can't keep that secret from me. That's not how it works down here. You'll be on my doorstep sooner or later." His smile was smug with confidence. "If your wine's good enough for me to bother with, that is."

Amy grinned. Skunk wine was going to go over big down here. *Not.* At least the local wineries wouldn't see it as competition. Maybe Alpha Wine and Spirits would be an important part of Rian's success down the road, but she was a long way away from that.

Rian took her next shot and missed the pocket by a hair. She looked at Kirk pointedly. "What I meant is that I'm still in the planning stages of the process. But I'm very good at keeping secrets."

Bonnie laughed lightly and glanced at her husband. "Then you don't know Kirk. Nothing gets past him." She reached for the glass she offered him earlier, took a sip before putting it back on the table. "If we're going to be neighbors, you'll have to come out to the ranch and ride with us. Do you ride?"

Amy shook her head and then realized Bonnie was talking to Rian. Rian didn't seem to notice since she was watching Kirk set up his shot, the ball flying into the pocket with a loud *thump*. And then suddenly Kirk was standing beside her. With Bonnie's hat still on his head, he seemed bigger and taller than he looked earlier.

"Mr. Waters," Amy said softly. "I want to ask you about Jerry Glen Villiger's connection to the Duke's. I understand there's some history?"

His back was to her, and it seemed he didn't hear her. His stroke missed its mark by an inch, and he spun on his boot heels to face her, jaw working, fingers tight on the cue stick. "I would have made that shot if you hadn't been yammering in my ear."

Amy felt her eyes widen. She pressed against Jimmy the gossip, who swayed slightly at the shift in weight.

"I know why you're here. I know what's going on," he said and thumped the butt of his cue stick on the toe of his shoe. "If she thinks she can cut me out of her market, she's wrong. Dead wrong. You can tell her I said that."

He turned back and Amy swallowed thickly. What was he talking about? She asked about Jerry Glen and got an earful of Katrina.

He turned to face her once again, his face so close now she could see the new growth whiskers on his chin. He grinned, but there was nothing jolly about it. "And you tell Villiger to keep his nose in his own business. I don't care who he thinks he is."

Amy felt a drop of spittle land on her arm. Out of the corner of her eye, she saw Rian take aim. The cue ball struck the eight ball, which shot past Kirk at dizzying speed, and slammed into the pocket with a loud *whack*. The cue ball struck the rail and bounced over the side, striking the empty glass on the table beside Bonnie. Kirk Waters watched as the glass shattered to the floor. He turned and glared at Rian.

"Look at that," Rian said looking Kirk in the eye. "Game over. You win." Rian smiled, and Amy saw that it, too, wasn't jolly. His face reddened with anger and then in a flash it was gone. He grabbed his cue stick case and walked out of the bar.

Bonnie turned to Rian and smiled. "Good shot for a newcomer." And then she followed her husband out the door.

Rian took the broom and dustpan from the bartender and swept up the glass. "Sorry about that," she muttered.

"Happens all the time," he muttered back.

Amy pressed her hands against her temples. "We need to find a motel."

"Not in this town," the bartender said, as Rian dumped the shards into the trash. "There's only one, and it's shut down for renovations. You'll have to go all the way to the interstate to find one. Don't you know anybody in this town you can bunk with?" He looked around the room.

Amy shook her head. How had they managed to let the evening pass without considering their options? The bartender may have managed to get them fed. But finding them a place to sleep was too much to ask.

His brow creased. "We close at midnight."

Rian frowned. "Can we get a taxi to the interstate?"

The bartender shook his head. "No taxi service here."

Rian looked at Amy and frowned. "Why didn't we ask Bonnie for a ride when we had the chance?"

Amy frowned back. "We didn't tell them why we were here. We never mentioned a flat tire."

The woman was gone from the table when Amy passed again. The bottle of wine was more than half empty, the steak on her plate was mostly uneaten. Amy noticed a business card on the table and palmed it without a second thought. She left the fifty where it lay.

Bethany Keller, the card read. *Sommelier in training, Alpha Wine and Spirits. Drink no wine before its time.* Her cell phone number anchored the bottom of the card.

Sommelier. Another name for wine snob with a pert little bun and boobs. Was this Pamela's competition? Because of the Duke? Or Jerry Glen? It was definitely the name Kirk mentioned on the phone.

"Got any good ideas on where to go?" Rian asked.

Amy palmed the card. "I can't believe I didn't think of this earlier. I have Pamela Duke's phone number. I could call her."

"We don't know Pamela Duke any better than our new friend Jimmy. What makes you think she'd come to our rescue?"

"Because one good turn deserves another," Amy answered. "Pamela asked for *my* help. Can't I ask for hers?"

Rian shrugged. "I'm game if you are. What's the worst that can happen?"

"Don't jinx us!" Amy squeezed her eyes shut. Dirty pillow ticking sprang to mind. And a sweaty little trailer in the woods.

Rian grinned as if she understood. "I was thinking more about having to sleep on a kid's squeaky bunk bed. If that's what we get, I call the top."

CHAPTER FIFTEEN

"You'll want to get your car to Teddy's first thing in the morning," Pamela said as she pulled away from the curb. Alligator Ray's neon blinked in the rear window of the car. "Otherwise, you'll be in town all day. There's not much to do but visit the winery or get a perm. I'll have coffee brewed early, so you can get on your way."

Amy was a little confused about how that would happen since her car was still on the side of the road, and they had no transportation otherwise. But she didn't want to push the hospitality further than she was already. Don't sweat the small stuff, Sparks. Things had a way of falling into place if you didn't stress about it.

Pamela may have been surprised to hear from her, but she came quickly to the rescue. They barely had time to pay their bill and add a healthy tip before Pamela was at the curb, engine running.

"I didn't realize you would be in town," she said, with a curious glance at Amy. "I thought that you would do your — you know, your thing — from afar. Do you use a crystal ball or the Ouija Board to access your psychic powers?"

Amy frowned. Genna had to stop spreading rumors. Amy glanced at Rian, who nodded. "I don't have psychic abilities."

"Oh? Your friend Genna claimed you saw the man with the smoking gun."

"Genna likes to exaggerate."

"Boy, does she," Rian muttered from the back seat.

"So, you don't actually see the..." she hesitated, "you don't see who does what to whom?"

"No." Her mouth tightened. This was not the tête-à-tête she wanted to have.

"Then what do you see?" Pamela glanced over at Amy. The lights from an oncoming car lit up her face briefly.

How could she answer that question? What did she see? They were like B-roll film snipped and dropped to the editing floor. Without the rest of the footage for context, she had no idea where her dreams would lead. As if they led her anywhere. She wasn't psychic. She wasn't a detective. She didn't know anything about crystal balls. Ouija boards were creepy.

"They're just stupid dreams," she answered, surprised by the harsh tone of her voice. She didn't mean to sound cross. "They don't make any more sense than other dreams do," she added.

Except they might actually come true.

"I misunderstood." Pamela turned the car into a driveway and opened the garage with a remote. Was that disappointment in Pamela's voice? Or was it relief? She glanced at her out of the corner of her eye. Pamela's face was impassive in the dark.

"I only have one guest room, but it has two beds. I hope you'll be comfortable enough," she added as the garage door closed behind them. "At least it's not a bunk bed."

Amy turned and grinned at Rian.

They exited the car and entered through the kitchen door. The room was tidy and smelled of lemons and lavender, and then Amy noticed the scented candle burning on the counter. A standard poodle bounded into the room, barked once, and then sat at Pamela's feet, a patient but hopeful look in her eyes. Her fur was a beautiful deep red.

"This is Claret. She won't bite. But she will pester you until you give her what she wants. I hope you're not allergic to dogs or anything."

They both shook their heads.

"Good, because she's allergic to grass. I can't even put her in the yard. She actually gets hives. I've seen her face swell up like a beach ball."

"She's gorgeous," Rian said, reaching a hand for the dog to sniff. "I've never seen a red poodle. I can see how she got her name."

The dog stuck her head under Rian's hand and nudged her fingers for more. She wouldn't have to pester Rian to get her attention. She already had it. She put a paw on Rian's leg. It was covered with a bandage. "Aw… you hurt your paw," Rian said in a voice Amy had never heard out of Rian's mouth. "What happened to you?" She looked at Rian with sappy brown eyes.

Pamela patted her fuzzy head. "She cut her foot on a piece of glass." Pamela frowned. "I think it happened in Bluff Springs, but I didn't notice she was limping until we got home. Doc had to sedate her to get the glass out. It was in pretty deep. Doc gave her a cortisone shot for her hives, too." Pamela looked at her and shrugged. "He must have let her out in the grass for too long. And he knows better."

No one corrected her tense.

Claret looked expectantly at Pamela and then at Rian, her brown eyes asking for more sympathy than she was due.

"Oh, you spoiled thing," Pamela said with affection. She reached into a cookie jar on the counter and pulled out a treat. Claret wagged her tail. She *woofed* once, accepted the biscuit from Pamela's outstretched hand, and cracked it between her teeth. It was gone in one dog-sized bite. She glanced up at Pamela expectantly.

"No more," she said, wagging her finger.

Pamela led them through a living room with a couch and an oversized chair facing the TV. The room looked like a home where a husband had left suddenly, with remnants of another life still hanging in the corners like cobwebs. The large leather chair sat squarely in front of the TV, positioned as if its former occupant had watched many a Razorbacks game and might come back for another. A plaid blanket thrown over the back hid part of a worn spot a back would make after years of laid-back comfort. She couldn't remember how long the two of them had been separated. Pamela had said he had moved out, but he obviously hadn't taken his favorite chair. Glancing at Pamela, Amy noticed how calm Pamela seemed, how unruffled by the circumstances in her life. The husband. The manly worn chair. Or even the uninvited guests standing in her living room. They followed her into the hall.

"There are fresh towels in the guest bath. I can dig out something for you to sleep in if you like. There are toothbrushes under the sink in the bathroom. I get one every time I see the dentist. Use whatever you need."

"Thank you," Amy said, now standing at the door to the bedroom where they would sleep. "We didn't expect this. We're really putting you out."

"Nonsense," Pamela offered as she flipped on the bedside lamp between the twin beds. "You're women in need. Friends needing my help."

Friends. Amy liked the way that sounded. Solidarity in action. Wheels on the ground. Things sure had an odd way of working out. Genna wanted to know why Pamela Duke was in Jerry Glen's political stump tour photos. Pamela wanted to know who killed her husband. In a twist of fate, she was now in the right place to do a little snooping. And by a little snooping, she meant nosing around in other people's business. The thought made her grin.

Amy heard the clatter of Claret's paws on the floor and voices in the background. She glanced at her hostess.

"Tilly and Gloria," Pamela said, anticipating the question. "They can't pass up a party. I told them about your predicament, and Gloria said she'll haul you anywhere you need to go tomorrow."

* * *

They settled in the living room — the five of them and the dog. Rian claimed the leather recliner, and Claret climbed up with her as if that was her favorite chair, too. Amy perched on the round ottoman next to the coffee table covered with magazines and a potpourri bowl. Tilly and Gloria cozied up on the couch, and Tilly put the throw over her tanned bare legs. Pamela sat in the accent chair that viewed the room from the opposite direction. The chair wasn't outside the circle, yet it was distant enough to make Amy feel that Pamela was distancing herself from the room.

"Some guy at the bar was talking about a TV show that starred Paris Hilton," Amy said, making small talk. "Paris and a friend. I didn't know anything about it."

"What was her name, Gloria?" Tilly asked. "Tiny little thing. Smart as a whip."

"Nicole," Gloria answered. "Lionel Richie's daughter. You know, *all night long*," Gloria sang.

Pamela looked sideways at Gloria. "I remember you on a karaoke stage singing that song while well into your bourbon, all night long. Weren't we in Little Rock that weekend?"

"I don't remember that."

"No, you probably don't."

The friends laughed, and Pamela poured a round of wine from a decanter on the table.

Tilly turned to Amy. "You never saw '*The Simple Life*' TV show? You must have been living under a rock."

"I haven't lived in Arkansas long."

"That might explain it," Gloria said.

"Those two girls turned our sleepy old town on its hind feathers," Tilly said. "Best entertainment we've ever had."

Amy sipped her wine. "What was it about?"

"It was supposed to be an experiment to see how two spoiled rich girls adapted to country life. You know, milking cows, hanging laundry, and flipping burgers," Tilly said.

"They were from LA," Pamela interjected. "California LA, not Lower Arkansas."

"Bless their little hearts," Tilly continued, an amused twitching in the corner of her mouth. "They were two pretty little guppies out of water. The things they had to do were just everyday things to us, but it was foreign to them. I'm surprised they even knew how to gas that truck without help."

"That was some pickup truck," Gloria said. "I wanted one just like it."

"How old were you when this was filmed?"

"Old enough to know better," Gloria answered with a grin. "We were still raising kids and kittens. Although, our kids were mostly grown by then."

"I wonder how hard it would be to find that truck," Rian asked. "You think it's still around?"

"Oh heavens, no," Tilly said. "They took it on the road with them for the second season. Dragged an Airstream behind it. They borrowed the truck from Jerry Glen and never gave it back. He was quite smitten with one of them.

"The truck started out blue, and they drove it blue for a while. Then all of a sudden... *Poof!* Barbie Doll Pink! I don't think he wanted it back after that. That pink truck used to mark the road to the winery."

Pamela laughed as if remembering, but Amy wondered if the mention of Jerry Glen smitten with someone else brought her discomfort.

"Paris always sounded like she'd sucked a helium balloon," Pamela said. "I'm sure some of it was staged for TV, but it was funny in a stupid way, and they were both cunning little pranksters."

Gloria nodded. "They worked for just about everybody in town for at least a day or two. Well, if you can call it work. That was part of the show, and they made a mess wherever they went."

"I think the sign was the straw that broke the camel's back," Tilly said and broke into a grin. "I can still see it."

She waved her hands in front of her. "*1/2 PRICE ANAL SALTY WEINER BURGERS.*' In letters as big as you can get on a Sonic drive-through sign." They all roared with laughter. "That politician had just come through town. His name was Weiner. We always wondered if the wording had something to do with him, but that never got addressed."

"*Life is good, wild, and sweet,*" Gloria sang.

"Those two irked a lot of townspeople, but they made friends, too," Tilly continued. "Everybody missed them when they left. Well, except maybe the mayor. And maybe the family they lived with. I don't think they missed them much. Bless their hearts."

"We got to be in the limelight for a year," Pamela added. "The city was supposed to get a new fire station out of it, but they only received a few thousand bucks for all their trouble. Everybody in town got free copies of Season One on DVD. I still have mine somewhere."

"Me too."

Tilly nodded. "And you don't know the half of it," she conspired. "We could tell you stories."

"Before we have more stories we need more wine," Pamela said. "Amy, can you give me a hand? I want to get some wine from the cellar."

Amy followed Pamela to a door that lead off the kitchen. It looked like a pantry door, but when Pamela swung it open and flipped on the light, the hairs on Amy's neck prickled.

"Watch your step," Pamela said and led the way.

The air was clammy cool as it drifted up from the floor below. Amy reached out to brace herself with a hand to the cold, rough stones on the wall to her right. By contrast, the wooden handrail on her left felt smooth to her touch. At the bottom of the stairs, an amber pendant light illuminated the landing. The halo cast over Pamela's head felt eerily familiar. Amy found herself counting the stairs as she descended behind her hostess.

Four, five… a row of pendant lights appeared, each hanging from the ceiling, with long cords and red metal shades. The ceiling of the cellar was the floor above, of course, and the wooden support beams crossed the room at eye level from where she stood on the stair. It was from the beams that the pendant lights hung.

Counting six, seven— she saw the wine racks that now lined the walls. The shelves swallowed two walls like a honeycomb, and bottles filled the shelves like a hive would be filled with bees.

"This is amazing," Amy murmured.

"Extraordinary, isn't it?" Pamela said over her shoulder. "There is wine here from every trip we made to vineyards around the world. France, Spain, Germany, Chile, Argentina."

She turned back toward Amy. The light behind her made a silhouette of her face. "We had not yet made a trip to Africa or Australia. But then, Donald thought their wine industries were still up and coming." Pamela smiled briefly and Amy saw the sadness gathering in her eyes.

Donald's the wine snob. She remembered Pamela's words.

"Those countries are on my bucket-list, too," Amy said, wondering if the look in Pamela's eyes was from a memory or from regret. The hair on her arms tingled as she drew deeper into the room. There was something familiar about the cellar.

When she saw the wine barrel table and the four stools encircling it, she knew why.

She closed her eyes expecting to hear laughter, expecting to see raccoons. But the room was empty of that — no laughter and no raccoons. Just the hum of the pendant lights that illuminated a room full of shadows.

Pamela's footsteps echoed sharply as she approached one of the walls of wine.

"Duke loved his wine collection more than he loved me. I should have seen that from the start, but I didn't. He was very charming, believe it not. He wasn't always so — well — I didn't see it, anyway. I thought he would change. But then, I—" She glanced at Amy without expression. "But then *I* changed. Once you turn that corner in life, you can't go back. Do you agree?"

Amy nodded. She thought of them as blind corners. You never knew what was coming at you from the other side.

As Pamela pulled a bottle from the wall and blew the dust from the label, a thin smile crept across her lips.

"Such irony that Duke loved his wine but could neither taste nor smell it. Honestly, he couldn't tell plum from pineapple." She glanced again at Amy. "I was the one who wrote all the wine tasting notes. I was the one who decided which were the best wines. He invented the origin stories, and I did the tasting. We made a good team — me and Duke. Well, until he joined business with Kirk. And then," Pamela sighed deeply. "And then I was no longer as useful."

She pulled another bottle from the hive. "I wasn't willing to be another object in his collection." She gestured to the bottles. "He counted them, you know. He counted them all the time."

Amy looked at the honeycombs and breathed the damp, still air. A nursery rhyme echoed in her head.

The king is in the counting house, counting out his money.
The Queen is in her parlor eating bread and honey.
And in her royal heart of hearts, she's happy as can be.
Isn't she?
Isn't she?

"He was so angry when I told him I wanted the house, the wine, *and* the dog. It happened fast, too. The papers were ready for his signature three weeks ago." She dropped her eyes. "It doesn't make any difference, now."

She didn't know what to say. Condolences? Congratulations? She couldn't think of anything profound in the damp of the cellar with its eerie light and raccoons chattering in her head.

"Where was he living?"

"At the office, I'm sure. There's a little apartment attached to the building. It's not much, but it comes in handy when they need to overnight a client who's had a little too much fun tasting wines. It's like a French *gîte*. A little shelter for wayward travelers. We're not big on hotels in town, as you found out."

"Did the four of you spend time together? Bonnie and Kirk and you and Duke?"

"We used to. Especially when social events called for husbands and their wives. We attended fundraisers all over the state. Alpha Wine and Spirts is a well appreciated sponsor. Charities raise a lot of money that way. A good bottle of wine is a good investment."

She sounded as if she was quoting a wine sales brochure.

"We would spend a couple of days, and Bonnie would shop. Bonnie is *always* shopping." Pamela smiled as if remembering, and Amy realized the life the Dukes lived was nothing like hers. They were socialites because of their business, and every opportunity to meet and greet was a chance to do business. Big money business, probably. The conference in Bluff Springs had been a monumental opportunity for her, but it was just another day in the life of Alpha Wine and Spirits, et al.

"Now, Bonnie spends most of her time at the ranch with Dot," Pamela added with a sigh. "I can't say I blame her. I haven't been much fun lately. I'm focused on other things, other passions."

"Oh? Is it something you can talk about?"

"No, not yet," Pamela answered quickly. "But it won't be long before we can share the big news." Pamela pulled another bottle from the comb. "This will do. Here, take this one." She held the bottle for Amy to grasp. "A special wine for a special occasion. I can't remember the last time I had company."

Stepping toward her, Amy felt something crunch under her foot, and kicked at the pebble with the toe of her sneaker.

"I hope this wine is not corked," Pamela said. "That would be a shame."

"What does that mean, *corked?*"

"It means the wine is tainted. And tainted wine smells awful."

Amy shuddered. *Don't mind him; he's corked,* one of the raccoons had said. It was a high-pitched falsetto, like a voice altered by helium. Amy shuddered again.

"It's chilly down here, isn't it?" She was watching Amy with dark eyes. "It's always cold down here in the cellar."

This will come to pass, Amy heard in her head. She knew Grandmother Ollie was right. She didn't want to admit it, but she was standing in the cellar of her dream.

* * *

"Tilly was just telling me about the doctor who was murdered in Ozark," Rian said as she and Pamela returned to the living room. "That's only a few miles from here."

Amy shivered and glanced at Pamela. Her face was flushed from the climb but serene. She blew the dust from the bottle and then wiped the label and foil with the tail of her shirt. Her eyes were dark, and Amy couldn't see her expression as she looked at the wine label in her hands. Was she entranced by the wine? Or was she thinking of her husband — soon-to-be ex-husband, now deceased husband — whose final exit was with a glass of wine? It was impossible to know.

Amy turned her attention away as Tilly continued with her tale. "No, the doctor was from Ozark. She met her end in Fort Smith but was found in Alabama. It was sad and horrible. It was a humdinger of a story."

Amy glanced again at Pamela, wondering why this topic wasn't uncomfortable. She felt a little uncomfortable herself.

"I was the court reporter for that case," Pamela said. Her voice had a faraway quality as if remembering another time. "It was one of the first cases I was assigned. I was petrified I would screw up, and that screwball would go free. He was such a low-life thug."

The cork made a pleasant pop as she pulled it from the bottle. She sniffed the wine cork and, seemingly satisfied, put the bottle on the table. "This one needs a few minutes to breathe."

"We tried so hard to get you to spill the scoop on that case," Gloria said. "You had all the details as the stenographer, but you wouldn't tell us anything the papers didn't report."

"I couldn't," Pamela declared. "If anything got leaked, they could call a mistrial." She paused as if remembering. "He never did take the stand. No one ever explained how he did it, not in the courtroom, anyway. Everyone had a theory, of course, but he never copped to any of them. To this day, we don't know what happened other than greed gone wrong. Isn't it always about greed?"

Amy's eyes widened. Why wasn't this topic taboo?

"Well, I'm not saying the good doctor deserved to die, but her greed got her in trouble in the first place," Gloria said. "May God rest her soul."

"Oh, she knew it was a money laundering scheme from the start," Tilly added. "She thought she was going to turn one million dollars into three. If somebody says they have the Midas touch, but they need a suitcase of cash to make it happen, you're both gullible and greedy."

"The world is full of robbing bandits," Gloria said. "It's a good thing we've got each other. We're always going to watch each other's back."

All this talk about murders and money laundering, and no one seemed bothered by the murder sitting right under their noses. Someone had put a drug in a bottle and given it to Donald Duke. Unless he was vengeful enough to plot his own death and take his wife out in the process, somebody had a secret they didn't want to be disclosed.

Greed? Revenge? Amy looked at the three friends. How far would they go to help a friend through a difficult divorce? She had been willing to do a lot to help her friend get through one. And then Zelda's marriage ended in what looked like a premeditated death.

Poison in the wine was definitely premeditated.

Amy glanced at Rian. She was aching to tell her about the cellar. Amy hadn't told her friends about the raccoon snippet, but the minute she and Rian were out of earshot, she was going to unload.

Pamela disappeared for a moment, and when she returned, she held a tray with five wine glasses. She set the tray on the table in front of her. "This wine deserves a fresh glass if we're going to be proper about it. This is a French burgundy from Francois LeClerc, a highly respected name in a little wine mecca called *Gevrey-Chambertin*.

Donald and I visited there early in our travels in the *Côte-d'Or* department in the *Bourgogne-Franche-Comté* region of Northeastern France."

Her pronunciation sounded competent. Maybe her husband hadn't been the only wine snob in the family.

"It was a little touristy, but we liked it. That year was an excellent vintage. The weather in the vineyard was perfect."

She paused and then began to pour. No one cheered or clinked glasses. It didn't seem proper, even though the rest of the presentation was. Pamela breathed the wine and sighed. Swirling the glass in her hand, she admired it — the color, the legs, the whatever she was looking for. Amy could see Pamela appreciated the vintage, while the rest of her guests seemed clueless. Amy held her breath as Pamela brought the glass to her lips.

Pamela smiled, briefly, the globe held aloft in her hand. "Yes, that was quite a year." The light of the lamp was behind her, putting her face in shadow, but Amy could see the smile lingering.

La mujer de cabello plateado. The woman with the silver hair.

What had this woman done?

CHAPTER SIXTEEN

"I'm grateful you're here to help," Gloria declared, her hands gripping the steering wheel of her Cadillac Escalade. She had volunteered to come back for them and take them to the mechanic in town right after coffee. Pamela apologized, but she was busy. Rian's eyes glassed over when she saw the Cadillac SUV.

"A hundred grand, easy," Rian quipped as the doors unlocked, and they climbed into plush leather seats. Rian would admire the car from her viewpoint in the back.

They had stayed up later than she thought they would, but she was entranced by their stories. It was well past midnight before they knew it. They had enjoyed two excellent bottles of wine — and she was glad she had nowhere to go but down the hall. Her bones felt like weights as she dragged herself to bed.

"We didn't talk about it last night, but it's not often your best friend is the target of a *homicide investigation*," Gloria said with emphasis. "I know they are only doing their jobs – but they're not even talking to that two-bit-bun who hung on every word Duke said. That's who they should be asking for an alibi. She's the one who needs to be answering questions. But, no, they have their eyes on Pamela, even though she had a rock-solid alibi. There's a bunch of us who can vouch for her whereabouts. The police told her they thought her alibi was thin."

"Thin?" Amy asked. "There were sixteen of us at Tiddlywinks!"

"They say that stuff could have been added to the bottle at any time. The whole state of Arkansas was in Bluff Springs that day. A lot of people could have had the opportunity." She glanced at Amy over her shades. "I won't say everyone had a motive. That would be unkind." She smiled sweetly.

"I'm beginning to think Duke had enemies."

"I'd say he had at least one."

She had to agree, except you didn't always know who your enemies were until they came out of hiding. On Zelda's birthday cruise, she misjudged many of the people she met onboard. She trusted others she shouldn't have and believed one lie right after another. That was the thing about people hiding secrets; just about everybody had one. People would go out of their way to cover their dark truths. Some would kill to keep them hidden. Had that happened here? Had Donald known a secret that got him killed?

"I know it doesn't help that they were going through a divorce," Gloria added. "If you've ever been in that position, then you know it's clearly motive for murder. I've always said that marriage brings out the bridezilla at both ends — before the wedding and during the divorce."

"It wasn't amicable, I take it?"

Gloria laughed and pounded the steering wheel with her fingers. "Amicable. That's funny. Chad, my husband, said Donald had a lot to say at one of their meetups about Pamela being out for blood and money."

"Are they part of a club or something?"

"You could say that. Some local doctors have a wine investment club that Donald and Kirk started. Every month they get together and drink wine. They get tips on what to buy for investment and which ones to drink." Gloria laughed again. "They call themselves the Cork Docs."

Amy laughed. Rian, seemingly still star-struck in the back seat, snickered. "Cork Docs. That's funny."

"Are there any women doctors in the club?"

"I don't know any woman who would want to hang out with these geeks. It's a grown up frat party. They drink wine, smoke cigars, and talk sports. Dot is not even interested."

"Did any of the Cork Docs have a problem with Donald Duke?"

"You mean, did any of them want to get rid of him?" Gloria was silent, as if guilt among the Cork Docs had just entered her mind.

"Well," she said after some time, "I don't know. Hank told Chad he was starting a Cork Jocks club because Duke wouldn't let him in the club. I don't think there are enough jocks in town willing to give up beer for a fancy bottle of wine."

"Were Donald and Hank close? They came to the social hour together."

"Good Lord," Gloria sputtered. "Close like fly and a fly swatter. Neither one of them thought their you-know-what stinks. They tolerated each other because they were men of influence. Hank has always had a soft spot for Pamela. I don't think he ever got over his high school crush."

"A crush on who?"

"On Pamela."

Amy sat back against the seat. She looked at the hills rolling by the car, the countryside dotted by hay bales and cows, and twisted grapevines lined up in rows. It was a beautiful part of the state, a sandy loam riverbed protected by the Ozark Mountains to the north and the Ouachita Mountains to the south. The Choctaw named the Ouachita for the buffalo that roamed there in another millennium. Now, if there were any buffalo left, they were on somebody's farm awaiting the same fate as cattle.

"What is Pamela's relationship with Jerry Glen?" Nothing like shooting from the hip when you aim for the heart of the matter.

Gloria took a sharp breath. "Are you asking me what I think you're asking?"

"Am I?"

"He wasn't the reason Pamela and Donald were over, if that's what you're implying."

"My friend Genna is running Jerry Glen's media campaign. In every newspaper photo of Villiger, Pamela is by his side."

"Oh," Gloria said and gripped the wheel with both hands. "I hadn't noticed." After a moment, she added. "You know Jerry Glen is my cousin."

"I remember him calling you cousin."

"And Pamela is my friend." She glanced at Amy, who nodded. "Then you know I can't say anything about that." Gloria turned and looked straight ahead.

Amy felt the disappointment in her gut. It was risky to ask such a bold question, but it seemed worth taking. Now, not so much. It could be challenging to gain Gloria's trust again if she thought Amy was fishing for a big lie with Pamela on the hook. She wanted to hear more about Jerry Glen.

"Genna's concerned that the person of interest in the investigation — and the victim's wife –- is also involved with her candidate. Genna's trying to make sure everybody looks good."

Amy glanced back at Rian, sitting quietly, not missing a word.

Gloria turned and faced Amy. "Let me tell you this: Pamela defended Donald at every turn, whether he deserved it or not. Duke liked power. And even though he was a country cowboy with too much starch in his jeans, he was still a man of standing in this part of the world. Pamela has always been a faithful wife. As my witness," Gloria added and touched the cross at her neck.

"When she said, *I do*, she did. And no one can say she was anything other than dutiful. She and Jerry Glen have been friends all their lives, but when he went off to college and left her behind, that was it. She moved on."

Wow. That put a stop to her query. She couldn't refute testimony like that.

"Do you know why Duke had such animosity toward Jerry Glen? He told me himself he wouldn't vote for him. Did it go both ways?"

Gloria shook her head. "Boys will be boys. Their feud has been long standing, but something happened about a year ago that refueled their dislike for each other. Or maybe it's more distrust. It was about the same time that Bethany showed up. She'd been away for a while."

"Bethany Keller? The sommelier?"

"How do you know Bethany?"

"I don't. Not, really. She was at the conference in Bluff Springs. I have her card." No need to expound on how that came to be.

"Well, if you have that you know all you need to know. She's after what Duke has. She wants the same bright spotlight that he's taken a lifetime to build. She follows him around like a lost puppy, all droopy-eyed and eager for any sign of affection."

"And how does Pamela feel about that?"

"You'd have to ask her. But if you ask me, she's playing Kirk and Duke against each other for a slice of the pie."

"Is that a bad thing?"

"It is if you're Pamela Duke, because she's in the middle of that pie."

Gloria braked quickly and Amy braced herself against the dash. Somebody begrudged Donald Duke because someone put the poison in his wine. His faithful wife? A candidate with a grudge? The sommelier with ambition? The pieces of this puzzle were still packed tightly in the box. She wanted to shake them out.

"I've talked to the business partner," Amy volunteered. "I was curious why he didn't think it was heart attack."

"Kirk gave you his minute by minute details, did he?"

"You mean about calling for help or his attempt at CPR?"

"He was beyond saving. May God rest his soul." She touched the cross at her neck. "Is that all you got from Kirk? He wrote it all down for the police. Bonnie sent us a copy and I've looked at it so many times, I have it memorized.

"At six fifty on the dot he called to discuss a business matter with Duke but didn't get an answer. At 7:24 he got a text. At 7:40 he went to Duke's room. And that's when called for help."

"That's very specific information."

"That's a bean counter for you. They cross every t and dot every i, or whatever the accountants do. Kirk is nothing if not specific."

"Did he mention that Duke was — uhm, naked when he found him?"

Gloria gasped. "Naked? Whoever said such a thing?"

"Two guys I overheard in restaurant. I guess they were mistaken. Did Kirk say what time the EMTs got there?"

"No, I don't think he said."

"Did he say if he moved the body to start CPR?"

"I don't think he mentioned that, either." She glanced at Amy and shrugged.

"It's a good thing Kirk didn't grab the wine and chug it himself or we'd have two deaths on our hands. I would certainly start chugging the wine if I came upon something like that."

Amy glanced at Gloria. Probably not. More likely, she'd be chucking her last meal in the grass. People imagined themselves responding quite differently in an emergency than they do when it happens. She had bumped into a body on the birthday cruise, and it had sent her to the rail.

"It made sense to him at the time, especially after Duke sent the text. He was fond of quoting John Wayne, you know."

Amy nodded.

She remembered when Pamela got the message at Tiddlywinks. She was relieved when Pamela ignored the call, stuffing it into her purse without responding. Only because she was eager to get the game started without delay.

She wondered how Pamela felt about it, now. If her husband's last text on earth was an SOS of some kind, it hadn't worked. If he was looking for sympathy, he hadn't found that either. Pamela had appeared ambivalent, if not a little perturbed by the interruption.

A thought wriggled in her brain, like smoke circling a spent match.

"It was an apology of sorts, but I've never heard Duke apologize for anything. There's always a first time." Gloria shrugged and glanced over at Amy. "I guess we'll never know."

Gloria wrung the wheel with fingers full of diamonds and rubies and sapphires. She had teased about Bonnie Waters about her bling, but she wasn't that far behind on glitz. Amy glanced at her face, at the taught, smooth skin and sculpted jawline. Lifted brows and eyelids made her look surprised, as if frozen in mid-life amusement. She looked flawless even after a slumber party with too much wine and talk of greed. There was much to be said for modern medicine and a skilled cosmetic surgeon.

"You're in luck," Gloria said as they pulled to the garage on the square. "It looks like Teddy's in early today."

"We appreciate the ride," Rian said, opening the door. "A really sweet ride." She patted the seat appreciatively.

Gloria smiled her Goldilocks smile. Not too many wrinkles, just the right amount. The perfect face for the ideal life. Another thought wriggled its way to the surface. What about the perfect crime? It was not out of the question. Pamela now had it all: the house, the wine… and the dog.

* * *

It turned out that Teddy had his own tow truck. Within minutes of arriving at the mechanic's grungy shop, the Miata was up on the lift in the garage bay.

"Punctured tire," he said.

No kidding, she wanted to respond but didn't.

"I know right where you've been."

"Pardon?"

"I said…"

"I heard what you said," Amy interrupted, suddenly cross at her predicament, "I just don't know what you mean by that."

Teddy smiled, and she was reminded of Clayton and his ruddy cheeks and friendly blue eyes. Unlike Clayton, whose nickname was Two Ton, Teddy was a stick in a pair of baggy gray coveralls. They were dark enough to hide most of the grease and grime.

"You were at Doc Dot's ranch," Teddy said.

Amy's eyes widened. "How do you know that? Did you see me?"

He shook his head. "Don't have to. Look at this." He held a piece of stone pinched in his fingers. "This is Bigfork chert and planerite. There's only one place around here that has this rock. See those sharp edges? It'll pop a tire if you strike it wrong. And these are not off-road tires you got on your little Miata."

He said *Mee-at-uh.*

She shook her head. "I still don't get it."

"Her entire driveway is full of this. It's cheap, hard, and doesn't throw dust. It was one of her husband's harebrained ideas. He thought it would be better for the potholes and cheaper than asphalt. Turns out it ain't good for either. You'd think she'd be inclined to have it removed and replaced — just like that last husband — but she says it's easier to buy new tires.

"Okay, by me. It's how I make a living. In fact, I changed the back tire on Bonnie Waters' car a few weeks ago. Her husband brought it on the spare. I knew she'd been out riding with Doc."

Amy accepted the rock from his fingers. It was sharp and hard. There were little flecks of blueish green in the stone.

"It's a pretty rock in the driveway," Teddy said, "and it's durable, I'll say that. But it sure chews up tires."

He glanced at her sideways. "Here's the other thing I have to tell ya. I don't have this tire in stock. I can have it here by the afternoon. Maybe a little after lunch."

Amy blew out her breath.

"You can wait in the shop, of course, but if I were you, I'd head for an early lunch at the winery. It's a short walk from here. Up the hill, there." He motioned, and Amy saw the signs directing tourists to the winery, tours, and restaurant. All things to all tourists stuck in wine country on a sunny day.

Rian was sitting in the sunshine on a park bench in the square, waiting for Amy. "I didn't realize this was going to be such an ordeal when I asked you to drive down," she said, as Amy joined her on the bench. "I had in mind a quick trip down and a quick trip back under a bright, moonlit sky."

Rian crossed her ankle over her knee. Her jeans were cuffed above her sneakers, and she had buttoned her buffalo plaid shirt against the cool morning air. They had taken showers at Pamela's but then put on yesterday's clothes. It wasn't ideal, but she had had much worse. By afternoon they would be on their way home to fresh clothes.

"He doesn't have your tire in stock, right?"

"Right. It will be here after lunch."

"I figured as much. We'll buy you a spare and finagle that baby into your trunk when we get home. I can't believe I sold you a car without a donut."

Amy didn't respond. Although always quiet and watchful, Rian had been less subdued than usual this morning. Maybe she would share what was kicking around in her mind. She didn't wonder long.

"It's not our business, and we have no reason to stick our noses in it. Except..."

"Except what," Amy said when Rian didn't finish her sentence and some time had passed.

"I can't get your snippet out of my head. I almost wish you hadn't told me. But then, I understand why you did. Like you said, you saw it in your dream. What if the raccoons represent the Six-Pack? What if they really did set up their trip to Tiddlywinks as an alibi to set this crime in motion? What if it was planned from top to bottom? That means they used us for the crime, and I don't appreciate that."

Rian uncrossed her leg. "I can't shake the feeling we're being played. Even now. As if someone is pulling strings in the background."

Amy nodded. "I don't know about strings, but the Six-Pack has my attention. This feels like *Deja vu*."

"You did go off on a wild goose chase when you thought we were guilty of murder," Rian chuckled and shook her head. "But really, it could have happened."

Amy showed her surprise.

"I'm only saying it *could* have. And that means the Six-Pack *could* have plotted this, too."

"But we shouldn't get involved. Right? It's none of our business. That's what you said to Genna."

Rian didn't answer, but Amy wasn't offended. It was Rian's way. She looked around the quaint little square where they were passing the time. It was typical old Arkansas. Four streets squared off a plot of land made into a park. There was a gazebo big enough for a band, with wooden benches set in an arc on one side. The oak trees were ancient and covered the park in dappled shade. A sidewalk led to a fountain where water trickled out a maiden's concrete pitcher of what Amy could only assume was sacramental wine. The statue, in her mossy laden robes, stood on a pillow of grapes.

Amy turned back to Rian. "I don't know how *not* to get involved," she said pointedly. "I'm tired of Genna calling me a psycho-detective, a mind reader, and whatever else she's spreading around the state. The truth is I *did* have a snippet. And it *was* about that cellar. A man *is* gone, and Genna is involved." Amy exhaled loudly. "If I don't do anything, I'll feel guilty. If I get involved, I feel like a voyeur. Like a creepy nightmare peeping Amy."

Rian grinned and slapped her hand on her knee. "Sometimes you have to stand up for what you believe in, even when it's not popular with your friends.

"If you want to hunt down the killers who show up in your dreams, do it. If you want to prove Genna wrong, do it. There's no sense pinning for something you *could* do and chose *not* to do. There's no shame in following your passion, your faith, or whatever else you believe in. Regret is for sissies."

Amy cocked her head at Rian and grinned — the words echoing in her head like the voice of a prophet. Rian had always danced to the beat of her own drum, and she was no worse for it.

"You're right! This happened on our doorstep. I *am* involved and I want to find out who killed Donald Duke. I do want to see justice prevail. And I need to put those crazy, laughing raccoons out of my head once and for all. I want to know that I did what I could."

Rian smiled warmly, brown eyes sparkling in the sunlight. "I knew you had it in you, Sparks."

"I want to know what kind of poison it was and how it got in the wine. Was it your everyday ordinary husband-killing rat poison? Or was it the prescription Kirk saw on the bottle?"

Rian leaned over and straightened her shoelaces, pulling sticker burrs from their walk on the side of the road. "You can assume the police know all of that by now. But if Pamela is their primary suspect, and they haven't arrested her, then they either don't have evidence, or they can't connect her to the crime anywhere but in their vivid imaginations."

She understood imagination. She had conjured all kinds of circumstances in her mind when she was digging through Zelda's house looking for clues. That had been last year. She had invented another reality when she saw Andrew with narco-assets on the ship. That had been last October. As it turned out, neither of her suppositions were anywhere close to a truth.

"How would we find out what the police know?"

"I shouldn't get in the habit of calling on Ben to snoop for us," Rian said, looking at Amy.

"It's not right to ask him to cross enemy lines every time we bump into in a murder. But maybe he'll overhear something he can share. He will be down here working on the cabin, so he will be in the places cops tend to hang out. I'll ask him to keep his ears open."

"That reminds me. I overheard something when I was in the diner yesterday," Amy said. "A couple of guys were talking about Donald Duke. They mentioned he was having money trouble."

Rian nodded. "See? Small town. Gossip grapevine."

"Speaking of grapes, let's go sample. The winery has a restaurant, too. It's a short walk, and you're buying," Amy added.

"But I paid for everything last night!"

"And you're buying again today. I had to spring for a tire and the tow charge, and I wouldn't be here if not for you!" And smiled to let Rian know she wasn't angry about it. Rian whistled softly as the two headed up the hill toward the winery. There was no Barbie Doll pink truck marking the way.

CHAPTER SEVENTEEN

Amy scarfed her caprese salad like she hadn't eaten in week. She glanced at Rian's plate and the crumbs left of her grilled cheese. Rian had been hungry, too.

"Another gorgeous day in wine country," Rian said, yawning. "Is the garage going to call you when you car's ready? It's going to take a while."

Amy nodded and Rian leaned back and inhaled the scenery before them. They were on the deck of the winery restaurant with a vista view of the vineyards, green mountains in the distance. The leaves on the grape canes were full, and the bumblebees buzzed in and out of the cover crops blooming at the base of the vines. The sky was cerulean blue, with white clouds high and drifting. They sat in the quiet, the rhythmic drone of the fans overhead and the buzz of the bees in the vineyard.

"I think I'll build a deck on the back of my new barn," Rian said. "I have a view like this one. I wouldn't mind sitting in the shade watching grapes grow."

"Are you going to move here?" Amy asked. "Give up your little cabin on the pond in Bluff Springs."

"Nah," Rian muttered. "I like where I live. Nothing wrong with having a place to escape to when you want."

Amy agreed. Maybe Rian would let her friends escape with her now and again, too. Amy pulled out the card she had swiped off the table at the bar and straightened the corners where it had gotten crumpled in her pocket.

"We should find this Bethany Keller again," she said. "I have questions."

"I bet you do." Rian grinned. "You think she's involved?"

"I know she's involved; we just need to dig a little deeper. Gloria wasn't flattering at all when she called her a two-bit-bun this morning. She mentioned something about a feud between Jerry Glen and Duke, and I gather Pamela thinks Bethany and Duke had something on the side and didn't like it."

Rian ate the garnish from her plate. "Is there an address on that card? We could stop in for a surprise visit. I know Waters would *love* to see us again." Rian grinned. "Well, probably not."

Amy nodded. "I'll ask for directions."

"I'll ask for directions," Rian countered. "You tend to get lost in a paper bag."

"I'll have you know I've never been lost in a paper bag, thank you very much."

Rian chuckled as she meandered through the maze of empty chairs to find someone local. She was only gone a few seconds. "Guess what? It's right up the road."

"You're kidding."

"Not kidding. We can't miss it. It's a wooden warehouse with a great big A painted on the side."

A is for Alpha. How quaint. That sure fit the egos of its owners.

The road looked like it went straight uphill, and Rian took off at a brisk pace. Amy hustled to keep up. The road was paved, but narrow, and the trees on either side had overgrown the road so much that they made a tunnel of branches. It was like walking in a fairytale. The road wound through the countryside just above the town, and it wasn't long before they passed a lone church on the top of the ridge. The church was made of native stone, with a bell tower that rose far above the trees like a beacon. They passed a graveyard at the back of the church property, and then the trees overtook their view once again. Every now and again the sky broke through the branches, letting in enough sunlight to splash the road in wide ribbons.

"I thought you said it was right up the road," she said breathlessly after a few minutes, her legs beginning to tire.

"*Up* was the operative word," Rian said, breathing just a little heavier than usual. "You can do it, Sparks."

They turned yet another sharp, shaded curve and a building came into view. "The big A," Rian said. "Can't miss it. No cars — doesn't look like anybody's here yet."

"That's good. We can look around without being noticed." She and Rian exchanged glances and Rian grinned.

The building was a two-story wood frame warehouse that looked like it had been in service for decades. The big A on the side was bright red against the dark wood, but it was fading where the afternoon sun hit it hard. There was a loading dock on one side with wide doors that slid open. Amy could see the padlock from where she stood. There were clerestory windows at the top, just under the eaves. She glanced around the back of the building, which was overgrown with weeds, the perfect hiding place for Arkansas' famous chiggers and ticks. She turned back.

On the side facing the deep woods of the property, there was a relatively new addition that jutted out like a tuber on a potato. Pamela had said there was an apartment onsite, and that's where she thought Duke had been living.

The welcome mat sported daisies in its design, and there was a wreath of faded field flowers on the door. Amy knocked softly. The door opened slightly to her touch. She looked at Rian with wide eyes, and Rian peeked around the door frame. There was no one standing there; the door had opened on its own. She pushed the door with her fingertips and then stepped inside. Rian was right behind her.

"What are we doing?" Amy whispered.

"Snooping," Rian whispered back.

"What are we looking for?"

"I don't know," Rian said and laughed.

"*Ssshh.* Be quiet."

"Why?"

"In case someone hears us."

"Oh, like that's going to save our skin. We're trespassing, pure and simple."

Amy ventured further into the room, knowing she was in the wrong. But hadn't Pamela asked for her help? After all, wasn't the business half Pamela's now? She couldn't help if she couldn't step outside the lines. Every step she took now was outside the lines any way she looked at it. But how else would she learn what people wanted to hide?

There was a lone lamp on the table by the couch. It shed light on a room that had obviously been hobbled together with cast-offs. There was a tan leather couch with a stone coffee table, a pair of blue and yellow floral side chairs, and a dinette with two cane bottom seats. The room had a studio kitchen that conjoined the living room. In one corner was a desk and a computer. A dark opening inferred yet another room beyond. A bath, perhaps, or maybe the bedroom.

Donald Duke was a tidier housekeeper than she would have thought. Even in the gloom, she could see it was clean and well-kept. There were dishes in the drying rack by the sink. One coffee cup. One plate, a fork, and one wine glass. She picked up the glass and looked at the rim. There were lipstick stains still on the side in a light shade of pink. She opened the fridge, and the interior light filled the room. There were leftovers in boxes. A bag of salad. A bottle of Ranch. A can of coffee and a pint of milk. Duke obviously didn't cook.

She glanced in the garbage beside the fridge. On the surface she could see another take out box and a cash register receipt. She reached into the bag for the receipt, and a postcard tumbled into view. The receipt was dated two days ago, and the postcard was an offer from a genealogical website. *Upgrade your membership now!* Amy turned the card over. It was addressed to D. Duke at Alpha Wine and Spirits.

Amy dropped the postcard back into the trash. Rian was looking at the pictures on the wall above the couch.

"One of the pictures is missing." Rian said, pointing to the wall. "There's a blank spot and you can tell there was something there before. This looks like a family tree and this other is a family crest, I think."

Rian peered into the framed glass. "General Fay Duke. Honorable Samuel Duke. Boy, he died an old codger. Hey, here's Donald Duke, born 1959. Looks like he's the last of his linage."

Amy crossed to the desk and lifted the pages on the surface with her fingertips. "I don't think he and Pamela had children. At least, I've never heard them mentioned."

"They'd be grown," Rian said. "In their thirties, probably."

Amy tapped the keyboard to the computer. The screen came up but then so did the password request. She shuffled the papers on the desk, a collage of pages, bills, and such. She riffled a little deeper in the stack and a picture slid from the pile. She recognized the label on the bottle of wine. It was a simple ivory-colored label, with a French country mansion on the front and the *Domaine Francois LeClerc* name in large, scripted letters at the top. It was the French Pamela had spoken to impress them. And she had.

Beneath it was another picture that looked like a copy. Side by side the bottles looked the same, until the nuanced differences came to light. There was an extra stroke in the roof of the mansion here, a shadow on the letter there, a stray mark in the name. She wouldn't have noticed the differences at all if someone hadn't circled them with red ink.

"Look at these," she said, handing them to Rian. "This is the same wine we drank last night. What do you think this is about?"

Rian shrugged. "I don't have any idea. I wish I knew what I was looking for. I do know that wine labels are a winemaker's signature, like the chop mark Chinese artists use to sign their work. I'm beginning to feel I may be in over my head in this wine business." Rian set the pictures back on the desk. "There is so much to learn."

Amy peeked inside the darkened doorway. The bed was made and plump with a pile of pillows. There were daisies on the duvet. Perfume pervaded the air, and she noticed the closet door was open. The clothes hanging in the closet were not a cowboy's. There wasn't a pair of pressed jeans anywhere in sight.

"If Donald Duke was living here, he wasn't living here alone," Amy whispered to Rian at her back. "This is not a bachelor pad."

"*Ssshh*," Rian said, her ears perked. "I hear somebody outside. Oh, Hail Mary! I hope they're not coming in here!"

They pressed against the wall inside the bedroom as they heard the front door open. "Bethany! You here? Bethany! I want you to run an errand! Pronto! Bethany!"

It sounded like Kirk Waters. She was getting to know that voice. Amy held her breath as the door closed. Was he inside the apartment now, or was he outside? She and Rian exhaled in unison and waited. They heard boots on pavement, and the footsteps moved away. Amy blew out another breath.

"That was close," she whispered.

They crept back through the apartment, opened the door, and then peeked outside. She expected to see Kirk standing there, waiting outside the door, but he wasn't.

A truck rumbled up the driveway, gears grinding on the incline. It passed them as they stood in the shadows and Amy saw that Alpha Distribution was stenciled on the side of the truck. The door at the dock slid open and the truck did a three point turn from the driveway before backing expertly to the dock wall. Two men got out and jumped up on the ledge, then disappeared inside the warehouse. Amy and Rian grinned at each other and then hurried to the building.

They could just see inside the cavernous interior from below the dock. If someone looked their way, they could easily duck below the wall and stay hidden. As it was, the two men were paying no attention to two women up to no good. One of them got into a forklift full of cardboard cases and began the slow crawl toward the truck. Amy heard Kirk's voice in the background.

They sprinted to the front of the building, opened the front door and crept in. If someone should ask, they were lost and looking for directions. But as it was, there was no one at the front desk, just an anemic looking Ficus tree sitting crooked in a large stone pot. There were two doors off to the right, and only one was dark. Amy darted to the door and poked her head into the room. She motioned for Rian to follow.

The room was empty of its owner. The name plate on the desk declared The Duke was the owner. One window, high up, made enough light to see the room without flipping the switch. Rian pushed the door closed with a soft *click*. An over the door hanger swayed slightly, and the wire hangers of pressed jeans and pearl button shirts swung softly with the *shoosh* of dry cleaner bags.

"What are we looking for?" Rian whispered.

Amy put a finger to her lips.

The space was quite large. There was a desk with a high top executive chair just off center from the door. A trim black leather couch sat against one wall, a table and lamp beside it. On the opposite wall was a built-in bookcase, with cupboards on the bottom. One cupboard door was crooked on its hinges so that it didn't quite close. Its contents were trying to spill into the room, and Amy opened the cupboard door. A bed pillow and blanket were stuffed in the space. She opened the other cupboard and saw a black gym bag crammed into the cubby. She slid the bag into view. It wasn't new, judging by the scuffs in the material. The handles were frayed, and the luggage tag was missing. The trefoil Adidas logo on the side was worn and faded. Amy slid the zipper and peeked inside. A hair dryer. There was a partial change of clothes — socks and tee-shirt. A zippered leather bag she assumed was a shave kit. A barrel-type corkscrew — the electric kind— and a loose stack of wine labels. Without a second through, she grabbed one of the labels and slipped it into her pocket.

I'll take *Things a wine merchant carries for $400, Alex.*

"Look at this," Rian whispered, holding a photo frame from the bookshelf. Looking over Rian's shoulder, she could see that it was a framed caricature drawing of the Duke, of Donald Duke, the kind

you can find at sidewalk shows and tourist traps. The artist had captured him with a giant cowboy hat and a cigar in his mouth. The likeness was uncanny. Beneath the picture the artist had written —
99% Cowboy 1% Neanderthal and Proud of It!

Amy resisted the urge to laugh. At least he knew where he stood in the evolution of man. Rian replaced the photo and Amy picked up the book beside it. *The Official John Wayne Handy Book for Men: Essential Skills for the Rugged Individualist.* It was a hardcover edition. *Step-by-step advice and real-world examples.*

Footsteps sounded in the hall, and Amy's heart thudded. Where would they hide if the door should open? She dropped to her knees and crawled to the desk, inching the chair out enough to get underneath the desk. Rian flattened herself against the wall behind the door. The footsteps faded and Amy relaxed. She pulled out one of the bottom drawers. It was full of files. Nothing caught her eye as she thumbed through the tabs. Upon opening the next drawer, she found pajamas, socks, and boxers in an untidy pile. The middle drawer was full of desk supplies and a little black book. Handwritten on the first page was Alpha1 - 257421. The rest of the pages were blank. She rummaged silently through the drawers with her fingers over the edge. There was one RX bottle. Atorvastatin. Generic for Lipitor. The prescription was expired.

The door swung open, and the overhead light flipped on. Amy pressed inside the desk cubby, hugging her knees to make herself as small as she could. The lights went out and the door shut again.

What would Kirk Waters do if he found them in Donald Duke's office uninvited and up to nothing honest? Especially after their little game of ego at the pool hall, she didn't want to tempt fate to find out. She glanced at Rian, who was still standing behind the door, and motioning with her head, the two of them crept on tiptoe to the door.

In the hallway, they could see two ways to go. One went past the front desk to the door they came in. The other went down a hall Amy hoped would lead to the warehouse proper. She could see a woman was sitting at the front desk now, and Amy thought she recognized the back of the bun. Bethany Keller, Sommelier in training. She shrugged at Rian. They couldn't very well approach her now, from this direction. Rian nodded toward the other way. It was easier to hide behind a stack of boxes than a Ficus tree that had lost half its leaves.

As they crept down the hall, Amy found herself wondering what saint or minor deity she could plead to help them escape without being discovered. She thought of a fantasy game they had played a few times, and Horsis came to mind. He was the ruler of espionage, spies, and secrets. A halfling who ruled the library of truths, he offered cover if you called him to the game. His sister, Ela, she remembered, was the trickster. She could turn herself into a tree if needed. People would never suspect a tree of eavesdropping.

They stood outside the door for a brief moment and peeked in through the window into the warehouse. She could see the forklift, piled with more boxes, headed back toward the dock. Another man with a clipboard was checking boxes in the queue. She couldn't see anyone else. Meaning — Kirk Waters. The one person they wanted to avoid.

Rian opened the door and slid inside; Amy followed behind her. They hid behind a stack of boxes, sprinted to another, and then another until they were near enough to the dock to shimmy down the wall on their bellies and then jump free.

"Hey!" one of the men yelled, as Amy stumbled and nearly fell to the ground. They didn't stop running until the big A was out of sight.

CHAPTER EIGHTEEN

Amy drove Rian to her homestead on the pond on the way into Bluff Springs. A few minutes before closing, she parked her car in her designated space behind the building. Tiddlywinks wasn't busy, surprising for a Friday afternoon. Suzie and Zelda were sitting at a table with a cup of tea when Amy walked in. Making a beeline for the front window, she swiped Victor from the back of the chair, hugging him so tight he squeaked. She loosened her grip and snuffled the fur at his neck. Nothing smelled as good as a fat cat sitting in the sun. He purred, letting her know she was forgiven. Victor's forgiveness didn't always come that easily.

"Well, hey, Sparks," Zelda said. "About time you made an appearance."

"It's been a long couple of days." Amy dropped her purse on the table with a heavy *thud*. "What have you been doing?"

Zelda grinned. "Hanging out at my bar."

"What bar?"

"The steel bar in my swimming pool. As it turns out, the pool boy teaches water aerobics at the Y. He showed me some exercises I can do in the pool." Zelda patted her hips. "I can already tell the difference."

Amy grinned at her friend. "What a difference a day makes."

"I'll see your sarcasm and raise you some sass," Zelda said. "You could use a few laps in the pool yourself."

"Thanks for the confidence boost."

Amy turned to the other woman. "You're a champ, Suzie. I appreciate you stepping in to take charge."

"It was a breeze. It's been steady all day, until now."

"What happen to you guys?" Zelda asked. "And why didn't you call me?"

"Battery juice," Amy said. "I had enough power to make two calls. I asked Suzie to clue you in."

"She did. But I want to know what happened. Details, Sparks. Details."

"I want a hot bath, fresh clothes, and dinner before I do anything else. Are you cooking tonight? Or should we treat ourselves to dinner out?" Amy hoped for the former — less effort and cheaper, too, but Zelda wasn't known for her culinary efforts. It would be Birdseye and Stouffer's at Zelda's.

"How about I pick up a pizza while you scrub off your road trip? I'll bring it up to your apartment."

"Perfect. You want to join us?"

"Thanks, but I have plans," Suzie said. "Do you want me to close up?"

"That, too, would be perfect."

The weight of the last 24 hours suddenly settled onto her shoulders. She imagined the sound of hot water running into her clawfoot bathtub upstairs, bubbles rising with the steam. Instinctively, her shoulders dropped from around her ears at the thought of a relaxing bath. Cradling Victor like the 17-pound fur baby he was, she left the Cardboard Cottage with its curlicue sign and climbed the stairs to her apartment above the shop. Twenty-nine steps. She counted them. Each one reminding her that home is where the heart is. Home is where you keep your bath salts and freshly laundered pajamas. She turned the key in the lock. It always felt so good to be home.

* * *

"A flat tire and a sleepover with husband-killing suspects," Zelda mumbled with a mouth full of pepperoni and cheese. "I admire your style. You live life dangerously."

She had told Zelda, between bites of pizza, of her and Rian's supposition about the raccoons and the Six-Pack. She had shared the details of her last snippet, endured a barrage of reprimands for not sharing it sooner, and recounted her trip down to the wine cellar with Pamela. It was the same as in her dream.

"So, you agree our suspicions are plausible?"

"Sure, I do. And those women could have tied you up with duct tape and left you in that basement to rot," Zelda answered. "You and Rian both!"

"They're more sophisticated than that."

"Oh, I see — sophisticated murderesses. That's generous, even for you."

"It seems that Donald wasn't a good husband, and he didn't hide it. He was trying to cheat her out of marital assets, too," Amy added. "It's no wonder she wanted him dead."

"She said that?"

"No, she didn't say that. I added that part. But you know, she's not the only wife on the planet who's poisoned her husband."

Zelda raised an eyebrow.

"Jacqueline Patrick served her husband antifreeze in his celebratory glass of cherry cider on Christmas Day," Amy offered, as she pulled another slice. "Lydia Sherman used rat poison on her husband. She served it to him in his hot chocolate with whipped cream and a cherry on top. And Heather Mook added rat pellets to her husband's Bolognese."

"Who are these women, and why do you know them?"

"I don't know them. I read about them. You never know when that kind of trivia wins the game."

"Factoids for fun, right?"

"My theory isn't solid yet," Amy added, ignoring Zelda's gibe. "We don't know how the poison got into the wine. We also don't know why Pamela is in Jerry Glen's press photos. Gloria clammed up when I asked about it, but she made it be known they were not having an affair. I wouldn't have believed her if she hadn't all but sworn on the Bible. So, they must have something else going on — Jerry Glen and Pamela — and I intend to find out what that is."

"Well, of course, you do," Zelda quipped.

"For Genna," Amy added.

"Oh, for sure. No one should ruin a good political campaign," Zelda said, her voice dripping sarcasm.

"I wonder if the *sommelier in training* knows anything about that."

"The someone, who?"

Amy fished the card from the table where she had emptied her jeans pockets before climbing into a steaming hot bath. Victor had perched on the clothes hamper to fill her in on his day. He enjoyed howling in the bathroom. He liked how he sounded, his version of soap on a rope or a lion caroling in the wild. She handed the card to Zelda, who held it out at arm's length to focus on the words, shrugged, and then handed it back. "What's she got to do with anything."

"I'm going to call her and find out. She works at Alpha Wine and Spirits."

Amy wanted to share the funny stories about reality TV, the Cork Docs, the Cork Jocks, and an Ozark doctor whose greed got her killed. She wanted to share their espionage adventure at the warehouse and their narrow escape, but the carbs were suddenly making her head fuzzy, her eyes heavy, and her bed a necessity in her most immediate future. She yawned deeply.

"I can see our gossip session is over," Zelda said, rising from the sofa. "I'm glad you are home safe. Listen Sparks, you know you don't have to prove anything. You can leave all this detecting to the detectives. That would *not* be a bad thing. It would be a safer thing, too. Don't forget about the Hummer. You could have gone up in flames."

Amy nodded heavily and then listened as Zelda clunked her way down the stairs in her Jimmy Choo shoes. She heard the click as the door shut and locked. Zelda was right. She didn't *have to*. But like Rian said, if you want to, *do it*. And besides, solving the mystery of her snippets was a lot like solving a riddle. Both would ping in her head until the answer was clear.

"Victor!" She called as she pulled back the bedspread. Victor bounded into the room with far more energy than she had left, circled the bed, then curled up in the crook of her arm. She snuffled his fur and yawned again. Home is where the cat is.

CHAPTER NINETEEN

Sunday afternoon couldn't arrive fast enough. On Sundays, the Cardboard Cottage and Company closed early when most tourists were on their way home. It was a welcomed tradition among most of the shopkeepers in Bluff Springs. After a busy week and weekend, the shop owners were ready for their own R and R. After the week she had, a few hours off the clock sounded like a dream vacation.

Amy glanced at the stack of rack cards Genna left at Tiddlywinks, declaring that Villiger was the right candidate for Arkansas. It also highlighted the infamous events colloquial to his voting district, along with his Big European Tour of Arkansas dates conveniently packaged to promote, promote, promote.

She studied it now.

The tourism conference had already happened, with mixed results. Jerry Glen Villiger had schmoozed the crowd. Donald Duke had been murdered. It wasn't the kind of draw Bluff Springs wanted for its tourism persona and not the best launch for the Big European Tour. There were still several events up coming.

Next on the calendar was a free chicken dinner at the corner Kum and Go in London, and then the London to Paris scavenger rally following shortly after. The city of Paris held its Butterfly Festival in June. The Altus Grape Stomp took place in July. Their harvest party was in October. Stuttgart was HQ for the World Championship

Duck Calling Contest held during Thanksgiving week, when the entire town celebrated its role in the movie *Mud* with Matthew McConaughey and Reese Witherspoon. Genna couldn't resist adding the World Famous Armadillo Festival (held in April). *Don't miss next year!*

She hadn't seen much of Genna lately since the Big European Tour kept her on the go. Even their last weekly domino game had been absent a player. Like the game of *Parcheesi* — the four players were separated at the four corners of the board. As they played the game, the players would cross each other's paths, often with a challenge or two on their way to home square. Game over.

She felt that way now. She and Genna had been busy with the conference. And then she and Rian attempted a quick road trip that got hijacked by crazy directions and a flat tire. She came face to face with her dream. The raccoons were involved in this somehow.

Today the four friends would finally gather poolside, where Zelda promised a Bloody Mary and sandwiches. The subs might be from the corner deli, but that was okay with her.

Glancing fondly at the stacks of games on the Tiddlywinks shelves, Amy admired the cardboard spines on the game boxes. This was the reason she named her co-op the Cardboard Cottage. It wasn't a house of cards. There was a cohesiveness to the shops under this one roof, and, like the games on the shelf, each played a little differently from the next. It made for a collection; a cottage styled collection.

As for Tiddlywinks, scouting for vintage games and their provenance was more fun than she wanted to admit. It was much like a children's treasure hunt. She knew game sellers made up stories about where the games came from to make what they had to sell more valuable. Much like Duke's wine origin stories. Undoubtedly, there was creative license involved. People made stuff up to make a sale. She might exaggerate just a little, and she wasn't against repeating what she'd been told. How was she to know if it was true or not? She had to pay the bills.

Pulling a cardboard box from the shelf, she opened it, reflecting how little the *Parcheesi* board had changed since her childhood. The game of *Pachisi* originated in ancient India. A pair of New York game makers bought the rights to the game and trademarked its new name in the mid-1800s. They called it the *Royal Game of India*. That was creative license, although it was pretty close to the truth, as far as she could tell. The kings of ancient India played *Pachisi*; only they played in their gardens with real people as pawns. The prettiest ladies and maids were staged as players in the courtyard, which was full of secret hiding places for stolen love and other dangers. And of course, there were knights on horseback to save the day. The goal was for one beautiful maiden to find her way to the center of the garden, where she was then declared the winner of the ultimate prize: the honor of serving the nobility. Servitude. Not much of a prize.

In the ancient game of *Pachisi*, twenty-five mauri or cowrie shells were used for dice. The number of shells that fell from the king's pouch on each play determined how many steps the maiden moved along the path. That was how the game got its name. *Pachisi* meant twenty-five in that native tongue.

The New York game makers replaced the living maidens with brightly colored wood coins and the shells with dice. In some modern versions, the players became the tiger, elephant, camel, bear, and buffalo. They hadn't played the game in a long time, but she always grabbed the elephant. Genna chose the tiger. Rian gravitated toward the buffalo, and Zelda switched back and forth between the camel and the bear. There were warmly held traditions in every game she and her friends played. Genna couldn't cheat at *Parcheesi*, although she had certainly tried.

Looking out at the sidewalk in front of Tiddlywinks, she noticed the street was sparse. Tourists were already on the road home on this sunny day in May. Tall stalks of purple, yellow and maroon iris marked the spring flowerbeds. Brilliant pink quince and the last blooming dogwood marked the wooded hills above the town. There was no fluffy cat in the window today. Victor had stayed home, but not by his choice. She wanted to lock up and go without the extra trip upstairs. Rian and Zelda left nearly an hour ago, and Sammie closed at noon on Sundays. All she had to do was get in her car and go.

Alone, now, in the quiet of the building, she breathed in the scent of the old wood floors and lemon-scented polish. The building had stolen her heart the moment she stepped across the threshold. It was silent without customers but far from feeling empty. She listened for the creak of the wood and the whispered air blowing through windows that never really sealed. Yes, this was Home Square. Her Home Square.

As she grabbed her swimsuit bag from behind the counter, she noticed the bottle of wine from the night an army of women invaded this space with their laughter. She slipped the wine into her bag. Today was as good a day as any to sample fine wine from the Duke's wine collection.

* * *

An hour later, sated by submarine sandwiches and a spicy-hot drink, Amy, Rian, and Zelda soaked up the sun poolside. She sat under her wide brim hat and cover-up, Zelda paraded in yet another new floral print bathing suit, and Rian wore her trusty one-piece Speedo. Genna was late.

Rian said, "Ben was working on his cabin yesterday and ran into a rookie cop. The two of them started talking when Ben told him he worked on the police force in another county. It seems this rookie has been itching to talk about a case and doesn't know who to talk to who's not off limits."

The comment made her think of Pamela and the greedy doctor's court case. Pamela kept the facts under wraps from her friends even under pressure. Ben was good at getting people to talk.

"This guy knew Ben's cabin. Said it was a favorite place to shack up. I think he meant like a *B52 Love Shack*. Although he's way too young to know who the B52s are."

Amy laughed. "Why does this rookie have information about the investigation from up here?"

"Do we care?"

Amy shook her head. Zelda laughed.

Rian slurped her drink, poking at the olives with the straw to move them out of the way. "He said Duke didn't die of Xanax overdose." She grinned at Amy with a coy sparkle in her eye. "The poison was injected through the cork. They found the tip of a hollow point needle in the bottom of the bottle. It must have broken off as it was pushed through the cork."

"A needle? How can that be? A cork is dense. Even a corkscrew needs some force."

"So, this was a big needle. An 18-gauge."

"I don't know anything about gauges on needles."

"The bigger the number, the thinner the gauge." Zelda interjected with a wagging finger.

Amy was impressed. "Why do you know that?"

"I flirted with the idea of becoming a nurse for a little while. I found it wasn't my thing."

"What are 18-gauge needles used for?"

"I think they get used everywhere," Zelda answered. "You've seen how nurses do it. They draw medication from a vial with a big needle and then swap that needle for a smaller one."

"But wait…" Rian added, "you know who else uses 18-gauge needles?"

Amy's eye widened. "Who?"

"Veterinarians. In particular, equine vets."

Amy fell silent. She pictured the gate at the DD Horse Ranch and Veterinary Hospital with its cowboy font and the crunch of Big Fork planerite under her tires.

"The Six-Pak!" Zelda exclaimed. "The vet is part of the Six-Pack!"

Amy nodded. Zelda had caught on quickly. "And what about the poison? Do they know what was used?"

"Barbiturate."

"What is that?" Amy turned to Zelda, hoping she'd have insight there, too.

Rian answered instead. "It's not poison. It's a drug. Barbiturates are used to put you in a deep, euphoric sleep."

"And too much will cause death," Amy added.

Rian nodded. "And this barbiturate is often used in equine euthanasia." Rian sat back and steepled her fingers.

"Jeez Louise," Amy said. "They don't shoot horses, do they?"

Zelda gasped. "They do, too."

"Well, this vet doesn't," Rian said. "And that's why this rookie wanted to talk. He rides rodeo, so he knows this vet. He knows she puts horses down with a barbiturate cocktail when their time comes. She has a history with the PETA people because you can't bury an animal if drugs are used. She's been getting around that for years."

"Gross," Zelda said.

"She's a devotee of Temple Grandin," Rian continued. "Ben didn't know who Temple Grandin was, but I do and so did this rookie kid. Doc Dot is passionate about animal welfare in equine sports."

"Like rodeos? And horse racing?"

Rian nodded. "She's the registered vet for the gay rodeo in Little Rock. She's one of their biggest supporters."

"Gay rodeo? But Dot's been married three times!"

"Well, the only requisite to gay rodeo is your willingness to get your ass kicked by a bronco."

"Are you saying this barbiturate came from Double D Ranch?" Amy asked.

Rian nodded. "It sure fits our Six-Pack theory. And if Doc Dot is passionate about animals, she would probably be compassionate about murder."

"You'll have to explain that one to me," Zelda said. "I'm not tracking here. A compassionate murder?"

"What's the most genteel way to kill someone?" Rian asked and then answered her own question. "Poison. Like a hush-now-go-to-sleep kind of poison. No suffering involved."

"A humane murder?" Zelda mocked.

"That's a stretch. Or maybe it's not," Amy added. "It does mean she didn't want the victim to suffer."

"That's how I see it," Rian said. "But it could also mean she used whatever she could get her hands on."

"Or it could mean she didn't want to get her hands dirty," Zelda added.

"Do the police have the evidence they need for an arrest?"

Rian shrugged. "That I don't know. The rookie didn't say anything about that. He was just freaked out about Doc. But without the drug vial and lot number — which I gather they don't have — they can't trace it back to its source. I don't even know if the police have put the vet and the drug together. But this rookie has. And everybody is so related that no one wants to raise alarm against one of their own. It's a look-the-other-way kind of place."

Look the other way. An Arkansas code, if ever there was one. Mind your own business, and I'll mind mine. She'd experienced that more than once dealing with the Arkansas hill folk.

Amy pulled the wine bottle from her bag and held it in front of her. She eyed the foil sealed over the cork. "Was the needle pushed through like this? Foil, cork, and all?"

"It wouldn't have to be pushed through the foil," Rian offered. "The foil cap can be removed and replaced. You can buy foil caps by the caseload. They come in red, green, gold, black, and silver. All you need to do is hit it with a hairdryer, and they shrivel and seal tight."

"A hair dryer!" Amy exclaimed. "There was a hair dryer in that gym bag in Duke's office." The bottle suddenly became suspect in her hands. What if Pamela had injected a barbiturate into this bottle, too? Amy put it away. No way were they drinking this.

"The hairdryer is a modern day tool of the trade," Rian added. "Or so I've gathered. I've been getting a Google education on wine bottling. There's a whole bevy of really cool wine-making paraphernalia out there."

"Paraphernalia is so your thing," Amy added, and Rian grinned.

Zelda laughed. "I heard about your skunk wine. You really think there's a market for that?"

"Once Arkansas legalizes it, there's going to be a market for anything and everything cannabis," Rian answered. "You just wait and see. I'll come out from hiding and into a full-fledged enterprise. I could make millions and retire. If I can get all the permits and stuff. If I can perfect the recipe."

IF was big gamble, even for Rian.

"What do you need with millions?" Zelda asked. "You buy your jeans and flannel shirts from the thrift shop, and you've been wearing the same high-tops for years. The only thing you change is your shoelaces."

Rian narrowed her eye. "A person can have a big impact on the world if she has money. Women would put it to use in totally different ways if we were in power."

Rian's tone surprised her.

"A person with influence can do important things. I'm not talking about the kind of power that dominates others, or the kind of wealth that just creates more greed. I'm talking about helping others get a start on their future. Where science and nature work on the same page so that we heal instead of harm. I'd like to see money used to encourage us all to be better stewards of the earth and the creatures who don't have a voice. Money is not about trinkets and travel and expensive swimming pools."

"Ouch," Amy said, with a glance at Zelda.

"Are you saying I'm shallow with my money?" Zelda asked.

"I didn't say that. It's yours. You do what you want. I'm just saying that if I had an excess of money and some power, I would use it differently."

Amy sat back and stared at Rian. She never dreamed Rian would want any kind of power outside of her private life. She was the queen of her own universe, and that was as far as Rian's reign needed to go, or so Amy had thought. Rian wasn't cheap, but she was frugal. Well, not so much that — she just didn't buy into the consumer ideal. Here she was making big plans in cannabis commerce. Maybe she was less like Jane Goodall than they thought.

"Well, I, for one, hope you achieve all of that," Amy said brightly. "Follow your passion. Do it. And I can't wait to try whatever you name your money-making cannabis wine."

Rian exhaled deeply and looked at Zelda. "Truce? I didn't mean anything personal by that."

"Truce," Zelda agreed. "I didn't take offense anyway. And you like my expensive swimming pool, so don't say you don't."

Rian grinned. "Then pour me another and pass me a sandwich. It's a good day to get a tan."

Just then, the gate swung open, and Genna pushed through, red in the face, bathing suit wrap flapping at the rapid rate of her approach.

"Guess where I've been for the past two hours," she demanded as she reached the table.

"Do tell," Zelda said as she poured a drink from the pitcher, sticking a celery and olive garnish on top.

"Getting grilled by the police. That's where I've been." She paused for effect. "Getting absolutely, positively mauled by the buffoon who runs *homicide* in this county." Hard h, the word drawn out with a southern drawl. "We've met before," she added. "And he didn't seem surprised to see me again."

"Oh, no!" Zelda said.

"Oh, yes!" Genna responded. "And let me tell you why." Again, she paused for effect, and sucked half her drink up the straw. "As I suspected, I was caught on camera at our dearly deceased Donald Duke's hotel room dragging wine — which was his mortal demise, I should add — but I was also accused of having motive and opportunity! Again!"

Amy tried not to smile. The image in her head was comical. But this wasn't funny.

"To add insult to my injury," Genna went on, her hands splayed in front of her, "Villiger — my overly ambitious Congress-seeking candidate — was seen arguing with Donald Duke like a frat-boy bully. The hotel staff were grilled about what they saw and heard that day. According to reports, a furious Jerry Glen was thrusting a bag at Duke with one hand and a bottle of wine in the other. Witnesses said he was making rather *assertive movements* toward Duke while mincing words loud enough for everyone else to hear."

"What did he—"

Genna cut Amy off. *"If you don't move forward on this, I will see that you never sell another bottle of wine in this state for as long as you live. And maybe that's one day too many."*

"Yikes!" Zelda said. "Is that a threat? A veiled threat?"

"Veiled!" Genna screeched. "He couldn't have been clearer if he'd written a memo on official stationery!" She slurped her drink to the bottom and slammed the glass in front of Zelda. "Another, if you please, Zelda." Zelda poured.

"Here's the cherry on the top of my Sunday fiasco," Genna added after another healthy sip. "Know what was also found in the hotel room?" She didn't wait for them to guess. "Jerry Glen's stump tour brochure. It was in the bottom of one of those decorative bags that wine comes in. It still had my chewing gum on the back."

"You mean the bag the wine came in? The poisoned wine?"

"I don't know if it was from that wine, but they asked if I knew it. I said of course I knew the brochure because I designed it, but I didn't know about the bag."

"Did they believe you?"

Genna didn't answer. Maybe she didn't know.

"So now we have a widow, a politician making a threat, a slew of newspaper photos that puts the two of them together, and a PR guru." She poked herself in the chest, "that's me—and I'm leading the lamb to slaughter. I may have been the one who brought the sacramental wine to the last supper and dropped Jerry Glen's calling card in the mix!" She raised a brow and pointed a finger. "And if you make a snarky comment, I will implode."

No one said anything.

"I don't think I can get that boy to Congress if he was the last man standing!" Genna exclaimed. "I had such high hopes. And now they're dashed on the rocks like grandma's dirty laundry."

Amy raised a brow. Grandma's dirty laundry?

Amy glanced at Rian. Should they tell her about the hollow tip point pushed through the cork, or would that make matters worse? Did she need to know that a powerful drug had taken Donald Duke out? Did Genna need to know what she overheard at the bar? That Jerry Glen and Duke had some deal going down that involved money and a sommelier? Or would that all be fuel for an implosion? She decided to let Genna stew in tomatoes and a healthy splash of vodka before saying anything.

Rian exhaled and broke the silence that had fallen over the festive table. "They may be trying to frame Jerry Glen," she said.

"They?" Genna asked pointedly.

"The Six-Pack," Rian answered.

"The who?"

"Not *The Who* as in Pete Townsend," Zelda schooled with a bite to her tone. Genna narrowed her eyes at Zelda.

"You met them at Tiddlywinks," Amy said. "The Six-Pack is Pamela and her friends: Gloria, Tilly, Bonnie, and Doc Dot. There used to be one more —that's where they got the name — but she's deceased. I don't know what happened to her, but I'm pretty sure it was a long time ago."

Genna shook her head in confusion. "I am not in any mood for all that kissing cousin crap!"

Rian interrupted Genna with a nudge to her arm. "Listen. They may be responsible for Duke's death. We think they planned this whole Tiddlywinks domino night to get rid of one husband and frame another for the crime. Jerry Glen could be up for the fall. We don't have any evidence, just Amy's…." Rian glanced quickly at Amy.

Amy inhaled sharply. "All we have to go on is another one of my snippets," she said quietly. "There were five raccoons in my dream.

And one of them was dead."

Genna shook her head slowly. Amy had no idea what would come out of Genna's mouth next, but she was pretty sure it wouldn't be good. "Before you say anything," Amy blurted, "hear me out."

Genna stayed silent while Amy told her about the dream and the laughing raccoons. The color in Genna's face drained even in the bright heat of the day. Her mouth was drawn in a tight line. The *Rose contra temps* on her lips looked garish against the pallor of her skin.

"Framing Jerry Glen for a murder," Genna said quietly as if musing over the possibility. "That would fit why Pamela is in his press photos. She could be trying to make it look like she and Jerry Glen are having an affair and got rid of her husband. A jealous lover! A thwarted triangle. Bad blood!"

Zelda slurped her ice. "What do they have to gain by it? The Dukes were getting a divorce anyway."

"Money," Genna answered.

"Money," Amy agreed. "Power. Politics."

"Puppets on a string," Rian added.

"Who are these Six-Pack friends anyway?" Zelda added. "You need to find out, Amy. You need to dig up their history. You said they've known each other all their lives, but not all memories are happy ones. I bet they have a secret they don't want anyone to know."

Zelda poured the last round from the pitcher, and Genna grabbed a sandwich. "We've got snooping to do," she mumbled between bites. "If they haven't arrested their suspect yet, that could mean they don't have the evidence they need. Not yet."

"Then we need to find some," Amy said. "We have to help Genna clear Jerry Glen's name."

Genna nodded and Amy continued, "It's possible the Six-Pack planned their trip to Bluff Springs because they knew Jerry Glen would be here. It's possible they created the alibi at Tiddlywinks for that very reason.

"If Genna hadn't made Villiger the star of the show, so to speak, it would have been just another conference on tourism. But he *was* the star. Somebody knew he'd be there. And somebody knew Donald Duke would be there, too.

"Pamela would know Duke's habits. She would know he'd return to his hotel room and uncork a bottle of wine to end his day. All Pamela had to do was get the poisoned bottle to his room. Pamela told me herself that she went to his room to walk Claret. She could have given him the poisoned wine then."

"It wasn't really a poison," Rian added and glanced at Genna. "It's a drug that vets use. We think that's probably where it came from. Maybe Dot injected the bottle herself before giving it to Pamela."

"Yikes," Zelda said. "You'd have to keep track of all the poisoned bottles. How would they know which wine was deadly and which wine was not?" She grinned. "That sounds a lot like which witch is which."

Amy nodded. "I'm thinking about the loose labels. They could have created a special label for a special wine. A wine that kills on demand."

"Pick a card, any card," Zelda added. "It's like that magic trick. The one where the queen of hearts disappears and then reappears somewhere in the room. I could see us coming up with something like that."

Amy frowned at her friend.

"What? Like you don't think we're smart enough to devise a plan like that? Wait a minute," Zelda said suddenly, wide-eyed and flushed. "What if the Six-Pack were planning on killing all the husbands? What if Donald was only the first to go?"

Amy gaped. "Why didn't I think of that? Those old crows at the diner said Kirk claimed Bonnie was trying to kill him, too. Maybe he also got a poisoned bottle of wine."

Rian whistled under her breath. "It's a black widow society."

"It's a killer *washund* club!" Zelda squealed. "I wonder what it takes to get a membership card."

"It takes a husband," Rian answered. "You need a husband and a killer bottle of wine."

"And poison," Amy added. "It's a wives-only wine club where the husband always dies."

CHAPTER TWENTY

A bit sunburned despite all precautions, Amy returned home to a hungry cat and a soothing bottle of aloe vera. Now curled up together on the sofa, she petted Victor absently as she stared at the business card in her fingers.

Sommelier in training. Drink no wine before its time.

How was Bethany Keller involved? Gloria seemed to think she was. She was connected, somehow. If things had worked out a little differently when they were snooping around the Alpha Wine warehouse, they might have been able to find out how she was involved.

A six-pack of friends. A needle in a bottle. A vet with a deadly drug. And another husband gone. A *wasbund* who didn't cheat or steal or make his wife unhappy. If Pamela and her friends were in cahoots, why had Pamela asked for Amy's help? Why would she take that risk? She patted Victor's flanks and pondered. He flopped over to expose his long underside, begging for more. She stroked the soft wispy fur of his belly and listened to him purr.

Why had Pamela asked for her help?

"Because she was fishing for information, that's why," she said. Victor seemed to agree.

If Amy could see the smoking gun as Genna had boasted she

could, she might see who had injected the poison in the wine. Or who placed the bottle in the room. And if Pamela knew that Amy could see that, she could confuse the evidence. She could scramble the facts. She could throw Jerry Glen under the bus. Or maybe Bethany. Was that what Gloria was doing? Throwing Bethany into the suspicion soup?

What was it about this *sommelier* that was so compelling? Which dot connected to another? It felt like a Twister game with too many arms and legs, too many cousins and friends.

Amy reached for her phone. How would she explain this call out of the blue? The woman wouldn't remember meeting her because they hadn't met. Once past that hurdle, what was she going to ask? *Do you know anything about Donald Duke's death? Did you know if Pamela Duke put the poison in the wine and served it room temp? Drink no wine before its time. What time was that?*

She had to do better than that.

The phone was instantly answered. "Bethany Keller," the voice said, sounding confident and eager on the first ring.

"This is Amy Sparks from Bluff Springs. We— uh— my company sponsored one of the social events at the recent tourism conference, and I was hoping to talk with you about — uh— about a wine investment."

"Oh!" The woman said as if she was out of breath. "Bluff Springs?"

"My friends and I want to learn more about wine."

"Are you a restaurant owner or a collector?"

Amy paused briefly. "None of the above, really. I'm a novice by all accounts. I'm looking for some tips to get started."

"Oh." Her tone dropped a peg of enthusiasm, along with the bulk of the dollar signs. No ca-ching. No interest.

Amy pushed on. "I heard you have experience with investment wines. That's what I'm interested in."

"Who told you that?" Her tone was wary.

"Donald Duke." She hoped the lie couldn't come back to haunt her.

Bethany Keller was silent on the other end.

"I'm really sorry," Amy said. "I know you worked with Mr. Duke." She caught the barely audible exhale on the other end of the line. "I know about his passing," she said quickly, "If you were close, please accept my condolences. I — I was hoping to talk to you about — "

"I wasn't anywhere near the hotel when it happened," the woman interrupted. "I answered all the questions the police asked. Yes, I work with Donald and Kirk. So, of course, I saw him that day. I saw him almost every day. But I won't answer any more questions about it. I just won't."

"I understand," Amy said. "This whole thing must have been a shock."

Again, the little scoff of a breath. "Mr. Duke was one of the most influential men I know. I thought he had everything he wanted at his fingertips and so I was so shocked when Mr. Waters told me. I just couldn't believe it.

"And now. I mean, why are they saying it's a homicide? What happened? Who wanted him ... you know.... *gone*...." Her voice rose and then trailed away into thin air. Amy listened for a sniffle. She could hear rustling and imagined a tissue being yanked from the box.

"If you don't mind me asking, are you still working with Alpha Wine and Spirits?"

The little breath came again. "Oh, yes! In fact, I got a promotion right before... before... well, Duke was so very pleased with the clients I was bringing in. He said I had promise in this industry and that I could make a name for myself if I wanted to. And that's what I want. That's all I've ever wanted. To be just like him." She paused for a moment as if collecting her thoughts.

"Kirk is not a wine expert even if he thinks so. He needs me now more than I need him, and I'm not going to schlep cases of Moscato for the rest of my life!" Her voice cracked with bitterness.

"Will you take over the Cork Docs investment club? You sound like you have a passion for it."

"What do you know about the Cork Docs?" Bethany's tone was sharp.

"I know it's a group of doctors who buy investment wines."

The scoff was audible this time. "Bunch of jerks with too much money. And it was my idea to begin with!"

"You mean they're not open to new members? I heard that from someone else."

"Not even in high heels and a mini skirt. Not even when *she* knows what's really going on."

That caught her attention. "What is going on?"

Bethany hesitated. Amy felt the tension.

"They don't know much about the wine they're buying, that's all."

"Ah, I see," Amy said, hoping Bethany could tell she didn't quite believe that was true. *I'll take lies for $400, Alex.*

"I shouldn't talk about the Cork Docs that way," she said. "I've already said more than I should. It's not professional to talk about this. Are you really interested in buying wine as an investment? Because once the audit begins, we won't be buying or selling anything until it's all over."

"An audit? What kind of an audit?"

"Oh, it's nothing. It's a standard operating procedure. Happens more than you think in our industry. Kirk says TTB will find everything as it should be — nothing squirrelly here. Everything is in order." She sounded like she was quoting someone else.

"What does TTB stand for?"

"Tax and Trade Bureau. It's the government's mothership to the Alcohol and Tobacco Industry."

"Uh oh," Amy said. "Those are the big dogs."

"Kirk is not worried. He's OCD about everything." Bethany took a deep breath and blew it out through the phone. "I hope so. Otherwise, it will be a circus."

Amy laughed, even though it probably wasn't funny to Bethany. Or Kirk. Or even to Pamela, since she was now probably part of the business, from a legal standpoint, anyway.

"Is Pamela Duke involved in the day-to-day operations at the company?"

Bethany snorted. "No, she's not involved at all. She's got her nose so far up Project X, she couldn't smell the bouquet if it would save her life. If Uncle Jerry doesn't win his campaign, she'll have enough egg on her face to scramble an omelet. And Hank will be the first person in line with a fork."

Again, she sounded as if she were repeating someone else's words.

"What's Project X?"

"I don't know. That's what Mr. Duke called it. He wasn't impressed."

"Where would I go if I wanted to learn more about it?"

"Straight to the horse's mouth."

"Oh! And would that Doc Dot?"

"Aunt Dot? What does she have to do with it?"

"That's why I'm asking."

"You sure ask a lot of questions for someone just buying wine."

Amy chuckled. Better ease off the gas. "You're right. Curiosity is one of my better habits. I didn't realize you were related to Dot."

"Who am I NOT related to down here?" Bethany made that sound again — a cross between exhalation and sigh of contempt. Or maybe it was boredom.

"Shall we set a time to meet?" Bethany asked in an entirely different voice. "We should review your likes and dislikes, goals, and budget. My fee is seventy-five for the consultation, but I'm happy to apply that to your first case of wine. I know you'll appreciate the discounts I can offer when you buy through me, and you'll get better value than if you try to scout wines on your own."

"Would you come to Bluff Springs?"

The woman was quiet for a moment. "I could," she said finally. "If you need me to. I have other clients I could visit with. I didn't have time to call on them last time I was there."

Amy heard pages ruffling. "Were you staying at the same hotel?"

The scoff got a little louder. "Kirk would have pitched a fit if I used the company credit card to book a room for myself without permission. My job is to make the reservations and check them in. I even had to make last minutes changes because of the dog. I didn't know Duke would be bringing her. Not every hotel allows pets."

Bethany paused for a moment. "I don't mean to sound ungrateful," she said quietly. "This whole thing has me so upset I don't even feel like myself. Like my feet aren't touching the ground. Have you ever felt that way? Like you can't get anchored to the ground?"

"I know what you mean," Amy said. "It's not a very pleasant feeling."

"No. It's not."

"I think they call that grief."

"I don't like how grief feels," she said. "I don't like it at all."

"Next time you come to Bluff Springs, let me know," Amy said. "My friend Zelda has a little cottage she rents out. She'd sponsor you for an evening. Maybe not for free, but probably for what she pays the cleaning team."

"She would do that for me?"

"Sure, she would." Amy hoped she wasn't opening a can of worms she could not close.

"Gosh," Bethany breathed. The scoff was gone. "That's really nice of you. I'll text over some options for our consult, and you can let me know what works for you."

"Good," she heard herself say. "I look forward to meeting you."

They hung up. What had she gotten herself into? Probably several hundred dollars' worth of wine, much like the Cork Docs but without a surgeon's salary. What had Bethany said? *They don't know what they're buying.* There was something about the wine investment club that Bethany wasn't sharing. She remembered the photos in the apartment. The one with red circles. Could this be what got Donald Duke killed? He was at the center of it, Jerry Glen was on the fringe, and Gloria knew much more than she let on.

Besides asking Pamela an out-of-the-box bold question, Amy had no idea how to unearth the details of Project X. Nothing came up with an internet search. X marked the spot where Pamela, Jerry Glen, Donald Duke, and who knows who else had focused their attention. Maybe X was the reason the Duke was killed. Power, money, and politics followed each other around. And that meant Hank Summerfield was involved somehow, too.

What was it, this Project X?

Since Jerry Glen was in politics, anything he put his name on— and maybe his money, too — had to be legit, squeaky clean. Project X could be a bill Villiger promised to bring to Capitol Hill. Project X could be anything.

Bethany implied the success of Villiger's campaign was essential here, and if Hank stood to gain if it failed — egg omelet and fork and all that, which side of the fence was Hank on? Was he pro-Jerry? Or pro-Duke? She knew he was pro-Pamela, but she didn't know anything else about him except by sight, only briefly. He had worn a ten-gallon hat much like Duke's at the social hour. And, as Tilly pointed out, a red bolo string tie. She hadn't gotten close enough to Hank to see the pulley clasp, but it was probably the Arkansas diamond. It would tie in nicely with the Diamond Auto Group.

As of yet, the character of Hank Summerfield was an unknown. Still, why would Hank sponsor the candidate's event at the conference if Donald Duke intended to prevent Villiger from getting elected? So many people, so many strings.

Amy stroked Victor's ears. He rubbed against her hand.

What a muck. What a cluster of things to hold onto in her head. If the dots between Duke and Project X were connected, there was only one way to find out. She'd have to dig until she hit gold. While Donald Duke was well-known, he was no longer in the picture. Like Bethany had said, he was the most influential person she knew, so the operative word was: *Was.*

If the tree is in the way, cut it down. She remembered Genna's words. Is that what happened? Had Pamela injected the drug in the bottle with a needle in the cork?

The cork.

Her heart thumped.

It all came back to the wine. Just like players come back to Home Square.

CHAPTER TWENTY ONE

The success of the Big European Tour of Arkansas felt like it was falling flat around Genna's ears. On the surface, Jerry Glen was doing well. The polls were showing good gains. He schmoozed, cajoled, kissed babies, shook hands, and talked until he was hoarse. He was getting lots of press, even if Pamela Duke was in many of the photos. Voters were wearing the campaign buttons she had ordered by the boxful, promising to show up at the polls. By all accounts, Genna should consider this a feather in her cap. But she didn't feel that way. Even the morning sun streaming in the windows couldn't brighten her mood. Her breakfast of coffee and Danish was being served with a side of newspaper — several newspapers, and every one of them held a similar headline.

Wine Pioneer's Death Ruled a Homicide

And just below that…

Candidate Launches Charity

A picture of Jerry Glen Villiger anchored that story. They didn't even bother to edit Pamela Duke out of the photo. The two were smiling into the camera as Villiger cut the ribbon. Genna opened the paper and shook out the fold.

She scanned the story, and the name Merriweather Hopkins jumped off the page like a rabbit out of the hat. Merriweather Hopkins!

Genna growled.

A local source confirmed Pamela Duke, wife of recently deceased Donald Duke, is actively engaged in developing a charitable organization with the help of U.S. District Representative candidate Jerry Glen Villiger. Project X will serve underprivileged women, offer legal representation for disenfranchised women and children, and provide educational and business resources for women without resources of their own.

Organizer Merriweather Hopkins of Little Rock said the organization has achieved non-profit 501(c)3 status and would soon be fundraising for their initial projects. Hopkins claimed the abandoned train depot near the town of Ozark was on target as an initial acquisition but could not disclose the proposed use until further inspection.

"Unfortunately, this historic building has fallen into disrepair over the years," Hopkins said. "Until an architectural review can be completed, and the property's historic preservation requirements are identified, we are still in the negotiation stage with the property owner."

According to the public record, the railroad property is owned by Diamond Auto Group. Neither the company's CEO, Hank Summerfield, nor U.S. candidate Jerry Glen Villiger was available for comment.

"Humperdinck," Genna said out loud. They could have left that tidbit out.

She moved on to the other story.

Wine Pioneer's Death Ruled a Homicide

The death of Donald Duke, a pioneer and prominent member of the wine industry in Arkansas, is now being investigated as a homicide, local authorities said. The cause of death was barbiturate overdose and was initially considered a self-inflicted poisoning. Authorities agree new evidence suggests foul play. Sources claim at least one person of interest has been identified. No additional details will be released while under investigation.

Duke was found at a hotel in Bluff Springs, Ark., by his business partner, Kirk Waters, on the evening of the 13th of May. Waters, CFO of the regional alcohol distribution company, reported that he performed CPR on Donald Duke until the EMTs arrived. Waters said that when he found

Duke unresponsive, he blamed the state of Mr. Duke's frame of mind for his assumption, which he shared with the emergency response team.

"It was an honest mistake," Waters claimed. "I was shocked to learn this is now being investigated as a crime."

Waters claimed he is eager to help authorities and has turned over evidence that may be crucial to the investigation. "We all want the best outcome possible as quickly as possible," Waters said. "The Duke was known as a pioneer in the industry, and I will do my best to honor his legendary exploits."

"They were such a nice couple," said Selma Lowell, age 72, a long-time neighbor of Donald and Pamela Duke. "Except for the holiday parties they threw yearly, they were quiet, respectable neighbors. I don't understand why people can't work things out."

That's because you weren't married to a jerk, Genna thought.

Genna frowned as she swigged now cold coffee. She slammed the cup into the saucer, splashing coffee on her robe. Coffee puddled around the Danish.

What a mess! What was she going to do?

Jerry Glen had not shared a peep about this charitable enterprise. It sounded like a worthy cause, and she could have used it to build on his public image. Instead, he took it undercover. Merriweather Hopkins had to be responsible for that. And why? Because Merriweather wanted the limelight. Because Merriweather was always trying to pop the big news out from under Genna's headlines.

"Well, Humperdinck," Genna said again. She had still been under the impression that Jerry Glen and Pamela were having an affair, and that's why they were photographed together. How utterly un-newsworthy! How was she going to spin this?

She forcibly ground her cigarette in the ashtray and grabbed another paper. The story was similar. Nothing new added to the pile up. Was there something to Amy's theory that Jerry Glen was being set up? She was beginning to think so. Was Pamela using Jerry Glen's Big European stump tour to plant that seed of suspicion? It sure looked that way.

Someone else could be behind it. Someone like Merriweather Hopkins!

If the story about Donald Duke hadn't taken precedent on the page, the pair of them would have gained the confidence of many. Without saying a word about their altruistic charity for women, without saying anything really, they were building a platform of trust in the public eye. They were building an *esprit de corps* that unified their interests. And once Jerry Glen made it to Washington, fundraising would be a snap. Pamela Duke was probably planning on being at his side there, too!

The plan was brilliant.

And then Donald Duke was murdered.

Genna felt anger twist her gut. She tapped the photo on the page. This was going to backfire on all of them. Why did Merriweather release the information about the charity to reporters? Why did she bring it up *now*? Was she trying to make matters worse? Or was she trying to save her own skin?

Genna bit her lip, her mind turning. Merriweather was trying to ruin Jerry Glen's chances to win. And once again, she had shown herself to be the enemy. The enemy of Genna Gregory. The one person Genna couldn't trust. Her stomach knotted as she felt the battle about to brew.

She had to be careful. A charity for underprivileged women was an altruistic endeavor. It was a good thing. And even if it wasn't her world, she knew it was much needed. Women were often mistreated by the law, by the system, and by the men who made the system. It was hard enough to get economic traction if you had privilege growing up. It might be nearly impossible without it. She had to be very careful. This charity could be a step in the right direction. This could ride Jerry Glen to the top. Or it could tumble down around his shoulders. *Her* shoulders. It was her job to make him win. How was she going to bail him out of this?

She straightened the pillows behind her, then poured fresh coffee.

Something unfamiliar crept into her belly. She tried to ignore it, but then she realized that she had always had this feeling. It was a feeling she had tamped down, snuffed out, and put out with the trash. The feeling was a guilty conscience, and it was a hard emotion to manage for someone who wanted to win no matter what. No matter the cost.

The question hung in her mind, now. What — exactly — had she won?

Money in the bank; true enough. Professional prominence. Clients who sang her praises. She was respected for her talents, maybe even a little feared. She could move mountains, overcome any obstacle. And she would do anything to win.

She felt another pang of misgiving.

It wasn't her fault women battled a no-win war. It wasn't her fault underprivileged women struggled. So why did she feel guilty about it now?

Because she hadn't bothered to notice at all, that's why. Because she had not stopped long enough in her own struggle to the top to notice all the others at the bottom. Because she had pandered to men in power. For power. Because she had pushed other women down to stand above them.

She bit down on this feeling of shame rising like the steam from her cup. Rustling the pages of the newspaper, she distracted herself with ads for cars and vacations and brand new smiles. None of these trinkets were out of her reach. She had not grown up underprivileged. She was given clout and told to use it. She knew no other way. It hadn't been easy, but it was how the game was played. So, what, she asked herself again — had she won?

Skin as thick as a hide, for one. She worked harder than anyone. She compared herself to everyone. And if a peer seemed to have *more* or *better*, it meant she had failed. Not only had she failed, but it also meant she was a *failure*.

Her truth, now becoming clear, told her she wasn't the champion she thought she was. And the truth made her ache.

She built a wall to keep people out — or at least at a safe distance. And in doing so, she had locked herself in. The knife twisted again. She chopped down on the Danish and felt her jaws clench until they ached.

She wasn't the best. Did best even exist? She was uncompromising. She was the loudest voice in the room. Genna's way was the right way. Even among her friends. The ache grew. Especially among her friends. The kind of friends you cherish with every inch of your soul. They knew she wasn't perfect, even when she couldn't admit it herself, but they loved her anyway. A tear squeezed from under her lids and puddled in her lashes. Surprised, she batted it away.

She had been so cruel to Amy. And why?

Because she felt ashamed. Because she believed she was right, and Amy was wrong. On board the Darwinian, she had dropped her wall. She put down her guard long enough to fall for tall, dark, and handsome. She let herself be used. She let herself be taken for a fool. And then she blamed Amy.

Amy had nothing to do with it.

Genna exhaled deeply, and the tears began to flow.

For the first time in a very long time, Genna did not feel confident of her convictions, nor right in her righteousness. She felt duped by her own blind delusions.

Time to retire, she thought suddenly. Time to lay down her self-appointed importance and take up a hobby. She could practice yoga and find religion. She could learn to knit and bake cookies and volunteer at the local soup kitchen.

If they would have her. They might not.

Her father's voice popped into her head. "Stop being such a sissy," she said out loud with her father's cadence. She wasn't raised to be a cry-baby loser. She was a Gregory; capable of anything she set her mind to do.

She wiped the tears from her cheeks, and settling her shoulders against the pillows behind her, she snapped the newspaper shut. If

Pamela Duke was going to be tried in the media for the crime against her husband, maybe Genna had an angle to work. First things first. She had to pull Jerry Glen out of the guilty heap and get him back on track.

Maybe Pamela was guilty. Maybe she wasn't. But she was not taking Jerry Glen down with her. Not on her watch. Villiger was winning a seat in Congress. There was no other way.

There was only one other person who could help save him.

WWGD? What Would Genna Do if the roles were reversed? Would she help a foe in need?

A Phil Collins song from her college days came to mind. *"If you told me you were drowning, I would not lend a hand."*

WWMD? Would Merriweather help Genna save Jerry Glen? Or would she smile while she and Villiger sank below the water line?

With a breath of determination, Genna decided what she had to do next.

If you can't beat 'em, beat 'em anyway. It was time to give Merriweather Hopkins a much overdue call.

CHAPTER TWENTY TWO

Amy read the newspaper story twice. *Wine Pioneer's Death Ruled a Homicide.* The morning had gotten busy, and she hadn't even noticed the other Cardboard Cottage shopkeepers arrive to open their stores. If Zelda had hollered her familiar, *"Yoo Hoo!"* as she passed Tiddlywinks, Amy hadn't noticed, but the people walking past with packages told her the two stores were open and doing business. She'd trot down the hall to get their reactions to the story if she could catch a little break.

According to the reporter, the investigation was ongoing, and the facts that could be published were few. But the word was out. This had been a horrible crime. Bluff Springs had its share of untimely deaths and counterfeit hundred-dollar bills. But not something like this. She should trust the detectives to solve the crime as they were trained to do. But Pamela Duke was already in the hot seat, and so was Jerry Glen. Genna would have to punt hard if her overly ambitious candidate was arrested. Until then, just keep on trucking, Sparks.

Except — except she couldn't get the snippet out of her mind. The cellar in her dream was at the Dukes. The raccoons represented the Six-Pack. So, why did this not feel like a foregone conclusion? Something didn't gibe. It was one of those picture riddles that didn't match. What was missing from this picture? Find that, and you find the truth.

What facts did she know? She'd snooped in an office. She'd overheard a conversation in a bar. She'd found things that didn't make sense. But facts and truth? Where were they? What part of her snippet could she trust? The thought landed with a thud in her chest. After all this time, she finally understood what Grandmother Ollie had tried to explain to a child, and then to a sullen teenager. And lastly to a stubborn young woman who didn't want to listen. *Better to ignore them, dear.*

Because they would consume every waking moment if you didn't ignore them! Snippets were a nuisance. An odd bit of this, a quirky bit of that, and a lot of imagination mingled in. But she didn't want to ignore them. Ignoring them felt like the wrong thing to do. *If you want to do it, do it*, Rian had said. *Regret is for sissies.*

She had to admit she didn't know how to solve a crime. She had no training. And yet, with not much more than tenacity and the fleeting parts of a dream, she had managed to protect the people she loved. No one was chasing them now. None of them were headed to jail. Not unless the police believed Genna delivered the poisoned wine to his door on purpose. Even that would be a stretch for a homicide detective. Hard *h*.

The obvious wasn't always so obvious, and yet, if she followed the one thing that didn't fit, until it led to another thing that didn't fit, and so on, maybe she could manage to do that again. What was wrong with the picture in her head? Four raccoons smoking cigars. That's what was wrong with the picture.

"Miss!" a woman said at her shoulder. Amy realized the woman had been trying to catch her attention for some time.

"I'm so sorry. I was light years away in my thoughts."

"I could tell," the woman said. "Can you help me?"

"Yes, of course," Amy answered, bringing herself back into Tiddlywinks body, mind, and soul. "You have my undivided attention, now."

"I want to find a game for my step-grandchildren. Something we can all play together when I visit. They play so many video games that I want an old-school game, but one they will enjoy. I want to hear our family laugh again. Especially because now that I have a new daughter-in-law, who already has children. I want us to have some fun together at the table — that's something the world is missing right now. We had so much fun playing games as kids."

Amy eyed the woman in front of her. She was like so many others she'd met at the store. It didn't matter how old or young, people wanted to connect with those they loved with laughter. Games could make that happen.

Amy smiled. "What are their ages?"

"Eight, ten, and *fifteen*," the woman said and grimaced. "Teenagers are so hard to please."

Amy chuckled. She didn't have a teenager in her world, but she had been one, recalling the sneer that took over her top lip during those years. Neither of her parents could do anything right until after college. It wasn't until then that she realized they were the same loving, intelligent people who raised her. It was she who had grown into less of a jerk.

Amy pulled several games from the shelves — *Uno, Guess Who,* and *Clue*. She added two games that had just been released, and while she hadn't played them yet, they both received excellent reviews. The women eyed the stack, nodded, then bought them all.

"It's good to have plenty of options," she added with a wink. "I'm not above bribing my way into my new family."

After processing the payment and sliding the games in a Tiddlywinks shopping bag, Amy smiled warmly at the woman. "Farewell and fond memories," she called as the bell jangled behind her.

Now, glancing at her watch, she was excited to see the time. The shop was closing for the day, and she hoped to uncork some details about the wine country. She might even score some tidbits on how to buy a good bottle of wine.

Amy recognized the slim figure as she walked through the door of Tiddlywinks. Her hair was piled in a bun as it was before. She wore a similar outfit, too, with a pale pink dress shirt open at the collar, a black suit jacket, and a matching short skirt. Her long legs were not in sensible shoes. A bottle of wine poked from the top of her big bag slung over her shoulder.

"Amy Sparks." She held out her hand to the woman. "I appreciate your willingness to meet us here instead of the other way around."

"Always eager to please," Bethany answered with a broad smile. Amy noticed that her lips were pink — matching her shirt — and her smile was warm. She also noticed the same shadows she saw in the dark of the bar. Part of it was eyeliner, but it looked like Bethany Keller wasn't getting enough sleep.

Amy motioned to a table where Rian and Zelda could join them. Rian came in a moment later in a camouflage tee-shirt that said, *'Don't tread on me.'* The picture of a coiled rattlesnake was well faded from washing. Zelda arrived shortly after on a breath of freshly spritzed perfume.

She introduced them to Bethany.

"Since we're a cooperative business, we thought we could buy wines cooperatively," Amy offered. "These are my business compadres. We're missing one, but we all share the same tastes in wine. Where do we start?"

"How about with a taste?" Bethany pulled the wine from her bag, a corkscrew, and four plastic cups. She opened the wine, explaining how the label gave all the information one needed — the varietal or type of grape, the appellation or region of origin, the vintage, and the vintner. In the hour that followed, Amy learned more about wine and her tastes for wine than she knew possible. They also learned that wine budgets could span from twenty bucks a bottle to thousands.

"Do you want to drink or collect?" Bethany asked.

Amy shrugged. "We drink wine at our weekly game night. One bottle doesn't go very far with four of us."

"I wouldn't mind collecting," Zelda said. "But I don't have a basement for a cellar."

"A wine fridge is a good solution," Bethany said. "I can send a catalog of quality brands that offer an industry discount through us."

After another brief wine education, they finally settled on two cases—one white and one red to drink. Zelda started her collection. Bethany seemed pleased.

"You will be happy with your purchases," Bethany said, beaming, the little knob of hair on her head bobbing as she spoke. "I will arrange to have this delivered from our warehouse cellar as soon as possible."

She held out her hand to shake Zelda's. "You've been such a pleasure. I hope we get a chance to do this again. I want to help more women grow their wine knowledge. And their cellar stock."

Amy saw her chance. She retrieved the bottle of wine Pamela left behind, turning the bottle forward.

Bethany eyed the bottle. "Where did this come from?"

"Do you know this wine?"

Bethany glanced at Amy and frowned. "Did you buy this locally?

"No," Amy said.

Bethany reached for the bottle. "May I?"

Amy nodded. Bethany turned the bottle in her hands, brushed the surface with her thumb, and then cradled the foil cap. It felt like a ceremony, something one might witness while serving Japanese tea.

"Was this a gift, by chance?"

"You could say that. It came from Pamela Duke."

Bethany's shoulders straightened.

"Is there something wrong with it?"

"No, but that explains it."

"Explains ... what?"

She exhaled, and Amy recognized the sigh slash scoff breath she heard on the phone before. It was habit. It wasn't about being bored or having contempt. It was just an odd habit of letting out air.

"This is one of the wines chosen for the Cork Docs. They each bought a case at five grand. And that's a bargain," she added, glancing quickly at Zelda as if to discredit any surprise. "They'll be able to sell a *single* bottle for five K in another few years."

Amy shut down her surprise. She didn't want to show her lack of knowledge or sophistication, but she couldn't believe Pamela had gifted her an expensive bottle of wine. The Cork Docs were serious about their investment. Mentally, she tallied what kind of profit Duke might be pocketing from this arrangement. Not to ignore the opportunity to add to his personal collection in the cellar.

"This is all legal?" Amy asked.

Bethany eyed her carefully. "Well, yes. With a few restrictions."

She handled the bottle again, her thumb rhythmic as she stroked the edges where the paper and the glass joined, then frowned. She glanced at Amy, looking over her shoulder.

"Is something wrong with this bottle?" Amy's mind was racing. What if this was one of the black widow wines? What if all the wines sold to the Cork Docs were poisoned?

"There's nothing wrong with this wine," Bethany said. "I'm just surprised that Mrs. Duke had a bottle and gave it away. I didn't realize there were bottles unclaimed. I didn't know there were bottles in circulation in our territory." She straightened her skirt and smoothed the points of her collar. "It's my job to check the cases and inventory the wine when it arrives at the warehouse. I check every bottle, the condition, the box's condition, and everything shy of opening it up and giving it a taste." She grinned. "I wish I could do that, too!

"When I inventoried this wine, which I knew was headed to the Cork Docs, I noticed the bottles in two cases had a slightly different look. Well, not different, just, you know... different."

Rian nodded as if she understood the lingo. She and Amy exchanged glances.

"I wasn't sure what to do," Bethany continued. "I asked Kirk what he thought about it because he was the only one in the office at the time. He said that it was obvious the cases came from two sources. He suggested the bottles had been kept in two distinct environments and that I should have figured that out independently."

"What happened then?"

"Well, nothing happened. Kirk was right. I should have figured that out. And then Kirk sent me off on an errand like he always does. I think it was dry cleaning day." Bethany shook her head. "I assumed the cases were delivered. Nothing else was said about it."

Zelda popped the table with her fingernails. "That would sure piss me off," she thundered. "I hate when they mansplain."

"I'm getting used to it." Bethany frowned and rubbed the bottle again. "I've learned a lot about the industry from Donald Duke, but there's so much to know. I'm still learning, and I haven't received my certifications yet." She looked up and smiled at the three of them. "But I'm getting there. I'm learning from the warehouse out."

Amy leaned in. "You thought something wasn't right, I can tell. You hinted at that on the phone when we talked about the Cork Docs."

"Did we? I don't remember."

But then, to Amy's surprise, Bethany nodded. She glanced again out the front window of Tiddlywinks as if looking for someone. Bethany brought her attention back to the table, poured another sip from the bottle in each of their glasses, then leaned forward. She was almost whispering.

"One of the club members told me he was concerned about some of the wine the Cork Docs bought. I thought he was going to say the wine was overpriced. Of course, it sometimes is. Investment wine is all about speculation, and that's the name of the game. Everyone who invests knows that. There's always an element of risk."

She took a sip and continued. "He said he'd been following an internet thread on how easily collectors can be duped into buying something less than stellar. I told him they were safe with us — with Donald— that they would never encounter anything like that with Alpha Wine. I told him that the Cork Docs would be fine if they stuck with what Mr. Duke recommended and he could put his suspicions to rest. Of course, I didn't want him to raise a red flag.

And I didn't want to get caught in the middle of that either.

"When I mentioned this to the Duke, he laughed at me. He chastised me for bringing it up!" Bethany frowned as if remembering.

"But then I overheard him and Kirk arguing about it later. Kirk wanted to fire me over that comment. He said I was misrepresenting the company's standards! Donald came to my defense. He was always coming to my defense. Kirk can be a tough boss. He likes everything just so."

"Can you tell a counterfeit by looking at a bottle?" Rian asked.

"Only if you know what you're looking for. And only if it's rather obvious."

Amy thought of the photos in the apartment, the red circles marking what wasn't obvious to the naked eye. She wished she had thought to take a picture with her phone.

Rian steepled her fingers. "Are counterfeit wines that common?"

"Yes and no," Bethany answered. "There are many kinds of wine fraud. Re-labeling fraud is one of the most common. High-dollar investment wines that are sold at auction houses like Christy and Sotheby are carefully vetted before they ever make it to the lot. Their provenance is carefully tracked. You only hear of a few bottles slipping by now and again. It's almost like an art forgery." Her eyes widened as if excited by the idea.

"*We* don't have the resources for that kind of wine — I mean, Alpha Wine and Spirits doesn't. We have access to some fine and even some rare specimens, but nothing to sell by the case and nothing that would fall into suspicion."

"Does this bottle fall into suspicion?" Amy asked.

Bethany shrugged. "You can't examine the cork markings before pulling it. There's no foolproof way to verify vintage or geographical provenance. You either trust or you don't trust. We sommeliers are trained to have an educated guess, but it's still only that."

Rian asked, "Has this bottle been manipulated?"

Bethany shook her head. "I don't think so. There are ways to make a bottle look like it's from an old cellar, but I think this is legit."

Amy leaned forward forcing Bethany's gaze. "Police forensics found the tip of syringe needle in the bottle that killed Donald."

"They found what?" Bethany's brown eyes widened.

Amy nodded. "The bottle was injected with a barbiturate. It's a potent drug; something used at a surgeon's operating facility."

"Or a vet clinic," Rian added.

"The drug was injected through the cork. Enough of it to cause a deadly overdose with a single glass."

Bethany shifted uneasily in the chair and raised the glass to her lips as if she could draw comfort in the last sips remaining. Her brow creased, and Amy wondered what thoughts were churning behind those confused brown eyes.

"Bethany," Amy said calmly. "You mentioned the TTB audit to me earlier. Do you think Duke and Kirk were counterfeiting wines to sell to the Cork Docs? Could that have been what triggered the audit? Did he confide in you?"

Bethany shook her head, and her top knot shook. The long strands in her bun drooped around her face. The corners of her mouth were tightly drawn, and Amy saw the tears welling in the corners of her eyes.

"Are you sure?" Amy asked.

"If the Cork Docs *were* being defrauded," Rian added, "your friend was right."

"Oh, no," Bethany breathed, her hands raking her bangs.

"That could be what triggered the audit," Rian said. "That could be what killed Donald Duke."

The table went silent. Bethany's lips were no longer pink.

"Who was the Cork Doc who mentioned the fraud?"

Bethany shook her head.

"Come on," Zelda said. "You can tell us."

"Chad Barling," she croaked from dry lips. "But it was Hank who told me."

"But Hank isn't one of the Cork Docs."

"No, but Hank and Dr. Barling play golf every week."

Amy licked lips that had suddenly gone dry, too, despite the lingering taste of fine wine in her mouth. Doctor Chad Barling was married to one of Pamela Duke's best friends. Pamela Duke's husband was out of the picture. He was out of the picture and out of the club. And now, maybe someone else was hoping for a chance at love. Someone named Hank.

CHAPTER TWENTY THREE

"*Nach a Mool*," Amy said as Bethany left Tiddlywinks and the door jangled behind her. Bethany was rattled by the news of the drugged bottle and the needle used to inject it.

"Hail Mary," Rian added.

"Men!' Zelda exclaimed. "They're always getting in the way of a good time!"

Amy nodded. "It sounds like the Cork Docs *were* getting defrauded. Hank was full of sophomoric rage because he didn't get the girl of his dreams. The wife had motive, opportunity, and friends to stage an alibi. If we're right, whose husband is next?"

"Kill two husbands with one stone," Zelda said.

"Or one needle," Amy added.

"There are only two husbands left in the Six-Pack," Rian added. "Chad Barling and Kirk Waters."

The three of them looked at each other, eyes wide.

"I'd like to know how their scam works," Rian added. "I need to know what counterfeiting looks like when people start ripping off my cannabis wine."

Amy grinned. No one was going to rip off Kool-Aid flavored bong water, but now wasn't the time to snuff out Rian's pipe dream.

"I compared the label I took from Duke's office to the one on this bottle. It's not the same. It's French, but a different wine. This bottle is the one that Pamela gave me and that is the same wine that went to the Cork Docs. The wine we drank at Pamela's was yet another French wine. Remember, it was the one that got all the pomp and presentation. That's the wine in the picture with the red circles. And in the picture without the red circles."

"Shew," Rian said. "Let me get this straight. You're saying the vintage we drank at Pamela's and the picture we saw in the apartment are the same wine."

Amy nodded.

"But they don't match the label you swiped from the bag."

"Right," Amy agreed.

"And the wine Pamela gave you is the wine that went to the Cork Docs, but something was off about it."

"I wish I had been paying more attention when I was in the cellar," Amy said, "but I crunched something under my foot and then Pamela was trying to hand me wine to carry." Amy gasped suddenly. "Oh, my! Guess what I stepped on?"

"Tell us," Zelda demanded. "We're not playing twenty questions for this."

"It was a piece of chert. The same kind of sharp stone that punctured my tire. I think it had the same green vein running through it, too. I didn't pay much attention to it then, but I am pretty sure it's the same chert from the horse ranch."

"Hail Mary," Rian said again. "From the horse ranch to the wine cellar. That's a direct path of evidence. What did you do with the rock?"

"Scooted it away with my foot. I had no idea it was relevant."

Amy looked up as the Cardboard Cottage & Company door jangled again.

Bethany stood in the doorway, her eyes red and filled with tears.

"What is it?" Zelda asked, rising to step toward her. "What's happened?"

Bethany shut her eyes and shivered. "I didn't know the wine was poisoned," she said with trembling lips.

Zelda put an arm around Bethany's shoulders and ushered her to the seat she had vacated moments before. She slumped down into the chair and lowered her eyes. The three of them waited. The confident woman who sold them four cases of wine was no longer composed.

"I put the wine in the room," she said. "But I swear, I didn't know it would kill him!"

"Whoa," Rian said. "Back up and tell us everything. But wait a minute." Rian left the room and returned with a bottle of Cognac. She poured a shot into each of the glasses they had abandoned after their wine flight. Bethany downed hers in one gulp.

"Start at the beginning," Amy said.

"I don't know where that is," Bethany wailed.

"How about you start with the wine in the hotel room," Rian said and poured another finger into Bethany's glass.

"I checked them into the hotel," Bethany said, her voice shaky. "Two gift bags were waiting for them at the front desk. The clerk said they were delivered for Alpha Wine and Spirits."

"By whom?"

"I didn't ask. It happens a lot. Reps are always trying to catch their attention."

"Why would you check them in? Can't they do that for themselves?"

"That's part of my job. I handle the travel."

"But you didn't book a room for yourself?" Bethany had been bitter about that, Amy remembered from their phone conversation.

"I didn't plan to stay overnight."

"You drove up for the day?"

"I drove up for the social hour."

"Why?"

"Because that's what I do. I fetch when they say fetch. And when Duke said Pamela was all over him about bringing the dog and leaving her in the truck, he wanted me to take her home with me or take her to the hotel."

"You had Claret with you?

"What? The wine we served at the party was a Pinot Noir."

Rian shook her head. "The Duke's dog. Her name is Claret."

"Oh, right."

Amy and Rian exchanged glances. Claret would be hard to forget.

"Did you let her outside in the courtyard at the hotel?"

"Outside?" Bethany echoed. "Why would I do that?"

Amy shook her head. "I'm just trying to fill in some gaps."

"I'm not much of a dog person," Bethany added and wrinkled her nose.

"I hear that," Zelda said. "The only fur I want in my house is fake chinchilla on a velvet hanger."

Rian shook her head at Zelda.

"What are you gawking at?" Zelda spat. "I'd never buy a real chinchilla."

"Tell us what you did next," Amy urged.

Bethany sighed. That bored, contempt sort of a snort flared her nostrils as she touched a finger to her pinky. "I checked them in." She touched her ring finger. "Then I took the dog — Claret to the room." She touched her middle finger, and Amy realized Bethany was ticking off her actions with her fingers. Everybody had a trick for remembering things. Her own habit of counting stairs was proof.

"I put the wine and the bag on the table so he would see it." She touched pointer finger to pointer finger. "And then I left the hotel. No, I took the other bottle of wine to Kirk's room. And then I left the hotel."

"Do you know what time that was?"

"Maybe four o'clock. Oh, wait, I have a receipt. I stopped to get gas on the way to the conference." She rummaged into her purse and pulled out a receipt. "This says 4:17." She stuffed it back into her bag. "I saw Jerry Glen and Kirk in the lobby at the conference. I hugged my uncle and gave Kirk the room key envelopes. Then I went into the party." Again, she ticked off her fingers on one hand.

"Why did you tell Duke he couldn't check in until five?"

Bethany frowned. "I never said that. I don't *think* I ever said that. I don't know why I would."

"When was the last time you saw Mr. Duke."

"After the party. I went to his room to… to … make sure he had everything he needed before I left town. I was hoping to talk to him about something important to me, but he didn't answer me. I was just entering the corridor, and he was already at his door. He didn't see me or hear me call out because he went into the room and shut the door."

"How did you know it was him?"

Bethany looked puzzled. "It was his room. I would recognize his hat anywhere. I knocked, but he didn't answer. The dog was barking."

"What time was this?"

Her jaw worked around the answer. "It would have been almost seven. A few minutes later, I got a text."

"A man's gotta do what a man's gotta do," Zelda said.

"How did you know that?"

"Pamela got the same text. Kirk did, too. Why didn't you tell the police about the wine?"

"I can't. I can't even tell Uncle Jerry! He would be so disappointed after everything he's done for me!"

Amy studied the young woman for a moment. Her distress was genuine. So, Jerry Glen Villiger was her uncle. That wasn't surprising, given the familial construct of the town. Duke had not been a fan. Not by a long shot. What was the reason for that? And how was Bethany wedged in between? Which one was she protecting?

Rian turned dark eyes to face Bethany. "What was the real reason you drove to Bluff Springs? You didn't come all this way to take a dog to a hotel."

Bethany raked her bangs and looked at Amy for rescue. "Look, it's not a perfect job, and I hate when it's 'fetch this and carry that' like a bellhop. I deserve to be treated better. I'm smart and I'm always trying to do my best." She glanced at the three of them one by one. "I want to be part of the company. A junior partner. And I had the money to invest. Everyone agreed on it. I know Uncle Jerry gave him the money, because Duke asked me to take the bag to the room. It was Uncle Jerry's gym bag. I know it because he's had the same one for decades. I didn't dare open the bag, but I knew what was in it."

"What was in it?" Rian asked.

"My entire savings and then some."

"In cash?"

Bethany nodded. "But now, I don't know what's happening! I think the police confiscated it and I'll never get it back!"

"Why was Villiger part of this?"

"He's been helping me with some legal matters. He's making sure that I—" She stalled and then glanced at Amy, who nodded encouragingly. "I have every right to be a partner at Alpha Wine and Spirits and he was trying to help make sure that it happened."

"Bethany," Amy said quietly. "What harm could possibly come to you for telling the truth? You could tell police about the wine. You could clear your name."

"No!" Bethany screeched. "I can't! They're going to say it was me! That I stole the money! That I killed him! The one person who knows I didn't kill him is dead!"

CHAPTER TWENTY FOUR

"What a player," Zelda said. "Do we believe her?"

"I do," Amy said. "She was in the wrong place with the wrong bottle of wine."

"Well, there's a snag in her story," Rian added. "She put herself in that room on purpose. She was at the social hour because she is one the company's wine reps. She didn't have to drive to Bluff Springs to rescue his dog. The dog was an excuse to get into his room."

"I don't see what you're getting at," Amy said.

"Think about it. You've had a rough day at the wine mine, and your angry soon-to-be-ex-wife yells at you about the dog. A politician threatens you in the hallway, and then his PR guru propositions you with a bribe. What's the first thing you do?"

"Take a shower and pour a drink," Zelda said.

"Or in my case, roll a doobie."

Amy grinned.

"But he didn't. Duke left the room and went somewhere — we don't know where — and returned just as Bethany was coming to his room. He was alive at six when Genna brought the case of wine on the dolly. He was alive when Pamela returned with Claret later."

"She says he was alive," Zelda added. "It's her word against a dead man's."

"That's one way to put it," Amy said. "I have it on a good authority that the maid let someone in the room. Evidently, she claimed she'd lost her room key."

"She?" Rian asked.

Amy nodded. "A woman with silver hair." Had Genna been in the room, three pairs of eyes would have turned her way. Genna had silver hair and lots of it. So did Pamela Duke.

"Did the maid describe her? Tall? Short?"

"Not that I know of. But then, that wouldn't help us either. Genna and Pamela are about the same height. But why would Genna sneak back to that room? That doesn't make sense."

"Timing is everything," Rian said as she poured a final round of Cognac. Squinting against the fumes, she took a sip and exhaled. "If Waters had the same wine in his gift bag, why wasn't he poisoned?" She paused for a moment. "I'll tell you why. Because I think Donald Duke let Bethany in when she knocked on the door around seven. I don't think he ignored her at all. It wasn't until *after* she left that he drank the poisoned wine. Maybe she poisoned the bottle when he wasn't looking. It only took that one glass to kill him. His death was quick."

"But what about the text?"

"Bragging rights," Zelda offered. "Texted to the wife and the business partner to rub salt in the wounds. Texted to Bethany to let her know, too. But I hate to break it to you," Zelda added with a flourish of rings and bracelets. "That's not even a John Wayne quote. Everybody thinks it is, but it's not. The only actor I know who said it verbatim was George Jetson."

"What are you talking about?" Rian asked.

Zelda nodded. "It's a quote from George Jetson in the '*High Moon*' cartoon."

"How in the world do you know that?" Amy asked.

"Husband number three was a John Wayne devotee." She grinned back at Amy. "We played cowboy and the cantina girl. We…"

"Nope," Amy interrupted, waving her hands in front of Zelda. "I don't want any details about the cantina girl. TMI."

Zelda shrugged. "I wasn't going to tell you *that kind* of detail. I was going to tell you we won a trivia game with that little tidbit. You'd think a John Wayne buff would know that."

"Thanks a bunch," Amy chuckled. "Now I can't hear anything in my head but the theme song from the Jetsons."

Rian nodded. "It's possible the text was about bragging, but it didn't come from Duke. I think it came from Bethany. I think she's the one who wanted to rub salt in the wounds."

"Holy cow," Zelda said. "She may be the last person to see him alive."

"She may be *why* he's not alive," Rian added.

Amy shook her head. "Well, maybe I can believe she's telling the truth but not the whole truth. I don't see any sexual vibe between her and Duke at all. She was trying to win his favor and earn a place in his company, but not in that way. I agree, something is missing in the middle.

"Murder by poison takes careful planning," Amy added. "That kind of person would have to be cunning and calculated. That person would have to be conniving and cold-hearted enough to believe they could get away with it."

"That fits all of them," Zelda mumbled. "I'm still a firm believer in the *wasbund* club. This has Six-Pack written all over it. If Bethany delivered the goods, she didn't realize it until you told her about the needle. That really freaked her out. She came back to make sure we knew that fact."

"We can't discount anybody's story or their alibi," Amy added. "The drug could have been injected into the bottle anytime, anywhere. All you need is a hairdryer to seal the foil; every hotel room has one of those."

Rian nodded. "And don't forget, there was a state-wide conference in town that day, so the field of suspects is huge. We know that Bethany, Genna, Pamela, and Kirk were in Duke's hotel room at some point, but that doesn't mean they're the only ones."

"Don't forget Claret," Amy said.

"And Claret," Rian agreed.

"Well, someone is guilty," Zelda added. "You just have to prove who."

"Me?" Amy asked. "Why me?"

Zelda grinned at her best friend. "Because you're the psychic detective. We just tag along for the ride."

Zelda and Rian left her then, locked up their shops for the night, and left the building. Amy tidied the leftovers from the wine and Cognac tasting. She straightened the shelves of games, dropped her deposit bag into her purse, and turned off the lights. It was not even seven, but the sun-cast shadows lay soft against the wingback chairs in the front window. Feeling the quiet settle in, Victor jumped down from his perch and ambled cat-cocky to her side, his tail waving like a wheat frond in the wind. He wove through her legs, meow-chirping as he circled. He was ready for dinner.

Amy looked up as the door opened, jangling for the nth time that day. It was a sound she was so used to that she looked up with a smile each time she heard the jangle of bells like a Pavlovian response. Her smile faded quickly. A man in a crumpled white shirt stood in the doorway, scanning the room.

"I'm sorry, we're closed." She spoke from across the room. "We open tomorrow at nine."

"Amy Sparks?" He asked when their eyes met.

His voice carried across the room, the tables, and all the wood planks between her and the door, between her and an escape. Panic rose from around her knees, and she felt Victor press close against her leg.

"What do you want?"

He didn't move. He stood in the doorway, not entirely blocking it but not advancing through it either. In this stance, he was silhouetted by the light behind him. She couldn't see his features or the expression on his face. Was he dark-headed or blond? Green-eyed or blue? Friend or foe? She had no idea, just a feeling. All she could tell was that he was tall and muscular and male.

"I'm a private investigator," he said finally. "I've been hired to look into matters that bring me to Bluff Springs, and you're on my list of people to see."

"Hired by who?"

"Now, that's client privilege. It's kind of like asking a banker how much money you have in your account." He grinned as if he knew how much money she had in her account. She gulped. She was still holding her purse with the green deposit bag poking out of the top, zipper side up.

"It's closing time. I'm ready to go home. You'll have to come back." She hoped she sounded convincingly authoritative.

"You're only climbing the stairs to your apartment," he said, motioning with his head. "It's not like you have a long commute or anything."

Her jaw dropped.

"I'll make it brief. I only have three questions."

She stared at him. She couldn't help it. Three questions? She'd never sleep tonight if she didn't find out what three questions. She would toss and turn and ruminate in bed until Victor stalked off in a huff for disturbing his beauty sleep. Besides, how did he know where she lived?

He stepped forward as if he saw her resolve waiver. She could see him more clearly, then. Dark eyes. Dark hair. It had been a while since he had a haircut and a shave.

"I'm harmless," he said. "Honest. I just look a little rough. It fits my PI persona. Would it be okay if I come in and sit down?"

She narrowed her eyes at him, and then Victor stalked over, his wheat-frond tail brushing the air. The man squatted on his haunches and petted the stripes on Victor's head.

"Traitor," she mumbled to the cat.

He grinned. "Yeah, cats like me for some reason."

CHAPTER TWENTY FIVE

"Do you have a badge or anything," Amy asked. They were seated at one of the game tables, with Victor perched on his lap, purring away as if the two of them were long-lost souls reunited. She had acquiesced out of curiosity and the fact that Victor had followed him in.

He grinned. "No, we can't carry a badge, wear a uniform, or pretend to be official. I don't even have a pair of handcuffs. Not on me, anyway." He grinned again. "PIs are not law enforcement. Usually, you don't even know we're there."

She raised an eyebrow. Then why was this man sitting in front of her?

"I didn't catch your name," she said.

"I haven't offered it."

"That was a polite way for me to ask: WHO are you?"

He reached into his back pants pocket, pulled out a worn wallet, and extracted a card. His fingers lingered just enough to resist Amy's effort to retrieve it. He waited for her eyes to lift to his.

"Sam Ford, Private Investigator," she read. "I like the fingerprint. Nice touch." She hoped he heard the sarcasm.

"My nephew is learning to be a graphic artist. He reads comic books. What can I say?" He shrugged, and Amy knew from the gesture that he was fond of his nephew, who probably thought his uncle was a hero. She followed his gaze as he looked over her shoulder at the shelves of games behind her.

"You make a living doing this? With people playing games?"

It wasn't said with rancor, just interest, or at least that's how she took it.

"I won't get rich if that's what you're asking, but it's a quirky, satisfying occupation. Was that one of your questions? You only have two left. And honestly, that one was a bit disappointing."

He laughed, and she saw the face behind the beard. He had laugh lines around his eyes, which were not as dark as they appeared in the doorway. Now they had an amber quality to them. Almost cat-like in color. She didn't want to look too closely, but they were attractive eyes, a feature she was drawn to in others. His nose had been broken at least once. Probably a casualty of his job.

"How do I know you're not just some crackerjack off the street with a calling card? Tell me something."

"You mean about you?"

She nodded.

He splayed his hands on the table in front of him. His knuckles were huge. He looked at Amy and smiled. "You live in the upstairs apartment. You like Stonyfield Vanilla yogurt. I mean, you really like it. You drink a moderately priced Pinot Grigio, and your cat eats Fancy Feast pate."

Her eyes widened.

"And you rinse before you recycle," he added, with a grin.

She laughed, and his grin grew wider.

"That's pretty creepy, but then, it was an easy catch if you dug around in the trash in the alley."

"I have been dumpster diving more times than I choose to admit. Especially to a woman with a contagious smile and pretty red hair."

Her hands flew to her head. She tried not to blush, but she did.

"Unfortunately, that's not why I'm here."

"Who are you investigating?" She asked.

"Ah, contagious *and* curious." He grinned again. "I said I only had three questions. That caught your attention, didn't it?"

Amy sat up a little straighter in the chair. She wasn't about to be caught off guard by some PI with great eyes and broad shoulders. "If you ask me, then I get to ask you."

He shook his head, and his voice deepened. "I can't answer questions — not about my client."

"Well, then you have only one question left," she said. "You better make it a good one."

"Just one? No!" He laughed. "How do you figure that?"

"I've been keeping track. It's kind of like counting cards. You have one left. That's it. Otherwise, you're back in the trash can."

He eyed her with amusement, then reached over to a deck of cards she kept ready for action. The motion upset Victor's perfect perch, and he jumped down. Sam Ford slid the cards out of the box and shuffled the deck. "I tell you what. We'll play a game of War. I win a war; I ask a question. You win a war; you ask a question. You game?"

Amy grinned. "I'm game." Butterflies fluttered through her stomach.

He dealt, they laid down their first card, and he took the pile with the jack of spades. They played another hand, and she took that pile with the six of diamonds. On their fourth hand, they declared War. He won.

"Why was Bethany Keller at Tiddlywinks?" he asked, sliding his spoils to his pile of cards. His eyes were focused on hers.

She blinked. There was an easy answer, and there was a not-so-easy answer. If she was truthful, she'd say Bethany Keller was at Tiddlywinks so she could pump her for information about the death of Donald Duke. If she was less than honest, she would say Bethany Keller was at Tiddlywinks to sell them wine. They were both true. Somehow, she knew he would know if she left one of them out.

"Careful," he said, watching her closely.

Her mouth was suddenly dry. If he knew Bethany by name, he

probably knew more about her than Amy would ever know. There wasn't much use in being coy.

"I wanted to know more about the inner workings of Alpha Wine and Spirits. After what happened, you could say we have a vested interest." She sat back, confident that she had answered truthfully without spilling more than she should to a stranger.

"You believe the gossip that she was having an affair with her employer." He was careful not to frame it as a question.

Amy motioned to the cards. "Was she?"

He grinned and threw down the ace of diamonds.

When she turned over the ace of spades, she wondered if he had some trick up his sleeve; some way to make war sight unseen. She had not watched his hands while contemplating her answer, so she couldn't tell if he was pulling a Genna Gregory cheat with the cards.

"Have you had physic visions all your life?"

She caught herself before she choked on her own breath. She glared at him, now feeling both vulnerable and irritated with herself. Genna had shared tidbits about her abilities at the conference. Probably elsewhere, too, dressing it up or down depending on her audience. The *psycho*-detective thing had stuck in her craw.

"I'm not psychic," she answered and pressed her lips closed.

"You have dreams and then it happens. Crimes. Murders." Again, it wasn't a question. He was good at this.

She glanced at the cards and then at him. "Sometimes." She'd give him that, war or not.

They played a few hands before a pair of twos came to the surface. She turned over the king of clubs and grabbed the pile.

"Why are you watching me?"

"I told you. I'm investigating a matter for a client."

"A *matter* or a *murder*?"

He shrugged.

Amy frowned. "Oh, come on, I gave you more than that."

He nodded, the corners of his mouth pushing his mustache into a grin. "We're not on opposite teams, you and me. We're both rooting for the good guys." He said it like he was offering up a clue. "Inner workings would be a good way to put it, and it's not the first time they've been audited. If you were asked to make a sizable investment in a company, you'd want to know the history on all the players, right? Past, present, and future. Especially when one of them winds up dead and fifty thousand dollars goes missing."

"Fifty thousand dollars! Who are you investigating?"

"Oh, you're way out of bounds, now, Amy Sparks, age 48, divorced. You're in debt up to your elbows. Although you are making all your payments on time. Title on your Miata's free and clear. Taxes are paid. You have no outstanding warrants here or in Florida. Your business seems to be running on the up and up, even if a lot of estrogen is involved." He shook his head.

"Your three closet friends — well, one of them has about as many unpaid parking tickets as you can have without serving jail time. One of them has a rather clandestine business. And the other one doesn't use her turn signal. Ever.

Amy glared at him. How long had he been watching them? Before today, she hadn't seen this man anywhere, yet he knew way too much about them. It gave her the willies.

"Your friend Sammie and her boyfriend have a bit of a checkered past."

"Sammie?"

"That's not her given name. Her name is one of those Irish names with lots of letters in unpredictable places. I can't blame her for changing it when she moved to the US. You know," he added with a cocky grin, "all these online DNA registries make the hunt for relatives and paternity claims a PI piece of cake. You can find just about anybody these days. That and insurance frauds are my bread and butter. I prefer to leave crime to the cops."

Amy gaped at him.

"I'm just a crackerjack with a calling card," he said. His eyes sparkled with amusement. He seemed to enjoy throwing her off center. She found it infuriating. "I still have one more question." He paused. "Would you have dinner with me? I believe Paul's Italian Eatery is your favorite restaurant in town. Spaghetti and meatballs with tiramisu for dessert?"

Amy could only stare at him in disbelief.

CHAPTER TWENTY SIX

Merriweather Hopkins answered on the fourth ring. Genna was about to hang up when the smooth, southern voice answered.

"Genna! So good to hear from you, dear. I wondered when I would."

Genna exhaled deeply. "No news is bad news, and bad news is worse," she said quickly.

Merriweather gave a little laugh. It was a saying they both knew well.

"You know why I'm calling."

"I assume it's about Pamela Duke and her affiliation with Jerry Glen Villiger, but I can't—"

"What you *can* do is shed light on this charitable project," Genna interrupted sharply. "Why didn't I know about it? Why is Pamela Duke in every one of his press photos? And why did you toss him under the bus with a front page caption about the murder of Donald Duke!"

"I didn't toss him anywhere. He got there on his own."

"I know you. You threw Villiger in the ring because I'm involved in his campaign!"

"As you are well aware of the process, the press release was already on the reporter's desk long before this… this unfortunate circumstance occurred. It's not my fault it landed on the same page simultaneously. You know how editors love a bit of scandal. We're both headed for a little back paddling. But if I were you, I'd be thanking me instead of, of... whatever *this* is."

"*This* is a demand for an explanation."

"We should talk in person," Merriweather said, seemingly unfazed by Genna's demands.

"Can you be at the Hilton in thirty minutes?" Genna said. "Meet me in the lounge?"

"Here in Little Rock? I'm busy until after five."

"No, not in Little Rock. I'm in Bluff Springs," Genna snapped.

Merriweather laughed politely. "Sorry, I don't have a *broom*."

Genna narrowed her eyes at the phone. Amy made a quirky comment at the conference about Genna's office being in the broom closet at the Cardboard Cottage. The innuendo didn't go unnoticed then, nor now.

"Oh, really," Genna drawled. "I heard you had the latest model."

"Do you ever get tired of being the one on top? Why not give people the benefit of the doubt?"

"Because that's how people get screwed with a capital *S* and a sharp exclamation point. You had my trust once, a long time ago."

"It has been awhile, hasn't it? We had the opportunity to reconnect at the conference, but you avoided me at every turn. I always hoped you would set aside your grudge someday."

"I'm listening," Genna said, her pulse finally slowing. "We don't have time to meet in person, so this will have to do."

"I have a meeting to get to," Merriweather said. "I'm afraid you'll have to take a rain check. I can try to call when I get free this afternoon. Is this the best number to reach you?"

Genna hung up the phone without answering. She regretted her action the moment the call disconnected. Her rude behavior wasn't winning her favors, answers, or a workable solution when there was so much at risk. She needed something from Merriweather Hopkins, not the other way around.

"Sorry," she said into the phone after the call connected to voice mail, and Merriweather intoned her polite message before the beep. "The phone slipped out of my hand at the most inopportune time," Genna lied. "I will look for your call after five."

Genna felt the sweat beaded on her forehead and lip. Her hands were clammy. The AC in the car was on full blast. She wiped her forehead with a tissue and then checked her look in the visor mirror. Was this change in perspective going to come with hot flashes, too? She hoped not. Sweat could ruin the best silk blouse.

She parked and drove to her favorite tapas and wine spot. She had time before she could engage Merriweather again, and she needed to regain her composure before facing her old nemesis, even over the phone.

Always the one on top. That used to be a compliment, but now it didn't seem so. She needed help and she would have to accept whatever was offered. All while being the same proud Genna Gregory, she told herself, as she entered the bistro, found a table for one, and ordered a tall iced tea.

CHAPTER TWENTY SEVEN

The four of them finished their meal and grew quiet. Amy watched the restaurant thin and refill with customers looking for a stack of pancakes and a slab of ham. She kept an eye on the door, expecting a tall man with shaggy brown hair and broad shoulders to slip in the door and sit close enough to eavesdrop. She was on to him now. She would be watching him should he still be watching her.

She wanted to tell her friends about Sam Ford, Private Investigator, and his visit to Tiddlywinks. She didn't want to freak them out about them being watched. It would launch Rian's paranoia into overdrive. He never explained why they were in his line of sight, other than his comment about vetting a company and some missing money. Was it Bethany's missing money? The police would have possession of that if it was in the room. She thought about pushing for details over dinner but decided that wasn't a good idea. She declined his invitation, although spaghetti and meatballs had sure sounded great.

A feeling tickled her spine. What came to mind were the laughing raccoons with their cigars and their friend paws up on the floor.

"Didn't your spidey-sense pick up on any of this?" Genna looked at Amy expectantly. "Where's that Dial-A-Psychic stuff when you need it most?"

She shook her head to answer. She wouldn't snap at the bait.

"So, Merriweather didn't call you back. Big deal," Rian said to Genna. "She'll call you when she can. There's no reason to make a scene about nothing."

"You're letting her push your buttons," Zelda agreed. "Don't let her get to you, Genna. You're still in command."

Genna nodded. "If you can beat 'em, beat 'em anyway. If anybody's going to dredge up dirt on my candidate, it will be me."

Genna reached into her purse and pulled out a map of Arkansas. She unfolded it with noisy fanfare and spread it over the table. Sticky notes with scribbles were stuck to the page in several places, and Amy noticed there were circles drawn on the map itself.

"Where are we going?" Amy asked.

"I signed y'all up before all this happened," Genna answered. "And that was good thinking because now this trip is timely."

"That doesn't answer Amy's question," Rian said, leaning over to look at the map. She tapped one of the notes. "What is this? Where are we going?"

"These are secret clues to secret destinations."

"I love secrets," Zelda exclaimed, putting a final fork-full of baked dough into her mouth.

"This looks complicated," Rian muttered, looking at the notes.

"Oh hush," Genna warned. "You agreed we needed a road trip. Now we have a good reason. Trust me."

"Huh," Rian grunted. "Trust is a sharp blade."

"Tell me about it," Amy added. "I remember a pair of bunny slippers in my not-so-distant past. Genna said something about trust then, too."

"Rian, you'll drive your Fiat. Amy can navigate. And if you keep the top down, Zelda can ride on the back like a prom queen."

"Drive the Fiat where?" Rian demanded.

"From London to Paris," Genna declared. "I told you I signed y'all up."

"When did you tell us?"

202 · JANE ELZEY

"A month ago."

"Like we can actually remember what you said a month ago."

"Team Tiddlywinks has an 11:22 start time tomorrow. Each car is separated by a seven-minute start, so don't be late."

Amy sat forward. "Wait! It's tomorrow?"

"Surprise!" Genna beamed, but Amy could tell the luster had worn off a little. She wasn't getting the enthusiasm she hoped for.

"Here's the address of the starting point." She pulled off one of the notes and handed it to Amy. "You'll get more instructions when you get there."

"You're not going with us?" Zelda asked.

"I'll meet y'all at the end. I'm in charge of the finish-line party. It's the last stump on Villiger's Big European tour. I'm willing to bet my Mercedes it will be a party you'll never forget."

"Your Mercedes got wrapped around a tree and now lives in the scrap yard," Rian remarked. "We know how you drive."

"Well," Genna huffed, "no need to get personal. Not everything goes off without a hitch one hundred percent of the time." Genna reached into her oversized bag and pulled out a rolled-up piece of vinyl. "One more thing." She handed the roll to Rian. "These go on your car doors. They're magnetic."

Rian sign and groaned. "No way," she muttered. "I'm not driving through Arkansas with political signs on my Fiat."

"Who do you think paid your three-hundred dollar entry fee? Santa Claus?"

"Three hundred dollars!" Amy exclaimed. "What kind of road rally is this?"

"It a see-and-be-seen road rally," Genna answered. "At least from my perspective, it is. You don't have to win … just get to the finish line and make sure everybody sees you. Or at least, the signs on your car. The rally goes right through the wine country, so keep your eyes open for anything that smacks of women railroading my client to the gallows!"

Genna zipped her purse and stood up. "Alibi schmalibi! I'll see you at the finish line tomorrow," she said to three pairs of stunned eyes, raised brows, and Rian's thin frown of disapproval.

Amy was still shaking her head when Genna walked out of the restaurant, leaving the tab for her friends.

"I don't have anything better to do," Zelda said. "Why shouldn't we go? She's already paid our entry fee, and I don't mind riding around like a prom queen."

Rian eyed Zelda suspiciously. "You're going get blown to bits in the Fiat."

After a brief discussion and enough elbow twisting to convince Rian that the rally would be fun, they decided to take two cars to London tomorrow morning. Zelda and Amy would drive down in the Miata. Rian would meet them at the starting place.

"I have a couple of stops to make down that way anyway," Rian said. "I might as well take advantage of a full tank of gas and a pretty day."

Amy grinned. "I thought Granny was out of business."

Granny was Rian's code word for cannabis.

"Depends on who's asking," Rian quipped.

Rian's pot trade to an elite clientele in Arkansas was put on hiatus when Zack got too close for comfort. She still made cannabis goodies but was wary about the re-launch of her covert — and still illegal — business on a full-scale. Besides, medical marijuana use was approaching the legislature in Arkansas. Rian claimed she'd never win a franchise license, even when — or if — the law passed. She invested the windfall from Zack's business and lived on her earnings from The Pot Shed at the Cardboard Cottage. She didn't have debt that Amy knew about, and she still bought and sold vintage cars on request. Cash never seemed a problem. Amy thought of Sam Ford. He probably knew all of that.

"What are you going to do today," Zelda asked.

"You mean besides go to work?"

"Oh, yeah," Zelda said. "There's that."

"I need to run an errand before I open this morning," Amy said. "I won't be too late."

* * *

As she stepped out of the car, she noticed workers gathered around a dumpster near the back of the hotel. She could see the workers behind the big green box that was not as camouflaged by the hedge as intended. A man in work overalls squatted beside something on the ground.

Another body? Please, no!

She quickened her step.

"Stand back," one of them said as she approached. "Don't get too close."

"What is it?"

"Rats in the trash," he said simply.

"You mean live rats?"

He shook his head. He held his arm out like a crosswalk guard at school, as if to keep her from danger. "Looks like they were poisoned."

"Poisoned!" She heard the incredulity in her voice. "Poisoned on purpose?"

He shrugged. "We just found 'em. They got into something in the trash."

Amy glanced around his arm to see, but he blocked her view. "You really shouldn't be here. We called the boss, and he called the police. They said not to touch anything. To leave everything as it is. There's one over there and four more in the bin. I'm not going in after them."

Amy did not have to ask why the GM called the police. Two poisonings in less than a month wasn't coincidence. Five raccoons in her dream. Five rats in the trash.

She stepped to the side, hoping to go unnoticed, and watched as the police drove in — no sirens — and parked to block off the area.

An unmarked car pulled up seconds later and an older man with a mop of white hair ambled out. She couldn't hear them, but she could see their reactions. The man took the stick from one of the crew and poked at something out of her range of view. She knew what it was. She wouldn't envy them wading through that for the proverbial needle in the haystack.

She clasped her hands over her mouth. The needle in the haystack! The syringe with the poison! Could the syringe used to inject the poison be in that nasty bin? Would they find the drug vial, too? Had the rats eaten something tainted with the dregs of the drug? Her heart pounded so hard she had to lean against the fence for support.

The policeman marked off the area with yellow caution tape, motioning the hotel workers to move behind it. This had to more than just rats in a trash bin. There had to be evidence in the trash that made this dumpster a crime scene, too. Crime scene number two. She watched as the yardstick rose above the bin bearing a filthy white cowboy hat. Was that Duke's hat? What was it doing in the trash?

Amy wondered what else they would find as she climbed the steps to the lobby. She found her friend Doris at the front desk.

"Surprise!" She said as Doris looked up.

"You have impeccable timing," Doris exclaimed. "I've been meaning to call you and now – here you are!"

Amy hoped she would share gossip about the garbage can.

"This may or may not interest you, but I'm involved in the capital campaign fundraiser for our chamber. We're looking for another fundraising team and I thought of your gals at the Cardboard Cottage and Company. If we hit the goal, we all get to visit Ireland on the chamber tab. Would you be interested?"

"Hmmm," Amy said. "Ireland?"

"The Emerald Isle," Doris agreed.

"We might be. Let me give it a go around the table and see what everybody thinks."

"Fair enough," Doris said. "You'll let me know soon?"

Amy nodded. "I will. And, uh, is there anything you want to tell me about the trash?"

Doris signed heavily. "We just called the police. They've found something in the bin."

"I heard," Amy said.

Doris nodded. "It's very disturbing."

"I hope you don't mind, but I have a couple more questions to ask about your hotel. You know, before we book our getaways."

Doris nodded. "Fire when ready."

"Can you provide complimentary wine to guests?"

Doris frowned. "No, I'm sorry, we don't have that service."

"You mean you don't provide free wine, or you don't have it on your room service menu?"

"We don't have wine at the hotel at all. We don't have room service. We offer a complimentary breakfast, and there's OJ and coffee. I hope that's not going to be a problem for your guests."

"Oh, not at all. They can bring their own wine."

"Oh, good," Doris said. "We want to be as accommodating as possible."

Amy nodded. She felt so guilty about pumping Doris for information, but if Doris knew she was asking about what happened in the hotel room, she'd clam up.

"I assume you use key cards for the rooms?" Amy asked. "What happens if someone loses theirs? Or says it doesn't work?"

"We give them another."

"Hmm," Amy muttered. "Do you keep records of that by chance?"

"You're fishing for something, Amy Sparks."

"With a bare hook," she agreed. "I need to know if someone requested a duplicate key for that room — you know, the room that doesn't exist — during the conference? And if so, was he wearing a cowboy hat? And maybe a red bolo tie?"

Doris sighed. She was alone at the front desk at the moment. "We don't keep track of that, I'm afraid. I couldn't answer your question anyway even if I did remember. Privacy rules, you know. But there was something I wanted to mention. I shouldn't of course, but…"

Amy waited patiently as Doris answered the phone and then returned her attention to Amy.

"When the police interviewed me, they asked what color gloves the staff use. I thought that was an odd question. Of course, I told them that we buy one brand, and they're black."

"You think they found a glove that didn't belong there?"

Doris didn't respond. But her eyes did.

CHAPTER TWENTY EIGHT

It was a perfect top-down kind of day. Amy felt the excitement of being on another road trip. They would meet up with Genna at the end.

"I've never been on a scavenger road rally," she said as they sped down the highway in the Miata.

Zelda grinned from behind her Fendi shades. "Girls just wanna have fun," she said, turning up the stereo volume. Annie Lennox was singing one of their favorites. "*Would I lie to you, honey…*" Zelda sang to the wind blowing through her hair.

The parking lot was full of cars when they drove in a little more than an hour later. "Wow!" Amy exclaimed at the Corvettes and Mustangs already in the queue. Thunderbirds were lined up in a pride-flag array of colors. A sky-blue Thunderbird caught her eye.

"Nice," she called as they passed the car. The couple inside waved. There were a couple soccer mom SUVs, too, with all five doors open and young legs swinging in anticipation. One corner of the parking lot looked like a vintage car show, with every surface bright and shining in the sun. The other side of the parking lot looked like a summer camp drop-off.

"This is bigger than I thought," Amy said. "There must be thirty cars here already."

"Where's Rian?"

"She better not bail on us," Amy answered.

Amy drove around the lot looking for a spot to park and then glanced in the rearview mirror to see Rian grinning at her from behind.

"Ha! She's right behind us."

Zelda turned and waived.

"I managed to get the scoop on this rally," Rian said, now parked next the Miata. "Here's how this works." Her eyes twinkled with amusement as she held out a booklet of strange-looking hieroglyphics. "Like Genna said, each car has its own starting time spaced seven minutes apart. That keeps things from getting congested."

Amy nodded and stared down at the book she was now holding. "What is this?"

"This is our instruction manual. Our map if you will. Those little hieroglyphics are called *tulips* in a road rally, and those are the directions. You can be the navigator, Amy, and Zelda, you're going to ride in back and keep an eye on our signposts. Each leg of the course has clues we need to solve. The answer will determine where we go and what item we need to grab. It's kind of like a scavenger hunt road rally. It's not about how fast you get there, but how you score along the way."

Amy glanced down at the first page. It was a crossword puzzle with seven clues in the grid. "We have to figure out where we're going?"

"I assume we're going to Paris," Rian answered, "but not a direct route."

Zelda frowned. "We have to decipher riddles?"

"Amy's good at puzzles," Rian said. "You keep your eye out for our rivals. And whatever else we're looking for."

Zelda frowned. "I thought we would be driving in a parade."

"You can take the Miata home if you don't want to come with us," Amy said. "I can ride home with Rian."

"Did I mention the grand prize is a thousand dollars?"

"A thousand bucks!" Zelda echoed.

Zelda stepped out of the car and put her hands on her hips. "And leave you two to have all the fun and win all the money? Not on your life, Sparks. I'm in for the haul."

"In for the haul," Amy echoed. "That's my girl."

Rian handed Zelda the swag bag, and Zelda plundered in. "Look at all this stuff!" She pulled out a kaleidoscope-colored monocular and placed it in one eye. "These must be things we will need along the way. The tools of the road as it were."

Amy glanced at her watch, and her stomach jumped with excitement. "We have less than twenty minutes to figure out where our first stop is. It's a crossword puzzle. Here's the first clue: *Most towns have one.*"

"Have one what?" Zelda grumbled as she pulled a sharpened pencil from the swag bag and handed it to Amy.

"Most towns have roads. Most towns have a water tower. And too many people..." Rian answered. "They have a police station, too."

Amy shrugged. "Ten letters. Water tower fits. Do most towns have a water tower?"

"We don't," Zelda said. "But most towns have a Main Street. The Cardboard Cottage is at the corner of Bluff and Main."

"Main Street," Amy answered. "It fits. At least until we figure out some more of these clues. Good thing we have a pencil with an eraser."

"I don't think that's by accident," Rian said. "I think Zelda needs to pay close attention to every item in the swag bag."

Amy cleared her throat. "*A red fruit.*"

"Apple," Rian said.

Amy shook her head. "Six letters."

"Pomegranate," Zelda suggested.

Amy glanced at Zelda and smiled.

"How about *cherry*?" Rian asked

"Bingo." She added the word to the grid. "Next clue is: *Like*

Grand Central."

"Noisy," Rian said.

"Hurry," Zelda said.

Amy frowned. "Hurry? That doesn't fit at all."

Zelda tapped her watch. "The clock is ticking."

"Oh! Ok. Grand Central is in New York. It's a shopping mall, isn't it?"

"It used to be a place to catch a train," Rian interrupted.

"A train!" Zelda yelped. "*Like Grand Central* is a train station!"

Amy counted the letters. "It fits! How about this clue: *'type of peach found here'*?"

"Fuzzy," Zelda said. "All peaches are fuzzy."

Rian nodded. "This is Arkansas peach country, but I don't know the names of peaches. Skip this one, and we'll return to it when we have more letters."

Amy read the next clue. "Early boy band named after animals."

"The Beatles," Rian suggested.

"It fits! No, wait. It doesn't. The *e* is in the wrong place."

"The Byrds!" Zelda exclaimed. "Oh wait, that doesn't even have an *e*, does it? Just skip it! Hurry!"

"Next clue: Take the last one. *Don't be slow, oh no, no, no.*" Amy chewed the end of the pencil. "Thirteen letters. Take the last what?"

"You take a train," Zelda offered.

"That does seem to be the theme," Rian added, and the three of them fell silent to think.

"Clarksville!" Amy sputtered. "Take the last train to *Clarksville!*"

Zelda gasped. "The Monkees! That's the boy band!"

Amy scribbled in the letters as Rian pulled her keys from the pocket of her jeans. "We're headed to Clarksville, ladies. It's only about twenty minutes from here. Maybe a longer since we're carrying a prom queen on deck. Amy, all those hieroglyphics tell you what turns to make, and we can figure out the rest of the clues on the way."

They scrambled into Rian's red Fiat and made their way to the drive-through of the old bank turned into city hall. At the window, a pleasant face snapped their photo, pushed a scorecard — with one hole already punched — through the metal drawer, and said, "Good luck! Good Rally!" And the Fiat sped off right on time.

"Hold on," Rian called, as the Fiat zipped down the street.

"Yippee," Zelda called as her dark hair fluttered in the wind.

CHAPTER TWENTY NINE

Genna tapped the steering wheel of her bright blue BMW, a four-door sedan with more horsepower than she would ever know what to do with. She'd never get the engine up to a roar in the quiet streets of Bluff Springs. Especially if that traffic cop who was always dogging her caught sight of her new car. She had spurred it to 85 on the expressway getting here, and she loved how it felt under her control. She'd only had the car a few months — her beloved vintage Mercedes being put out to pasture, so to speak, after a collision with an oak tree in a poison ivy patch. She had to admit there was a lot to be said for new, shiny, and fast. The interior smelled terrific.

She was stopped at the one and only traffic light in the town of Ozark. The red light caught her just as she was approaching. There wasn't another car on the road. She looked around, thinking she could easily edge through the red-light with no one looking, when her attention was drawn to the parking lot across the street. There was no mistaking who they were. Merriweather Hopkins and Pamela Duke stood under the eaves of the building, animatedly engaged in conversation.

"What is this?" she said as she muted the radio.

She zipped through the light and cruised into the parking lot on the opposite side of the building, drove around the back, and edged the nose of the car as far as she could without being seen. She was a few yards from the two them but still hidden behind a bush if no one looked. They didn't seem to notice the car idling there. She powered the window down to listen, but their voices were too low to hear. She watched them for a few minutes in silence, hoping to remain undetected.

Why were they in Ozark of all places in a secret rendezvous? Well, not exactly a secret. They were in a parking lot near the town stoplight. That wasn't discreet.

Genna had left several messages for Merriweather in an I-mean-business voice, but the calls hadn't been returned. The two of them had been close once – peers in the same firm, confidants, ready to take on the world. It had been almost a decade since Merriweather's name was dropped from her daily vocabulary. Now, Genna ran into her everywhere. She was at the conference. She was quoted in the newspaper. She had weaseled her way into Jerry Glen's camp with this Project X business, and now she was standing on the corner commiserating with a suspect!

Could it get any worse than this? It could. Merriweather could foul it all up and serve it to Genna on a platter.

Pamela Duke was in his press photos. Donald Duke got himself killed and Jerry Glen was caught making threats in the hall. These were facts that needed sorting.

Donald Duke didn't kill himself. Twelve women from the wine country didn't show up at Tiddlywinks on a whim. Merriweather and Pamela weren't just hobnobbing on the corner in Ozark. Of that, she was sure!

A twinge of revenge kicked up the corners of her mouth. If she could catch her in something nefarious, that would be icing on the cake. But she didn't want Jerry Glen popping out of that cake like a party surprise.

Talk about timing. What could they possibly gain from all that press and exposure? And Villiger with much to lose.

The idea landed as she stared at the two women. Maybe this was about Merriweather and Jerry Glen. How would she extract Villiger's campaign from this steamy stew?

She lifted her foot and let the car roll slowly forward another few feet. She still couldn't hear them. Merriweather raised her cell phone to her ear. She turned, and Genna could see the back of her head nodding as she listened to the caller. And then, the two of them got into one of the vehicles and drove off away from town.

Genna didn't hesitate. She pulled the car into the same lane and followed. They were now headed toward the town of Altus, a short drive on a two-lane blacktop even if you were behind a slow tractor full of hay. Merriweather's car slowed a mile down the road, and Genna braked gently. The car turned into an abandoned car wash, the bays empty, and the roof caved in on one end. Genna watched as they drove to the back of the lot and pulled up beside a green SUV.

She recognized the car. He had taken the magnetic signs off the SUV doors, but it was the candidate's vehicle. He sat behind the wheel, waiting. Jerry Glen, Merriweather, and Pamela Duke — in a clandestine meeting at the derelict Wash-N-Go.

Genna sped on. She had been about to cross the bridge that spanned the Arkansas River when this happenstance derailed her and captured her not-so-idle curiosity. Her destination had been the park outside of Paris, where the Big European Tour of Arkansas would end with a final *hoorah*!

The two cars pulled out behind her, and she kept her eyes in the rearview mirror.

CHAPTER THIRTY

Zelda pointed to the sign as it zipped past. "Hey!" She called from her perch on the back of the Fiat. "Clarksville! Home of the Elberta Peach! *Elberta!* That's the peach we're looking for."

Amy nodded and scribbled the letters into the grid. They had passed acres of flowering trees, and although picking season wasn't until July, the astringent scent of the peach blossoms filled the air along the curvy country roads. It was up to the players to figure out where to go. Using the theme, they had already solved the remaining clue left in the crossword puzzle. They would get their scorecard punched at the ticket window at the train station in Clarksville, which were the words in the crossword puzzle. Then they would get their next clue for the rally.

"Cherry Street!" Zelda called as they passed the street sign. "There's the water tower," she announced like a sentry on the lookout. "Look out for the dog," she hollered as a blonde cur ambled across the road seeking shade.

At the intersection of Main and Cherry Streets, Rian turned the Fiat into the train station lot and parked. Festive peach-colored balloons were tied everywhere: Johnson County Peach Festival, July 22, floated the message for all to see. A group of kids hurried over to the Fiat, handed a balloon to Amy, giggled, and ran off. The three of them entered the train station, curious about the next leg of their journey.

"Time for a loo break," Zelda said, eyeing the door of opportunity. When she returned, Amy handed her a frosty peach Bellini in a plastic champagne flute.

"It's a virgin," Amy said. "But it's delicious."

"Mmmmm," Zelda murmured through the straw.

A pretty Miss Peach — dressed in a peach-yellow evening gown, sash, and all -- smiled from behind her tray. "We can't have y'all drinking and driving now, can we?"

Another character dressed for the occasion motioned them over. The crowd gathered around him as he began to tell the story. Amy stayed to listen, and Zelda wandered off in search of food. Rian went to the ticket window with their scorecard.

"The railroad at Clarksville had nothing to do with the Monkees, except the song *Last Train to Clarksville* was released in 1966 and Arkansas started teaching the theory of evolution in schools. Sugar was thirty-nine cents for a five-pound bag back then, and you could buy a car for five hundred bucks.

"By then the local peach industry was well established. The yellow-fleshed Elberta peach variety that came from Georgia — named after a peach of a wife," he winked at a young girl. "The Elberta peach was slower to ripen than other varieties, so transport by rail was not only possible; it was the big buzz. *It was the buzz on the fuzz.*" The crowd laughed.

"In 1910, the train station at Clarksville was built to haul peaches. To this day, we celebrate the Elberta peach and the oldest festival in the state. Governor Bailey started the festival in 1938 and crowned the first Miss Elberta festival queen." He smiled at the woman with the frosted drinks. She waved to the crowd with a gloved hand.

Amy sipped her frozen peach concoction, smiling as Zelda joined her.

"These are pretty good," Zelda whispered. "Too bad they're missing a shot of wine."

"Looks like we have our next riddle," Rian said, returning to join her friends. "We have the next clue." She held up the bottle with a scroll inside.

"A message in a bottle?" Amy asked. "How do we get it out?"

"Wait," Zelda said, munching noisily on pecan pralines. "There's a corkscrew in the swag bag."

"Time to scoot," Rian said, leading the way back to the car.

Amy directed them south, following the tulips.

Zelda pulled the corkscrew from the swag bag and uncorked the bottle. She fumbled for the paper inside until she slid it out and glanced at it briefly before handing it over to Amy. Zelda didn't have on her glasses.

"It says, *Don't be late to the garden gate. Don't wear your fancy shoes.*" The car hit a bump, and the paper nearly blew from her fingers. She righted the page and read on. "*You'll need the neck. You'll need the heel. You'll need the body, too. Gladness starts with a wholesome stomp when all your team is in queue.*"

Rian grumbled and swept a curl behind her ear. "Neck, body, and heel are parts of a wine bottle. We're going to be stomping grapes."

"Oh, for Heaven's sake," Zelda said. "What has Genna gotten us into? I'm not squishing grapes with my feet. I just had a pedicure!" She pulled a lipstick case from her jeans pocket with an attached tiny mirror that was slightly cracked, and as she was poised in the mirror to freshen her lips, she yelled, "Wait! There goes Genna right now!"

Rian glanced in the rearview mirror and swerved without warning. Zelda slid from one end of her makeshift seat to the other, almost catapulting out of the car. She yelled and grabbed the air, taking a wad of Amy's hair in her fist as she grappled for a hold.

"Ow!" Amy yelled, trying to free her hair from Zelda's grasp. "Stop! Stop!"

Rian slammed on the brakes. Zelda shot forward into the front seat, the stick shift coming to rest between her knees. She held a hank of red hair between her fingers.

"Ow!" Amy yelled again, rubbing a spot on her head. "You pulled out my hair!"

"Why did you stop?" Zelda yelled. "You could have killed me!"

"Didn't you hear her yell, *stop*?"

"That would be the one time your hearing is on point." Zelda snapped. "If you're going to drive like that, I've had all of this prom queen business I can stomach!"

"Yeah, I forget I was carting royalty," Rian muttered.

"What happened, Rian?" Amy looking at her friend with concern.

"You said to stop!" Rian pulled her ball cap down over her brows. "We're going the wrong way if we passed Genna. She's supposed to be at the finish line, and I know for a fact it's not in that direction."

"She's lost just like we are," Zelda bellowed.

"We're not lost," Amy yelped. "I know exactly where we are!" She punched the tulips with her fingertip. "We're right here!"

Zelda huffed. "We might as well be lost!" She glanced at herself in the rearview mirror. "Look at me! No, don't look at me!" She grabbed at her hair. "I look like a TV reporter braving a hurricane. And my lipstick is smeared everywhere!"

Rian glanced at Amy and then at Zelda. Zelda narrowed her eyes. "Don't you dare," she said. "Don't you dare laugh at me!"

Amy bit her lip, but she couldn't hold it back. She pulled a headband from her bag and handed it to Zelda. The corners of Rian's mouth curved into a smile and then a snicker, and then, under the weight of the bright blue sky, she burst into laughter.

Zelda pulled the material over the fridge of her bangs. "Such a big help," she said, her tone dripping sarcasm.

"Genna's the one going the wrong way," Amy said. "I know exactly where we're going."

Rian edged the car back onto the road and then glanced at Zelda in the rearview mirror. Zelda's scowl was firmly in place.

"This isn't right," Amy said to Rian as she rattled the book of clues. "You're not following the directions."

"We're taking a much needed detour," Rian said firmly. "We need a break. I'm taking us to my new favorite place. I want to show it to Zelda."

"Your new vineyard?"

Rian nodded. "I haven't come at it from this direction, so, I hope I can find it. I need to hang a marker at the road."

A grain silo covered in kudzu vine came into view, and Rian turned the Fiat onto the gravel road. They drove on the bumpy road, Zelda grumbling in the back until they stopped at a gate.

"Shoot. Wrong turn," Rian said.

"Wait." Amy motioned to the gate. "Drive on through." She recognized the arch and cowboy lettering. The iron gate was open, and Rian drove up the driveway, stopping beside a gray SUV. It wasn't Doc's. At least, it wasn't the car she drove the night she helped Amy find her way to Rian.

"Are you going to get us shot on sight?" Rian asked. "Who's place is this?"

"Doc Dot's," Amy said and got out of the Fiat. She followed the sound of voices. Rian and Zelda followed.

Dot and Bonnie Waters sat beneath an apple tree in full sun. They were on a little patio made of bricks, a cold fire pit in the center, and a horse trough full of muddy water at the end. Next to the trough, marigolds were bursting out the seams of an old water bucket.

"Hey!" Amy called as she approached, hoping they wouldn't shoot and ask questions later.

Doc looked up, surprised. "Look who the skunk dragged up," she exclaimed, looking to each in turn. "Good Lord! Y'all look rode hard and put up wet. Are you lost again?"

Bonnie glanced at Doc and then back at Amy, and then as her eyes landed on Zelda, she grinned. Amy raised her hand in greeting. She hadn't seen Bonnie since that night at Alligator Ray's. Today she was in jeans and a paisley pearl-snap western shirt, the bling on the belt was shiny with studded rhinestones.

"You remember us?" Amy asked.

"Sure, we do," Doc answered. "Sit," she ordered and motioned to a stiff-legged bench made of rough-hewn cedar. The seat bench was splattered with bird poop. No one sat.

"Your ranch is the only place I can find down here. I get lost, and then, bingo … here I am!"

"All the way from Bluff Springs?"

"We're on a rally today, but we took a detour."

"I'll say." Dot glanced at Bonnie again. "I forgot the LP rally was today." She looked at Amy. "You look like you've got something on your mind."

Amy bit her lip. "We were trying to find Rian's vineyard, but we took the wrong turn. Again."

Dot nodded. "I think so."

"But it's nice to see a familiar face."

Dot nodded. "Sure enough."

"And we also were hoping to find Bethany."

"My niece? Why would you be looking for her here?"

"Doesn't she come here?"

"Not much anymore. She hasn't worked for me since, I don't know — since last year sometime."

"Bethany worked for you?"

Dot laughed. "I'd say she grew up out here mostly, after her mamma died — my sister. Well, my half-sister," Doc corrected herself.

The other member of the Six-Pack! Amy sat down in the bird poop and crossed her legs. "Remind me of who her father is? I forget now who she said he was."

Concern flashed through Doc's eyes and was gone. Something rigid and unyielding stayed behind. She crossed her arms and leaned back in the lawn chair. "She didn't tell you squat," Dot said evenly, never taking her eyes off Amy's.

"Poor thing doesn't have a father," Bonnie interjected. "Does she, Dot?"

"None to speak of."

An uncomfortable silence fell over the group. Amy wished she hadn't been so careless with her question, but she remembered Bethany lamenting: *Who am I NOT related to?* It struck Amy as histrionic then, but an idea had begun to creep around in her head. It had started after playing War with a stranger who tracked down family and cheating husbands. She was beginning to wonder if maybe Jerry Glen wasn't really her uncle. Dot's reaction had said a lot, even though Dot had said very little.

Amy tried to relax against the rough wood. The purple-tinged blooms of the apple tree above them were just popping out in the dark branches. They reminded her of orange blossoms back in Florida, but with a bit more spice. In the fall, the branches would be full of this native fruit known as the cabernet of apples because of their dark skin. Rian had a stand of Arkansas Black apples. Crabapples, too, because the two flourished when grown together. And Rian made a tasty apple pie.

"What kind of horses do you raise?" Rian asked, motioning to the pasture where horses were grazing.

"I don't raise horses; I mend 'em, "Dot said. "I take care of their needs when their owners can't. But if I was to raise them, the Quarter horse is the best."

"Hmmpf," Bonnie uttered. "I'll take a Missouri Fox Trotter any day."

"Well, you would," Dot said. "You like that gait. That hunk of meat and two potatoes kind of gait."

"To ride one is to own one," Bonnie said and grinned. "You're never going to win this argument, Dottie Daniels."

"And you're never going to win a race against me, Bonnie Blue," Dot shot back. The two of them smiled, and Amy could see the argument was a playful one that had spanned years of friendship.

"I haven't ridden a horse in years," Zelda piped up. "I don't think one forgets how. Although I might have forgotten how to get up on one."

"Do people come out here to ride?" Rian asked.

"It's just the two of us most of the time."

"Kirk used to ride with us, too, but he doesn't anymore," Bonnie said. "He says it makes his butt sore."

"That's because he's a *wuss*," Dot said. "And you can tell him I said that. He didn't even ride the last time he came out to the ranch with you. Made a big fuss about spraining his ankle."

"He's going through the male equivalent of menopause," Bonnie said. "I wish they had hormones for that." She laughed. "He's gotten some strange ideas in his head lately."

Like you were trying to poison him, Amy didn't say out loud.

Bonnie laughed again, and Amy noticed how the sound matched her voice. It was smooth and sweet, not at all like a woman who could plot murder and get away with it.

"What an idiot he is," Bonnie continued. "I saw him pour a whole bottle of wine down the drain. He thought I didn't see him, but I did. I know exactly what he was thinking. Like I'm that dumb."

Amy looked at Bonnie out of the corner of her eye. She did not look like a dumb blonde.

Rian looked at Bonnie and then at Doc. "Where would a person get sodium pentobarbital anyway? Like if they needed to manage an animal on the farm?"

Amy shot her a curious glance.

"Beats me," Bonnie answered with a shrug.

Dot looked at Rian. "What are you, the Spanish Inquisition?"

Rian grinned. "Just curious."

Amy glanced quickly at Zelda and then at Doc. "We're just trying to help Pamela stay out of trouble. She asked for my help and that's what I'm trying to do.

"When my best friend wanted her husband gone, she asked for our help. She was struggling toward divorce, like your friend, Pamela. But then he was run over in a parking garage, and I was convinced someone close to her had planned that hit and run to help her out. Someone like a tight clutch of friends. Tight, you know, like your

Six-Pack."

"Are you accusing me of ridding Pamela of that menace?

"Am I?"

"Are you nuts?" Dot bellowed. There was spittle in the corners of her mouth.

Bonnie looked at Dot with surprise in her eyes. Dot turned and pointed a finger at Amy. Her knees would be knocking if she wasn't seated.

"There's a long line of Duke-haters ahead me. He didn't do right by Bethany, and he was screwing Pamela out of her fair share. But I wouldn't risk two nickels on that man, let alone my soul."

Doc narrowed her eyes at Amy. "I don't appreciate you accusing me of murder. And you're trespassing on my property!"

Rian stepped forward. "Somebody was willing to take that risk," she said calmly. "Think about it. The trail led us here and we can't be the only ones wondering if the drug came from your ranch. Somebody thinks you'd make a good scapegoat. Or the equine equivalent."

Dot shot upright, towering over Rian. Amy saw the muscles in Rian's arms tense and flex. Bonnie rose and stepped closer to Dot. She laid her hand on her arm, and the tension eased. There was no collusion in Bonnie's expression, just a little confusion and a lot of concern. Dot's face was clouded over with anger, but underneath, Amy saw that Rian's words had made an impact.

"Are you saying my friends are trying to frame me for murder?"

Rian nodded. "If you didn't put the drug in the wine, who did?"

Dot turned to Bonnie. Amy could see her jaw working. Maybe it was working on a question she didn't want to ask. Dot turned away from Bonnie and without so much as a second look at the trespassers, stalked off toward the barn.

"You got a lot of nerve," Bonnie said between clenched teeth. The sweet was gone. "There is not a kinder soul on this planet than Dottie Daniels!" Bonnie turned and followed Dot's tall, lanky strides. Amy could hear a little jingle to Bonnie's step, as the bling jostled and finally disappeared into the barn.

CHAPTER THIRTY ONE

Genna couldn't believe her eyes. She trailed the two cars on the two-lane road without them noticing, and then they led her here. Jerry Glen, Pamela Duke, and Merriweather Hopkins pulled into the funeral home and parked.

She left her sunglasses in place and entered a few steps behind them. Hoping they'd be preoccupied with their task — whatever that was — she was going to take full advantage of the opportunity to find out what was going on. She hoped they wouldn't see her because she couldn't pretend to be shopping for a new lipstick if they saw her. But if put to the ringer, she'd say she was shopping early for Kingdom Come.

As it was, the three of them disappeared behind a closed door, and Genna put an ear to the panel. She could hear murmuring but not much else.

"Are you here for the vigil?"

She jumped at his words. She hadn't heard the attendant approach.

"Yes, I am," Genna lied, not knowing what vigil or for whom.

"This way," he said. "If you'll follow me." He paused at a podium where a guest book lay open. He motioned to the pen. "Please let the family know you've come to pay your respects."

She nodded, took up the feathered pen, scribbled *B. Alice Walton*, and walked through the open doors.

The paneled room was straight out of a 1980s funeral parlor catalog. A pair of beige and blue striped velvet chairs made a grouping slightly off to one side. Rows of straight back chairs stood on the other side. Wall sconces on either end of the catafalque directed the light up — appropriately, she thought — to hide the faces of the bereaved.

She didn't recognize anyone, not even the smiling memorial picture of the deceased on the easel. The picture looked like it was the 1980s, too. At least, the mustache did. She stood and stared at the coffin, but the stained glass window is what caught her eye. The window was above the platform and the glass depicted an ascending dove holding the branch of peace in its beak. As she watched, reflected light bounced across the window, and the dove flew across the wall in shadow form.

It caught her breath. It caught more than her breath. She fled the room, and finding the restroom, gathered her wits. She removed her shades and tidied her look in the mirror. She was frustrated with the newspaper story about Project X. She was angry at being dismissed by Merriweather, who couldn't even be bothered to return her calls. She was confused about a host of unfamiliar feelings swirling in her gut. And a dove of peace had just flown across the room.

The bathroom at a funeral home wasn't the place to unpack these feelings, but sheer determination held her feet to the ground. She needed to finish what she started — and that was to get Jerry Glen elected to Congress.

She heard the bathroom door opening and stepped into a stall. She waited until the person left before exiting, and then stopped abruptly. Merriweather Hopkins stood in the hallway, in the little alcove furnished with a pair of wingback chairs. She sat just as Genna tried to pass by her unseen.

Merriweather's eyes widened. "What are you doing here?" she whispered. "Are you stalking me?"

Genna shifted her purse on her shoulder. "Mohammad, mountain. Something akin to that."

Merriweather looked right and then left as if waiting for Mohammad's army to descend. "I'm sorry I didn't call you back. I was afraid …." She didn't finish the sentence and Genna shifted her feet, her gaze never wavering.

"You can't avoid me forever."

"I knew it had to happen sooner or later," Merriweather said, her voice plaintive. "I knew I would have to face you to make amends."

Genna's eyebrows shot up.

"I apologize for what I did that created this terrible rift in our friendship," Merriweather blurted. "There, now you know."

Genna shifted her weight again. "A riff? That's what you call what you did?" She hissed in a throaty whisper. "You made up lies about me. On paper. For everyone to see. You left copies in the trash by the copier so everyone could read them. You said I embezzled campaign funds. You said you had proof."

"That was Phillip!" Merriweather cried. "Philip, the intern."

"That snooty little creep who listened at the door jambs?"

Merriweather dropped her eyes. "That's not true. I told everybody it was Philip. I blamed it on him, and I used him to ruin you. I took all of your accounts when you left so abruptly."

Genna rocked on her feet. Merriweather motioned to the seat beside her.

The alcove was pleasantly dark, the wall sconces directing light upward, away from their faces.

"I'm sorry, Genna. I am sorry for what I did."

"You're sorry!" Her voice broke with a wail. "We were friends!"

The man in the dark suit appeared as suddenly as before, giving them a compassionate, yet disapproving look before disappearing again. Merriweather signed heavily as if a huge weight was lifting from her core. Genna could see tears in her eyes.

"I'm not proud of what I did. It was egregious and I've regretted it every single day."

"I don't understand why you did that to me," Genna said, shaking her head.

"I — I thought that was the only way I could get ahead in my career. I wanted your influence. I wanted your power. I wanted your job. I wanted to be you!" She paused briefly with her eyes cast to the floor. "I thought it was the only way I could win. I thought if I didn't beat you to the winner's circle, you would beat me. And there wasn't room for two."

Genna's nostrils flared. The knot in her stomach tightened. It was like the alchemy of emotional pain and suffering and guilt all melded by horrendous heat. The kind of heat that changes a thing forever. What Merriweather did was not all that removed from what she did to others. Dog eat dog. It was how the world worked, wasn't it?

If she was honest with herself, right here right now, she would not hesitate to do the same thing to Merriweather if she felt the need. Hadn't she thrown the first punch with a dig at the benefit auction?

"In the end, I almost ruined me," Merriweather continued. "I didn't know how to approach you with the truth, so I did nothing. I let you suffer. I let Philip suffer. Although he might have deserved what he got." Merriweather grinned. "I don't really mean that."

"He really was a creep." Genna said softly.

Merriweather nodded and brushed at her cheek. "I wanted to make it right, so that's why I suggested Jerry Glen consider you as his campaign publicist. That's why I made sure Tiddlywinks and the Cardboard Cottage received good exposure at the conference. That's why I…"

"You are the reason Villiger hired me?" Genna interrupted.

Merriweather cocked her head. "No, *you* are the reason Villiger hired you. *You.* I just made sure your name was in the hat. He chose you for a reason. You're the best of the best."

"Now, who's putting a spin on it?"

"Good Lord, Genna, I'm baring my soul, here. Have some faith."

"Faith? How can I have faith in *you*?" Genna looked away and then looked up. The light shining through a stained glass panel on the other side of the room grabbed her eye and held it. It wasn't a dove. The glass had varying hues of brilliant blue, with a translucent cross in the center that gathered light with such intensity it seemed to glow. She couldn't pull her eyes away. She could hear Merriweather talking beside her, but the light was the only thing she could see. The only thing she could hear. It was as if the light was speaking to her in a voice she had never heard.

Merriweather touched her arm. "Are you okay?"

"Yes," Genna said. "I am okay."

Merriweather reached out, and their embrace was brief, but Genna had never felt such peace.

"We believed it because we were taught to believe it," Genna said. "Women were taught that cut-throat competition was a good thing. It's not unique to women. Men are competitive but women are better at it. We believed that fighting cunning and ruthless for a job, or a project, or a promotion, or even a *man* — was good strategy. But it wasn't healthy competition. We saw every woman as our nemesis. Our kryptonite. We believed there was only one seat at the table. And that, my friend, was a lie."

Merriweather steadied her gaze at Genna. If there was one person who could match her own tenacity, it was this woman looking at her with an unrelenting gaze. Genna blinked. She had said some hurtful things to Merriweather back then, and she hadn't had the gall to apologize, either. Subdued by this walk down memory lane, she had few words left, but she wished with all her heart that she could hit rewind. She wished they could rewind all the way back to the beginning and start over with what they knew now.

"I've been holding a grudge all these years for something I would have done."

"Isn't that what most grudges are about?" Merriweather asked quietly. "Our own guilt and shame?"

The two of them sat quietly in the alcove for quite some time. When she started out this morning, Genna had no idea the day would take this direction. It was a curve she hadn't anticipated. Like the roads through the mountains headed home, switching one direction before switching to another, she realized that life journeys were not traveled in a straight line. Such was the school of life. Such was the joy of life, too. She was human; and flawed; and humbled. The wall she had built was crumbling. And it felt good to see it crack.

Merriweather shifted in the chair, shouldering her purse as if to rise.

"Wait," Genna said, putting a hand lightly on her arm. "Please don't leave. I need to know what's going on with Jerry Glen and Pamela Duke. You're in this picture, too."

Merriweather seemed to gather her thoughts. "Before I talk about Project X, I want to tell you the story of Ana Marie Villiger."

CHAPTER THIRTY TWO

Amy felt shaken by the encounter at the ranch. She and Rian had all but accused Dot Daniels of injecting poison into the wine that killed Donald Duke. It was a wonder Dot hadn't shoved them headfirst into the muddy trough.

"How did you know about the sodium pentobarbital?" Amy asked.

"An educated guess," Rian said. She had both hands on the wheel as the car bumped over the road. "Dot knew that drug came from her ranch. That's what put her ire up. But I agree with Bonnie. She might bend for love, but she would never break."

"Did you see the way she looked at Bonnie? I think in that moment she suspected Bonnie."

"Somebody close to her knew her way around the vet drug cabinet," Rian added. "And I bet she knows where Dot keeps the key."

Amy had switched places with Zelda and was now the one perched in the back of the Fiat. Zelda's hair was still a wild mess, her lipstick smeared nearly ear to ear. She had the visor mirror open and was trying to wipe the mess from her face with a tissue.

Amy leaned forward. "Is that Genna's missing lipstick?"

Zelda snapped the visor shut.

By the time they arrived at the square with its fountain statue in her mossy robes and grapes, Amy was so thirsty she could have lapped at the water in the fountain like a dog.

Rian parked but left the engine running, as if undecided about what to do next. A country band played on the gazebo stage, with people listening from the benches below. Two couples were dressed as if they had just filmed a Bavarian beer commercial. They were dancing do-si-do in the grass, skirts twirling and boots stomping to the twang of the fiddle. It looked like fun.

A temporary stage now stood near the fountain, with three wooden barrels big enough to bathe a dog. A wrought iron garden gate covered in clumps of plastic grapes stood between the stairs and the stage. The sign below it said, *Heart of the vine!* And above it, *Gladness starts with a wholesome stomp.* In matching purple t-shirts, the crew stood on the ground, keeping time with the band, but they glanced at the stairs as if waiting for the next scavenger rally victims.

"This has something to do with our next quest," Amy said with a nod toward the stage. "One of those quotes is from the riddle in the bottle." She held up the wine bottle and the note they rescued.

"Let's skip this part and get a beer at Alligator Ray's." Rian looked over at Amy. "I really need to whet my whistle."

"What do we tell Genna when we don't show up at the finish line?"

"We tell her we couldn't solve the riddles and had to give up. We can say that's why we didn't make it to the finish line party."

"She'd never let us live that down," Amy said.

Rian turned off the ignition and pulled the key. "She said we didn't have to win."

"Yeah, and wine is *win* with an *e*," Zelda said. "Just saying."

"We should at least have a libation to honor the vine," Rian added. "And a little *win* with an *e*."

"It's the least we can do," Amy agreed. "The riddle led us here to wine country, and it would be wrong not to honor Dionysus. If you're Greek," she added, "Or Bacchus if you're Roman."

"Or Saint Vincent if you're Catholic." Rian grinned.

"Don't forget the Krewe of Barkus, "Zelda added with a chuckle, as a dog trotted by on its leash. "That's if you're from New Orleans."

"You're not from New Orleans," Amy declared.

"No, I am not," Zelda stated, with a defiant tilt to her chin. "But my first husband was. *Bon temps!*"

Amy grinned and then caught the expression that settled quickly over Zelda's face like a sweet, sad poem.

"A mutiny won't offend me in the least," Zelda rallied. "Besides, I see a salon, and I need help." She stuck her fingers in her windblown bird nest.

"Yeah, you *do* need help," Amy said, grinning, as she untangled herself from the Fiat.

* * *

The smell of ammonia and nail polish greeted them as they opened the door to Patsy's Beauty Salon, stenciled on the door in pink. The whirr of women talking stopped as they entered, and all eyes looked their way. A matronly woman in a pink smock and dark hair looked up from the counter near the door.

"Oh, sugar," she said, her eyes on Zelda. "Whatever happened to you? Did you wrestle with a big handsome bear or something?" She winked at the innuendo.

Zelda patted her bob gone wild. "My two best friends put me in the back of a convertible and then drove like Dale Earnhardt after a pack of Winstons."

"Rian warned you," Amy mumbled. "She said you'd be blown to bits."

Zelda narrowed her eyes. "She should have said she was going to try to kill me!"

The shopkeeper's eyebrows rose inquisitively. Her dark bird nest looked purposeful, the piled-high bouffant style as out of date as the linoleum floor. "You want to make an appointment?"

"Can't you squeeze me in now? All I need is a little wash and dry," Zelda complained with a sweet smile.

The woman put her hands on her hips. "You are a fright. Let's see what I can manage." She untangled her glasses from her backcombed bangs and settled them on her nose. "We rushed a half dozen regulars out the door not ten minutes ago. There's a funeral today and the church ladies put on the repast. They all needed a wash and set beforehand."

Zelda tugged on the ratted ends. "You have to help a sister out of this rat nest."

The woman smiled at Zelda. "If I skip lunch, I have time before my next gal gets here. Are you worth me skipping lunch?" She teased.

"I *am* worth it." Zelda declared with another smile. "I am an excellent tipper."

"What about you," the woman said to Amy.

Amy's hands flew her to the bun at her neck. It held up in the wind as well as it could until Zelda grabbed it like a door handle and pulled.

"I can do it," another woman said. "I wasn't planning on lunch anyway. I'm leaving early."

Amy settled into the chair beside Zelda.

"Caped and draped," the stylist said, with a friendly pat on Amy's shoulder and a spin to face the mirror. The three dryers in the reflection from across the room were full, and while the ladies under the bonnets were holding magazines, they weren't reading. They were more interested in reading the room and the two new patrons.

"Are you part of the scavenger rally?" Amy's stylist asked as she pulled the bun loose.

Amy nodded. "But we decided to take a break." She motioned with her head toward Zelda. "She was getting cranky."

"I was not being cranky," Zelda muttered. "My entire life was in danger."

"She's kidding," Amy said quickly. *Cranky,* Amy mouthed silently.

"I heard that," Zelda said.

Amy and her stylist exchanged looks.

"We haven't had time to watch the grape stomp today, but it's always a lot of fun. Especially when they slip in the grape must or dive into the barrel like Lucille Ball after an earring. Now that's a stain you can't *Shout* out."

The matronly stylist grinned, "Yeah, but today the stomp seems out of place. I think they should have cancelled it. Let's get you washed."

They walked to the basins, and Amy melted into the chair as the stylist ran warm water through her curls. She glanced over at Zelda, not but three feet away. Zelda's eyes were closed, but her mouth was open, ready to overshare. It wasn't long before Zelda had recounted the mishap in the Fiat to everyone who could hear. She glossed over the part where they had accused the local vet of poisoning Donald Duke, but Amy had a feeling it would pop up somewhere between the hot towel conditioning and the blow dry.

"We are supposed to meet our friend at the finish line, but we can't figure out the clues, so we have no idea where we're going," Zelda said as if testing to see how the excuse sounded out loud. It needed some work. Genna would never buy the excuse as it was now.

"You're going to Paris," the other woman said as she massaged the shampoo into Amy's scalp. "You get a key to open a lock at the Eiffel Tower. There's only one Eiffel Tower in Arkansas."

As if there should be one on every corner. She had never seen the real one, either. She opened one eye and looked at the woman above her. "Where do we get a key?"

"They give you a key after your grape stomp."

Amy frowned. "We're not doing that."

"Then, just ask, they'll give you a key anyway."

"How do you know about this?"

"They do this same event every year."

"Oh," Amy said and settled into the salon chair.

"You want me to blow dry it straight, or would you prefer a

scrunch-and-go?"

Amy grinned. "I'll take the scrunch-and-go." At least the tangles were gone, and the scalp massage had been heaven.

"Then how about a facial while you wait for your friend? It's just a quick little mud mask, but it does wonders."

Amy nodded and closed her eyes.

"So, where are y'all from, anyway?"

She hesitated a moment. "We're from Bluff Springs."

The gasp from across the room was audible. Amy opened one eye and looked in the mirror. The woman raised the magazine to hide her face, then peeked over the top.

"Did you know Mr. Duke?" the stylist asked with sad eyes.

Amy was surprised by the leap. "Actually, I did know him, but not very well."

Was that true? She felt like she'd been following his trail for weeks, starting with a chance encounter on the sidewalk at the conference in Bluff Springs. Was it coincidence that his wife booked game night with the Six-Pack at Tiddlywinks? Was it kismet that got her stranded just so she could visit his cellar? She knew him as a man who was passionate about wine and honored his southern family roots. A man who thought he was John Wayne and slept in his office so someone who liked daisies could use the apartment. The *gîte*, as Pamela called it. That was no bachelor pad. Did she know the man who was brash, and bold, and powerful enough to spur change throughout an entire industry? A man who was not as honest as he could be? Who didn't seem to have much respect for women? Didn't she know Mr. Duke?

"I'm dry," the woman called as she patted her curlers. Amy glanced at her in the mirror and saw she had shifted from under the bonnet to the edge of her seat. "Everybody's going be there today, especially under the *circumstances*," dryer woman said knowingly in an Arkansas southern lilt.

Amy and Zelda exchanged looks. "What circumstances?" Amy was pretty sure she knew.

"Well," dryer woman said as she leaned forward. "She blew in off the street like a tornado, I hear. Papers flying everywhere!"

"At least Mrs. Duke had the decency to hold a vigil for him, even if it was at the funeral home," the other stylist said. "Duke looked just like himself. Even that big ole' hat of his. They had it resting right in his hands."

"Just because they pay their respects doesn't mean they have some," dryer women said.

"Hush that," the matron said with a warning smile. The matron in pink turned off the handheld dryer and the salon got quiet. "I was working on a patron in the back. I'm the mortuary cosmetologist, too," she explained to Amy and Zelda in the mirror. "I was working on a decedent when I heard a bit of commotion. It's not a big place. It's easy to overhear things."

"What happened?" Amy asked. "Who blew in? What happened to Pamela Duke?"

"Oh, it wasn't about her. It was about Bethany Keller. She crashed into the funeral parlor with a fistful of papers and started hollering and crying about her daddy."

"Her what?" Zelda squawked. Amy snapped her jaw so hard her teeth ached.

The matron nodded. "She claimed she had DNA proof that Donald Duke was her father. That she had a right as his next to kin make sure he received a proper Catholic burial and a place of honor in the cemetery on the hill. This was just the vigil, mind you, but she was screeching at the top of her lungs that Pamela Duke wasn't even his widow!"

"That's not right," Zelda said. "Their divorce proceedings would have been terminated at his death. Until the papers were filed with the court, she'd be his widow and not his ex. I know that from personal experience."

"You may be right about that," the matron said, "but Bethany claimed the deed had already been done. She rattled a handful of papers in Pamela's face. She said she was the lone heir of his estate.

That the divorce papers had been signed. She found them in Mr. Duke's desk drawer at the office. In an envelope under his socks." The matron paused and shook her head. "Strange, I know, but that's what she said."

Amy knew exactly where he kept his socks.

"No one else knew the papers had been signed. Well, except the Duke himself," she added.

"I thought Mrs. Duke was going to faint on the floor, but then she grabbed Bethany by the bun and tried to rip the papers out of her hand! They were clawing and screaming like banshees."

The woman shook her head again. "I will say — those funeral folks are well schooled. They're trained for all kinds of grief-laden chaos. They just swooped right in and got everybody settled into a private room. I could hear them screaming at each other behind closed doors."

Amy's head was spinning. The pieces clicked into place like a Rubik's Cube. She closed her eyes as the stylist coaxed the mud from her face with a warm, wet cloth, and then opened them and stared at her reflection. There were two mud circles around her eyes staring back.

Of course! Hadn't she noticed the dark mask around Bethany's eyes? Donald Duke had the same feature. Her DNA game never failed her, and yet, she hadn't put the two together. The raccoons *were* part of the murder! Just not in the way she thought.

Did the Duke know about Bethany and keep it secret all those years? Is that why he was bringing her into the business? Did anyone else know?

Dot knew. Of course, Dot knew. She may have been the only one. The raccoons in her snippet could be the Six-Pack. They could be responsible for Duke's death, and they may have tried and missed the mark with Kirk. She had seen Dot's sudden realization about Bonnie.

Bethany hadn't just delivered a bottle of wine to Donald Duke's room. She had taken one to Kirk's room, too. And he was still alive.

No wonder Kirk thought Bonnie was trying to poison him. No wonder he poured the wine down the drain. Which *wasband* was next?

Before she could contemplate the answer, the door opened, and Genna Gregory appeared.

"Ha! I found you!" Genna exclaimed. "In a salon of all places! I parked next to Rian's Fiat, and I've been looking for the three of you in every store on the square. Rian's at the pub playing pool, and here you are getting styled!"

Every eye in the place was on Genna. She was dressed in a pair of skinny jeans and a blue checkered gingham shirt knotted at the waist, her version of Daisy Mae. Even as thin as Genna was, she took up a lot of space.

"Genna!" Zelda exclaimed. "I knew it was you we passed on the road. See!" Zelda turned to face Amy. "I knew I was right."

Genna plopped down in a vacant chair.

"I was distracted, and I got derailed, but now I am found." She spun to face the mirror, stroked her ponytail, and smoothed her brows with a fingertip.

"The bad news is that Rian is bailing on you and the road rally — no real surprise there — so I'm taking the two of you with me to the finish line."

"Oh, good," Zelda said. "Honest to goodness, Genna, we couldn't figure out those clues. We had no idea where we were supposed to go next." She gave Genna the side-eye. "I was anxious about how we would find our way to your party."

Zelda patted her hair, now returned to order, although it looked nothing like what her stylist in Bluff Springs would finesse. "I'm not riding in the back of that convertible *ever again*," Zelda said, adding lipstick to finish her look. "Not unless it is a real parade, and *I am* the prom queen."

Genna peered at Zelda in the mirror. "That wouldn't be *mine*, would it? "My missing *rose contre temps*?"

"Oh, is this yours? I got it from Amy."

Amy grinned and didn't bother to defend herself. She wouldn't win, anyway. *I'll see your sarcasm and raise you some sass.*

CHAPTER THIRTY THREE

The decision to bail had been easy, especially when Genna showed up unexpectedly. She felt bad about nearly tossing Zelda from the car. Zelda could have been hurt. It was foolish to perch Zelda on the back like that. Illegal, too. She was trying to figure out what to do about the three's-a-crowd in the Fiat situation when the answer walked through the door. Genna offered to take them off her hands.

Now traveling solo, she found the right kudzu-covered silo this time. She drove up to the barn and was surprised to see Ben had arrived ahead of her.

He jumped down from the barn's shaggy loft. Her smile told Ben she was happy to see him. His smile said he was up to no good.

"I've got a little surprise for you," he said and hugged her tight. She resisted slightly and then relaxed against his chest.

"I'm not sure I want any more surprises today."

His handsome face sobered.

"But I could try," she said. "Just for you."

With his hand behind her back, he led her into the barn.

She sniffed. "Smells like musty hay and aftershave."

Ben laughed and pulled a corkscrew from his pocket.

Rian eyed the tool. "Is that a corkscrew in your pocket, or are you happy to see me?"

"Look at this!" Ben motioned her to a hay bale that had lost its rectangular shape. Directly above the bale, a hole in the tin roof let in a steady stream of sunlight. Tall stalks of hayseed sprouted from the surface in all directions. Ben bent down and uncovered a case of wine.

"You brought a case? Most guys just bring one bottle to the party."

"I didn't bring it. It was already here. I uncovered it when I was poking around. And look." He pulled a bottle from the dusty box. "It's highly drinkable. It's a fancy French wine."

Rian accepted the bottle from his hand. The label looked vaguely familiar and Rian grimaced.

Ben's face fell again. "I thought you'd be happy."

She pulled at a curl, and Ben followed the gesture with sad eyes.

"I would be happy, except if we drink this, we might die a horrible death."

"You mean like Romeo and Juliet?" Ben looked confused.

Rian grinned. "You are a romantic despite your tin star badge and big book of rules. How do we know this wine hasn't been poisoned like the wine that killed Donald Duke? Maybe somebody left it here for us to find. And drink. And die."

Ben chortled through closed lips.

"What's so funny?"

"You're up to your eyeballs in paranoia," Ben said. "I bring you many glasses of jubilation, and you cast it aside as poison. I, Brutus?" He poked himself in the chest. "Okay, for one, this looks like it has been in the barn for a long time." He peeled the foil from the neck. "And two, the only wine used to kill anybody is in police custody."

"How do you know that?" Rian asked, lifting a foot to the hay bale.

"Because I have connections who have connections," Ben answered. "From what I understand, they have a suspect on the hook, and they're just doing the bloodhound work to find the trail of evidence. I think it's a safe bet that Donald Duke was the target and the only target."

"You don't mean actual dogs on a lead, do you?"

Ben grinned. "No, that's police jargon. They follow the trail of evidence until they find what they need to make the arrest stick. Like what we did on that mountain side. We found evidence that day. Remember?"

Rian nodded. She had been frightened by what they discovered in the weeds. She tried to hide her fear from Ben, then.

"Do you know who the suspect is?"

Ben shook his head. "I have no idea. Our unit is not involved."

Rian hadn't told Ben about their theory of wives' killer wine club and now didn't seem the time to bring it up. "I wonder why this is here?" She pointed to the wine still in his hand. "Maybe Katrina will know. I'm not drinking it until we know it's safe."

"Can I come with you to walk the vineyard?"

"Can you? Are you able?"

"Rian, I am always able. *And* willing."

Rian socked Ben in the arm with a lightly balled fist. "You know that would have hurt if I wanted it to."

"I know," Ben said and grinned.

They stepped out into the daylight just as a beat-up old Jeep came rattling down the hill. They set out on foot, walking the row of vines to the meeting place she and Katrina had arranged by phone.

"How's the green Gremlin," Rian asked as Katrina dropped to the ground. She had long legs with sunburned knees in western denim shorts and a dusty pair of boots on her feet.

"She's great," Katrina answered and pulled off her ball cap, rubbed her head, and snugged the hat back down on salt and pepper hair. It was almost as short as Ben's. "But you're right. I will have to get used to that honk on a right-hand turn. Even Teddy at the garage can't figure out why it does that."

"Even mint condition has a few caveats," Rian said.

"It's no big deal. The car is sweet and a deal is a deal. I like what you've got in mind for this place. If you need help, ring me up.

Growing grapes is not as easy as most folks think."

Rian laughed and nodded. She introduced Ben, the boyfriend, as Officer Ben Albright, and Katrina's eyebrows rose above her shades.

"You have a bodyguard?"

Ben grinned. "Sometimes I think she needs one." He stepped closer to Rian and let his arm touch hers. He knew better than to make any claim of intimacy in public. Rian glanced at him and back at Katrina.

"You got a sample already?" Katrina pointed at the bottle in Rian's hand.

"This was in the barn. I was wondering if you knew why it was there."

Katrina lifted her sunglasses and settled them on the brim of her ball cap. Rian noticed the logo for her winery stitched onto the hat, which was about the same color as her Jeep.

She looked at the bottle with surprise in her eyes. "Where did you get this?" The look on her face made Rian uncomfortable.

"It was in the barn."

"Just sitting out in the open?"

"It was hidden under a hay bale with an old feed bucket on top," Ben answered. He stepped forward and Katrina looked at him and nodded. He was handsome, muscular, and had dimples in all the right places. Rian was certain the woman had just given the whoo-he's-fine-look. Rian couldn't agree more.

Ben, unaware as usual, said, "I was nosing around while waiting for Rian. There is a case of it. It looks like it's been there awhile. Do you think it's safe to drink?"

"Finders keepers," Katrina said after a long pause. "It's your barn now. Is it drinkable? Wine gets better with age, and there's only one way to tell if it's corked. Pop the cork and pour."

Katrina set off at a fast clip, still gripping the bottle in her hand. She detoured to her Jeep and stuck the bottle under the seat. "You don't mind if keep this, do you? Good old nostalgia?"

"By all means," Rian said, feeling a little confused, as she and Ben caught up.

It was easy to see why so many generations of European winemakers farmed the plateau. The Boston Mountain range stood to the north, the Ouachita Mountains to the south. In the plateau in between, warm air and sandy loam came together like poetry. Gravel, loam, and acid earth made for the perfect pairing for growing grapes. The vines reached for the sunlight in neat little rows, their broad ragged leaves sheltering the grapes that grew fat in the summer heat. Rian felt the gravid quiet as if the land was whispering to her about its duty in place and time. The vines seemed simple and humble, and yet grapes could be transformed into something magnificent — a journey where water became wine like the first miracle performed. Every plump orb, tendril, and cluster in the vineyard hoped for such glory. Rian breathed in the sharp terpenes of the wood and fruit and heat.

Katrina grabbed a handful of dirt and let it sift through her fingers. "When we were kids, we played in that barn. We stashed all kinds of things in there, but never wine." She chuckled to herself. "Bonnie kept a suitcase at the barn because her mother was strict about what she wore. You know what they say… a strict parent creates a sneaky kid. She was a fashionista long before she was a Rodeo Queen."

"Rodeo Queen? Bonnie Waters?"

"Well, she wasn't Bonnie Waters back then. We were in high school."

"You all rode rodeo?"

"Not for long. It hurts when you hit the turf. Dot got her heart broken when a friend fell off his horse and broke his back. Bonnie went on to reign as the National High School Rodeo Queen. I think that was 1988, '89. Something like that. She had the biggest rodeo belt buckle I've ever seen."

Rian laughed, picturing a young Bonnie. "Do you still ride?"

Katrina shook her head. "I don't have a horse, and I don't want one. These grapes take enough of my time as it is."

"Have you ever had trouble with counterfeit wines?" Rian asked.

Ben was trailing a few respectful steps behind the two women, his eyes taking in the width and breadth of the land. Katrina stopped abruptly and turned toward Rian. Ben bumped to a stop.

"Why would you me ask that?"

Rian shoved her hands into her pockets. "Idle curiosity?"

Katrina tipped the bill of her hat back and looked at Rian. "I doubt that, but there are thieves in every industry and wine is no exception." Katrina turned and walked on. Rian followed.

"But how would you know if your wines were being counterfeited?"

Katrina stopped again. "If you've got a question about my wine, you'd do better to come right out and ask it. Are you insinuating something?"

"No!" Rian said, startled by the turn. "I'm asking if you've had an experience with your wines being counterfeited."

Katrina pulled off her cap, swatted at a bee cruising by, and then snugged the hat back down over her eyes. "I didn't mean to bark at you. I'm sensitive about it. I had just taken over the business from my grandfather. I grew up around the vineyard, and I wanted to step into his shoes like I knew what I was doing." She smiled. "Obviously, I didn't know what I was doing."

"What happened?" Ben asked.

"Someone told the feds that my wines were adulterated. The feds tried to shut me down." Katrina frowned. "Adulteration means that you've either diluted, added to, or substituted a lesser quality of wine, mislabeling the bottles to mislead the buyer into thinking they're buying something they aren't. It's a breach in wine production. It's a serious offense with the feds.

"I hadn't done any such thing, but the damage was done. I was younger and quite naive as you can imagine, and the alcohol bureaucrats stomped all over me. They aren't a warm and fuzzy lot, even when you're toeing the line."

"What happened?"

"They couldn't find the evidence they were looking for, but they confiscated an entire harvest anyway. Every single case I bottled that year was tossed." She kicked at the dirt with the toe of her boot. "That was the worst year of my life because I was humiliated in front of my grandfather. And I almost bankrupted the company. Kirk Waters was my CFO at the time, and I couldn't afford to keep him on. He left the company and went to work with Duke, and I started all over from square one."

Katrina's jaw was tight. "It's all wine under the bridge now, as we say down here. My grandfather's gone and I learned some valuable lessons."

"Did you find out who did it?"

"No, but I've always had my suspicions."

"You said Kirk Waters worked for you?"

Katrina nodded. "I inherited him from my grandfather. He started working for him right after college."

Rian wondered if there was more to the story. She wouldn't repeat what Kirk had said at Alligator Rays that night they played pool. It sounded like private business between two competitors, but it was obvious that he still held a grudge. If something like that happened to her when her grandfather was alive, she would have been humiliated, too. She thought it spoke to Katrina's character that she brought the company back from near ruin.

"Have you heard of counterfeit swapping?" Rian asked.

"Oldest trick in the book. Counterfeiters take a good wine and slap a nice foreign label over it. Not many would notice the difference. Are you saying you've seen such a thing?"

"No, not sayin' I have."

Katrina looked at Rian over the top of her shades. "But you're not saying you haven't."

"Who would I ask if I wanted to check authenticity? Around here, I mean."

"Donald Duke for sure. But he's passed on. You heard about all that?"

Rian nodded.

"The Duke could tell you anything you wanted to know about the industry, whether you wanted to hear it or not." Katrina grinned.

"You know Pamela Duke?"

"Of course, I know Pamela Duke."

"Was she part of your group from the barn?"

Katrina chuckled. "You could say she moved in, and I moved out. Duke had his eye on Pamela, and she had her eye on Jerry Glen. He had his eye on Mary Beth. And then Jerry Glen went back to college for the second time, and Mary Beth had a baby."

"Was it Jerry Glen's?"

Katrina arched a brow at Rian. "We all thought so. But Mary Beth never would say. She went to her grave with that secret."

Katrina glanced up at the blue sky and then back at Rian. "Why am I telling you all this? I'm not usually so sentimental. Giving up that old barn is dragging these memories to the surface."

Rian nodded. There was always a place where the light got in and feelings got squeezed out.

"He's been good to Bethany," Katrina said. "Jerry Glen has. He always helped where he could."

When they circled back to the Jeep, Rian was surprised that almost two hours had passed. Katrina walked her through the lay of her new acreage, and she had talked about the earth itself — filling Rian and Ben's palms with dirt while she talked grit and moisture, pesticides and pruning, and a myriad of other things now swirling in Rian's head. There was a lot to learn about growing grapes. It wasn't going to be anything like growing weed. More legal, perhaps, but a whole lot more work.

When they returned to the barn, Ben found an old irrigation head, and after a few manly pumps of the handle, the water that flowed tasted like a cold, fresh spring. They washed the vineyard dust from their mouths before picking up where they left off — with the case stashed in the hay.

"I think this is safe to drink," Ben said as he pulled the cork from the bottle with a healthy *pop*. Pulling a paper cone cup from his jacket pocket — the kind of cup you find at a water cooler — he straightened out the wrinkles and poured. He sniffed the bottle and then the cup. "Bouquet of... of grape and wax paper," he said with a grin, handing her the cup. "Ladies first."

"You go first," Rian said. "I promise to call 911 if you drop dead."

Ben touched his lips to the liquid, tipped the cone, and gulped it down. He squeezed his eyes shut, grabbed his chest, and thrust his tongue out of the corner of his mouth. Rian gasped, and Ben opened one eye.

"You rat."

"It's not bad," he said, refilling the cup.

Hesitantly, Rian let her lips touch the liquid. As her nose entered the cone and sniffed, she realized it smelled okay. There was nothing odd about it. No chemical odor that shouldn't be there. The wine smelled like fermented grapes and wax paper. She took a sip, then another.

"*Hunh*," she said finally. "It's poignant but not overbearing."

Ben laughed. "We aren't going to die today, my sweet Juliet. But we may get hammered."

"Hammered is so much better than driving a prom queen."

Ben's brow wrinkled. "What?"

"Never mind. I'm glad I'm here. I'm glad you're here. I'm glad I didn't have to call 911."

"Ditto."

Ben looked sleepy in the dappled sun coming through the roof. He had his back against one of the hay bales, his legs crossed at his ankles. The neck of his shirt was open a button or two, and Rian had to work to keep her mind on track.

"We have a theory about who killed Donald Duke," Rian said. "Can I run our scenario through your head? Just to see how it sounds to someone outside of our circle?"

He eyed her warily. "That's what's on your mind? You want to talk about that? Now?"

Rian grinned at him. It wasn't exactly like that. She plopped down on the hay bale beside him, tucking her head against the hollow of his shoulder. "No," she murmured against his chest, "that is not at all what I had in mind."

"That makes two of us."

Rian's pocket vibrated. She ignored the cell phone message. There were other things more pressing.

CHAPTER THIRTY FOUR

After lunch, the three friends planned to continue their journey to the finish line. Genna occupied the conversation, still glowing about her encounter with Merriweather Hopkins at the funeral home. The attitude toward Genna's old nemesis was so drastically 180 that Amy thought it best to leave the newest details of their discovery off the menu. There would be plenty of time to share what they learned from their time spent at Patsy's Beauty Salon, stenciled on the door in pink.

"I want to tell you the story of Ana Marie Villiger," Genna began. "She was Jerry Glen's great grandmother. She was from a family of money growing up and married an influential man. Even though she was a woman of economic privilege, she struggled to live in a man's world."

"Imagine that!" Zelda added and was shut down with a look.

"Ana Marie had big ideas, but she was thwarted and ignored, and soon realized that things were not equitable between men and women. She vowed to make a change. She couldn't understand why men talked down to women, and she couldn't tolerate the way women besmirched other women."

"It's still happening today," Amy muttered.

"Ana Marie believed that even though she couldn't change how women were received in her own time, she could seed change in the future."

Genna slurped her iced tea through the straw.

"She and her cousin, Hannah Summerfield — which is where Hank got his namesake — were close cousins. As widows, they established a trust that has been building equity for decades. Enter Pamela Duke and Merriweather Hopkins."

Genna nodded at their surprise. "I know, right? Their plans are grand and wonderful and complex," Genna continued, "but that is Project X in a nutshell."

"Why X?" Amy wondered.

"X is for the female chromosome."

Zelda grinned.

"Hank Summerfield inherited a piece of property that included an old railroad station. Project X wants that to be HQ for the organization. They see the train station as a symbol of transition from one place to another — or, if you will, from one era to the next. I think it's brilliant."

"But there was a hitch in their plans," Amy suggested.

Genna nodded. "Pamela Duke was trying to persuade Hank to donate the property. Merriweather would make it worth his while from a PR angle. Hank thought Donald Duke was a false prophet behind the project, trying to take the building for his own gain, so he hiked the price of the property out of reach."

"And then the Duke is murdered."

"And the Hank dropped off the radar. Merriweather said his secretary said he's gone fishing in Louisiana and can't be reached."

"It's all going to turn out the way it should," Amy said. "I can feel it."

"Oh, is your spidey-sense telling you that?"

"Yes," Amy said to Genna with a proud tilt to her chin. "My spidey-sense is telling me exactly that."

They left the square in Genna's new car. Zelda settled against the leather seats. "This is so much better. I can't believe I agreed to that nonsense in the Fiat."

"The scavenger part was fun," Amy said. "We solved a few riddles, learned some history, drank a peach Bellini."

"A *virgin* Bellini," Zelda interrupted. "Next time you want to spend three hundred bucks on a road trip, Genna, make sure there's food and wine aplenty."

"For thirst is terrible thing," Amy added with a smile.

Genna nodded absently. They were sitting at the intersection just off the square, turn signal blinking, while waiting to get onto the two-lane highway.

"Look at all this traffic," Genna said impatiently. "The line has to be two miles long! And why are they going so slow?"

She floored the BMW, merging into a spot between two cars, and then braked to avoid the bumper in front. She reached the next intersection, only to face a policeman motioning her to turn up the steep incline. She shook her head at him. He motioned her into the turn. She motioned her intention to drive forward, and he shook his head, signaling for her to turn. Finally giving in, she turned and followed the cars up the hill.

Amy glanced at the line of cars behind, low beams burning. When they approached another turn, a man dressed in a dark suit motioned them to park.

"I don't understand what's going on," Genna said.

Zelda lowered her shades. "You're may not like this, but we're at Donald Duke's funeral."

"No!" Genna looked at Zelda. "Today is the funeral?"

"To be accurate, it's the committal," Amy said, "the Internment of Ashes. They already held the vigil and such."

"And that went over so very well," Zelda added with a grin. "Bethany turned that into a circus."

"Which one is Bethany?"

Zelda took a deep breath. "Bethany is the long-lost daughter of Donald Duke who discovered the divorce papers that were already signed and hidden in drawer, and now there's going to be a lot of lawyers trying to figure out who's who and what's what."

"And you know this because?"

"Because if you want to know the gossip in a small town, the salon is the place to be." Zelda turned to Amy in the back seat. "Isn't it amazing how we got the low down on everybody and everything, and no one even exchanged names?"

Amy nodded. Anonymity made people feel safe. It wasn't all that different from the semi-clairvoyance she called tele*pathetic*. If she mocked it, she didn't have to own it, and then she could pretend to be normal. And yet, that was as unlikely as anything else. There was no normal. No one had dibs on that.

She touched the knot and peridot at her neck and felt a familiar warmth.

"Listen," Zelda said as they exited the car. "The bells in the tower are ringing."

Amy stood on the edge of the mountain with the church behind her. From this vantage point, she could see the town below as picturesque as a postcard. The square with its gazebo stage and flowing fountain were tiny objects from here, but they were there. Music rose up the mountain from the band in the park, and the clang of the church bells overpowered the melody. Fiddle and steel. Like fire and ice. She smelled the green and floral spice of the hedges along the road. She felt the breeze gently lifting the leaves of the trees, brushing past her on its way down the mountain. She sensed the finality of the day, the sun sinking closer toward the horizon.

She turned away from the slope. The church was the jewel in the crown of this mountaintop. It was a beautiful, time-honored setting built with sweat and faith. The settlers of Europe came here to grow grapes. And then, stone by stone on the highest point they could reach, they anchored their community with a church. It was their sacred commitment to the ever-changing cycle of the harvest and the insurmountable desire for the resurrection of Christ. She couldn't claim to be a religious person, but it was impossible to stand here and not feel the glory of God.

She followed what appeared to be the last person to arrive. There was something familiar in the way he moved.

CHAPTER THIRTY FIVE

A tent had been erected to give mourners a bit of shade, but it wasn't nearly big enough. It looked as if there were a hundred people there. Maybe even more. The mourners were everywhere: family and friends, townsfolk, business peers and clients, the faithful, the curious, and those who needed closure. The pageantry of a Catholic funeral that was not quite on point, for a man who had pioneered big ideas and then almost fell from grace, was more of a draw than most could pass up. Amy, Genna, and Zelda stood as close as they could and hoped they didn't look like graveside stalkers. It felt like they were stalking. They probably were not the only ones. She had texted Rian from the car, but there was no sign of her yet.

She moved so she could see the faces of the bereaved. Even in profile, she recognized the Six-Pack. Pamela was flanked on one side by Tilly and Gloria, on the other side by Dot and Bonnie. Kirk stood behind Bonnie. Standing beside him was another group of men. Chad Barling and the Cork Docs, she assumed. Hank had obviously resurfaced from his trip to the Big Easy, and he was now standing behind Pamela. He had taken off his hat and was spinning it absently in his fingertips.

Bethany stood off to one side with Jerry Glen. For once, should the press snap a picture, Pamela Duke would not have been at his elbow. Merriweather Hopkins was in the arc just behind them, along with many others Amy didn't know.

She saw him then. He stood several feet behind Genna's candidate. His white shirt was pressed today, and he had been to a barber. It was Sam Ford. Their eyes met, but she didn't smile, and neither did he.

Behind him on either side were two men with aviator shades and thin ties. She felt herself stiffen, as she realized she was not just at a funeral. She was in the presence of the killer.

Amy looked at the mourners closely.

Pamela and her friends had every opportunity to stage the crime and the alibi. They went to a conference, then to Tiddlywinks where they made friends and alibis. Each of them had a place to be and someone who could vouch for her whereabouts. They had access to wine, and to the drugs at the vet ranch. They had a motive. Who didn't want a bad husband out of the way. One down, two to go. Amy wondered if Dot's husbands were still alive.

She glanced at Bethany. She had access to the vet clinic, too. She knew her way around the ranch because she lived there at one time. She had as much opportunity as any of them and maybe even greater motive. She wanted to be part of Donald Duke's life and his livelihood. He didn't treat her like a daughter. He treated her like a hired hand. He certainly didn't act like she was the junior partner in the biggest wine distributorship in the state.

Bethany had been used to deliver poisoned wine, but was she as unaware as she claimed? Or was she as guilty as the others? Had she managed to fool them with her theatrics?

Amy focused on the dapper politician with his trim build and graying temples. He was close-knit with Pamela. He was family to Bethany, even though he wasn't her uncle. He was a politician earning his way to the top. Had Duke tried to ruin his chances to win? Was Duke removed to clear the way?

Over my dead body.

If a tree is in the way, cut it down.

Both had come true. Genna would be devastated if her candidate was guilty, and Amy felt an ache squeeze her chest.

Hank cleared his throat, and Amy turn to watch him. Hank Summerfield was the wild card, here. Once upon a time he wanted Pamela for himself. Had he grown tired of waiting for Duke to get out of the way? Murder by poison didn't seem to fit the M.O. of a big guy like Hank, but maybe the means was about the wine. Amy followed Hank's gaze. He was watching Pamela, his cowboy hat spinning in his fingers. Love was a crazy motive, and Hank sure wore that boy-in-love look on his face.

Amy studied the man behind Gloria. The Cork Docs had access to drugs. If not the kind a vet would use, they had drugs just as dangerous. A wine scam that duped them out of thousands could set off more than an audit. That could be motive. The Cork Docs stayed in the background, and maybe that's where they wanted to be. She looked at the four men. Somber and composed. Any one of them could have injected the drug and known what would happen.

But why only Duke? Kirk and Duke were both involved in the scam. She was pretty sure of that. Kirk had avoided his poisoned wine. Was it luck? Or had he been tipped off by someone? Did he know what was going to happen?

Amy watched him now. He looked at the ground in front of him, his jaw working. The beard had grown back in. There were thick gray whiskers around his mouth. His hands were at his sides, fingers flexing open and closed. He was the one who found his friend and business partner. The Rolls to the Royce. Kirk had responded to a text that had made him uneasy. He went to see what was troubling him. But he hadn't hurried. The EMTs wouldn't hurry, either. Kirk said it was a self-inflicted overdose in the 911call.

Amy watched him. He was breathing heavily, his chest visibly moving under his jacket. Had he performed CPR? She remembered the wheezing on the phone. Would he have the stamina? CPR took a lot more effort than most people realized.

Amy looked from Kirk to Pamela, who was standing as still as the statue in the park in town. Maybe Kirk knew what was going to happen to Duke? Maybe he was part of the plan. The one whose role in the crime was to discover the body. That one person waiting in the wings. Waiting for what? A sign? A signal?

La mujer de cabello plateado. The woman with the silver hair.

Amy drew her breath in sharply. Pamela claimed Duke was asleep when she returned Claret to the room. The TV, she said, was blaring as usual. She didn't have a key to the room, and she had to ask the maid for access. And why didn't Duke open the door when she knocked?

Because he wasn't sleeping.

Amy drew another sharp breath.

Zelda nudged Amy with her arm. "What's going on?" She whispered.

"I think I know who killed Duke."

Suddenly phones buzzed and chirped and jingled.

Amy grabbed her phone, horrified that she had forgotten to turn it off. She had texted Rian about the funeral and here she was finally responding. But it wasn't Rian. It wasn't even her phone. She looked up to see Pamela, Kirk, Bethany, Jerry Glen, and Hank all scrambling for their cell phones. She glanced at Sam Ford, and this time he smiled.

Her phone vibrated in her hand. Amy looked at the text.

A man's gotta do what a man's gotta do.

Pamela and Bethany screamed. Hank dropped his hat to the ground. Jerry Glen Villiger stepped back as if lightning had struck the ground at his feet. Kirk raised his phone and stared at the message. He raised his eyes to Pamela and then back to his phone. He glanced behind him at the men in shades and thin ties, and in a flash, Kirk was holding a gun in one hand. His other was around Bonnie's neck. He was pointing the gun at Pamela, but it was clear Bonnie wasn't safe, either.

"I knew you were up to something," he thundered. "All this pomp and circumstance for a man you didn't even want! All this pageantry for poor, pitiful Duke! You didn't want a funeral, you just wanted me to suffer through it!"

Amy saw the men moving into place behind Kirk, but he was so full of rage he didn't notice them. A twig snapped underfoot, and Kirk turned. Hank stepped forward and kicked at Kirk's legs, sending him tumbling to the grass. The gun flew out of his hand and landed with a thud at Bethany's feet. She picked up the gun and leveled it at Kirk. Her eyes narrowed at the man on the ground. Her hand trembled under the weight of the gun and the hatred in her eyes.

"You killed him!" Bethany screamed. "It was *you* I saw in the hat. That's why you shaved your beard. He told you, didn't he? You wanted me to think he was ignoring me. You wanted me to think he'd rather kill himself than admit I was his daughter! You wanted me to think he'd rather *die* than claim me as his own."

Bethany trained the gun at Kirk Water's head. She grabbed the gun with her other hand to steady it.

"You poisoned the wine I gave to my own father, you filthy thieving coward! He may not have wanted to claim me, but I am claiming him. Donald Duke was my father! And I will have justice!"

Bethany swung the gun and shot Kirk in the knee.

He screamed, and his face went white.

The mourners had dispersed when Kirk fell to the ground, much like water moves outward when a rock is thrown. They were still there, watching, mouths agape, but from a safe distance. Within seconds both Bethany and Kirk were surrounded by the men in thin ties, and Amy could hear the ambulance sirens already on their way.

CHAPTER THIRTY SIX

They were on the back deck at Genna's house, their favorite haunt, with peepers making a loud racket from somewhere unseen. Genna claimed that a creek ran through the bottom of her property, but since none of them were fool enough to traverse the slope and ticks that hid in the brambles, they took her word for it. Amy cocked her head to listen to the sound. Peepers and water. Like game night with friends and wine. The cases from Bethany had finally arrived.

"It feels like we haven't been together in weeks," Zelda said.

"We see each other every day," Rian said. "We work in the same building."

"Well, Amy's eating a lot of spaghetti and meatballs with that guy, you're making wine in the basement, and Genna's still traipsing all over make-believe Europe trying to get her politician elected."

"He's going to win," Genna said. "I have no doubts. We only have five months to go."

"We didn't really solve the crime," Amy said, "but then, we didn't have to. No one was trying to kill us this time. "

"Are you disappointed?" Zelda asked

"Not in the least."

Zelda nodded. "I'm glad the Six-Pack wasn't guilty. I like them. I think we'd have fun road-tripping down to see them. We can camp in

Rian's barn."

"We might have to raise bail if we do that."

"That would be okay by me," Zelda said. "I'd rather have fun than follow any rules."

"No, I mean we really might have to raise bail. Seriously"

"Okay, Rian, I'm not following your lead. Mansplain it to me."

"Ben and I found a lot more than one case of wine in the barn. Someone used the barn as a safe house and all the wine that was confiscated from Katrina was in the barn the whole time."

"Did she know about it?"

Rian shook her head. "She thought the wine had been destroyed. We gave her a bottle and she had it analyzed. She'd always suspected Kirk had tried to put her out of business. She suspected Kirk and some goons with fake badges were behind the raid. The feds were never involved."

Amy glanced quickly at Genna. They knew all about badges.

"Once he had embezzled her entire vintage, he planned to soak off the labels and replace them with something high dollar French. At least, that's what Katrina thinks he was attempting. Who would know the difference, right?"

"What happened?"

"Something happened. Because the cases were abandoned and covered over with hay. Katrina said she hadn't been in the barn for years.

"The case Ben found was the only one with the labels already switched. Kirk must have gotten spooked and aborted his plan. It was about the time she let him go and he joined with Duke. But he must have kept the labels, and he put a stack of them in the bag in Duke's office to make it look like a guilty trail for the feds. The real feds."

"Bonnie hadn't been that far off when she said Kirk cooked the books. Once a thief, always a thief. Will you have to turn the wine over to the feds?"

"Not unless someone squeals. That's sure not going to be me. I asked Katrina if she wanted the wine back. She said, '*not if it was the last drop on Earth.'"*

"Why would we need bail money?" Zelda asked, still confused.

Rian grinned. "There is a lot of wine in that barn. I mean a lot. And vintners make blends."

Amy laughed. "You're going to make skunk wine with it."

"Bingo," Rian said. "And *that* is not yet legal."

Amy had brought the Parcheesi board for tonight's game. A healthy change of pace. They were already halfway around the board. As usual, Genna chose the tiger and Rian picked the buffalo. Zelda grabbed the camel, and she chose the elephant in the room.

"I gather the police fingered Kirk as their person of interest the whole time, but they were waiting on DNA reports. He left a piece of a glove behind when he set up the scene. He must have gotten in a tug of war with Claret. There were glass shards under the bed. That's probably how Claret cut her paw."

"How did you figure it out?" Zelda asked. "You said as much when we were graveside."

Amy nodded. "It was the bit with the hat. I was watching Hank twirl his hat, and it clicked. We were all thinking Duke was alive when the texts were sent. That Bethany saw him go into the room right before that. But when they found the cowboy hat in the trash, I realized it might not be Duke's cowboy hat. His hat would still be in the room.

"Pamela said Duke was asleep when she returned Claret from their walk. Duke didn't answer the door and that's why she had to ask the maid for help. I realized then that he wasn't asleep as Pamela thought. He was already *gone*."

"I knew it was all about timing," Rian said.

Amy nodded and continued. "That meant someone pretended to be Duke and that someone sent the texts. Duke told me he only had one password. I think it was in the little black book in his office. Alpha1. It fits alphabetically or numerically. On a cell phone it would be numerical. 257421. That's all you'd need to get into his phone and send a text. I think Kirk, Bethany, and Pamela would all know that code. But Kirk said he didn't.

Pamela was at Tiddlywinks when she got the message, so unless she had some magic texting tool, it had to be either Kirk or Bethany."

"I thought it was Bethany who did it," Rian said.

"Me too," Zelda claimed.

"I'm just glad it wasn't Jerry Glen," Genna added.

"I knew that text wasn't from a John Wayne fan! Didn't I say so?"

"You did," Amy agreed. "We didn't understand its importance. I agree that Bethany was after something, but Duke's death wasn't it. She was trying to get close to him. Like father-daughter close. She mistook Kirk in the cowboy hat because she felt deflated and defeated. She didn't know where she stood with Duke, and she let that color everything. Kirk thought he had a fool-proof plan, but it wasn't the perfect murder."

"Oh, yeah," Zelda said. "And then Kirk gets arrested in front of God, and Jesus, and the entire state of Arkansas. They'll be talking about the Duke's funeral for years. We thought Paris Hilton was a big deal in wine country, but this steals the cake."

Genna grinned. "I made Jerry Glen explain his relationship with a game of truth or dare. He took truth every time."

"So why was he involved? Is he really her uncle?" Zelda asked.

Genna threw the dice and moved her tiger. "No, he's not, but for a long time he thought he was her father. Mary Beth wouldn't say who it was — now we know why— but Jerry Glen played the uncle role because he felt duty-bound. The two of them are really close.

"When he decided to run for office, he said he had to know the truth once and for all. He didn't want it cropping up during his campaign." Genna grinned. "Like that didn't happen."

"Anyway, he told Bethany about her mother, and they agreed to do a DNA test. He wasn't the father, but evidently Donald Duke has been all over the genealogical registries, and Amy's PI pulled up the match. Mary Beth died without giving up the father's name."

"She told Dot," Rian said. "Dot kept it a secret."

"I wonder if the other members of the Six-Pack knew or had an inkling?" Zelda asked.

"It's possible, but I think they were okay thinking it was Jerry Glen."

"I think it's not only possible, but probable," Zelda amended. "Close friends tell each other everything."

There was a silence that grew around the table then. They were sipping their wine appreciatively, admiring the color in the globe in the afternoon sun. Amy glanced at Zelda, who always pretended to be an open book. Close friends tell each other *almost* everything. Everyone had at least one guilty secret they were not willing to share with anyone. It was part of the human genome, the guilt gene that made humans uniquely human. Even her game of who-begat-who and who's-related-here didn't reveal that kind of secret.

"Jerry Glen gave Duke fifty thousand dollars at the conference to make Bethany a junior partner in Alpha Wine and Spirits," Genna continued.

"Well, he put in forty. Bethany put in ten. He was trying to use his influence to make a partnership deal for Bethany. A little too much influence if you ask me. He could have gotten himself railroaded to jail.

"Jerry Glen asked the detective about the money and learned it wasn't found in the hotel room, which meant someone else took it. That gave the detectives another piece to their case. He had the serial numbers from the bank, of course, and after that they found the bag in Duke's office at Alpha Wine and Spirits. Kirk buried the cash under a Ficus tree in the front office."

Rian and Amy grinned at each other. No wonder the tree was distressed.

"Whatever happened to the rally prize money? We never made it to the last leg of the rally," Rian admitted. "Did you make the last stump tour?"

Genna shook her head. "The same team wins every year, anyway. I was banking on Team Tiddlywinks to steal their thunder. Neither he nor I made it to the finish line, but he got great press anyway. I'm sure no one missed listening to a politician in the park."

Amy grinned. No, no one missed that.

"Bethany should have stuck with Villiger," Zelda said. "He was much better father material."

"I don't think it works that way," Amy said. "People have a strange and untethered longing to find their tribe of origin." She knew all about the need to belong. This was her tribe. This was her sisterhood. Even if they weren't blood kin.

"Jerry Glen hired him to find the money. According to Sam, anyway," Amy added.

"Sam, the cute new PI guy," Zelda teased.

Amy blushed. "He's teaching me a few PI tricks."

"Oh, right. Teaching you new tricks."

Amy's blush deepened.

"You know who else has a date?" Genna asked. "Hank!"

"With you?"

"No, silly, with Pamela," Genna answered. "He said he would donate the train station to Project X if Pamela would go on just one date with him. They've already been on three."

"Awww," Zelda cooed. "Isn't that sweet? He's waited a long time for love."

"Speaking of sweet," Genna said. "I know I'm not the easiest person to get along with. I am going change that. From now on, I'm a different Genna. I want my friends to know how much I love them, and I don't tell you that enough."

"Ever," Zelda said with a grin. "You've never told us that."

Rian looked over at Genna, her brows knitted. "You're not sick, are you?"

"No, but I did have a come to Jesus moment," Genna ventured. "I see now that it is better to forgive and forget, turn the other cheek, and then turn all the water into wine. I saw the light and it was blue. Now I know enemies are made of our own misdeeds and not raised on a farm with the fishes." She paused and smiled. "I think I'm waxing poetic and *paraprosdokian*."

"Pair of what?" Zelda asked, moving her camel toward Home.

"*Paraprosdokian* is a figure of speech," Genna said flatly.

"Of course, it is," Zelda retorted. "Knowing what we know about you."

"Where did you have this meeting with Jesus," Rian asked. "In case we need to send you back for another go at it. Attending church doesn't make you redeemed any more than standing in a garage makes you a car."

Genna flipped her ponytail from her shoulder. "I deserve that. I deserve worse. But when I was sitting in that funeral parlor listening to Merriweather Hopkins bare her soul, I saw the light and it had redemption written all over it."

"*Nach a Mool*," Amy muttered under her breath.

Genna eyed her askance. "I've been holding a grudge against Merriweather Hopkins for a long time, but I was really holding a grudge against myself. A grudge for my wounded pride. A grudge for not thinking I'd ever be good enough. I've hurt people doing that. You're one of them, Amy."

"Oh," Amy said quietly.

"It's not that I was doing it on purpose…"

"No backpedaling," Zelda said firmly. "Once you apologize for a wrongdoing, it cannot be brought up again. It's a rule. If you're talking about what you said on the ship, you know how we feel about it. Amy was the hero, and you were the heel. We're over it."

Rian bit into her sandwich. Zelda had won the last game of dominoes, so playing by the rules that the winner served the food while the losers brought the wine, Zelda was serving them canned pimento cheese on white bread.

"Aren't we still trying to figure out who killed the raccoon?" Zelda asked.

"Could have been this pimento cheese," Rian muttered.

Zelda made a sour look at Rian. "We also never figured out why the *Parcheesi* postcard was clutched in the Duke's hand."

"That's a puzzle we may never solve," Amy said. "I think I'm okay with that. Some things remain unexplainable. I choose to believe he was reaching for the square in the center. You know, Home Square."

Zelda smiled. "That's such a sweet thought. He was going Home."

THE END

Acknowledgments

Sometimes it happens: A writer falls in love with a title for a book and then begs for the story to follow. Such was the reality of *Poison Parcheesi and Wine.* Without the insightful help of my friend and fellow cozy writer, Susan J. Clayton, I might have given up. I hope my angst behind the scenes will be no more evident to you, dear reader, than all the other tricks used to hide clues and keep you reading. I am learning how stories have their own unfolding, with the writer ever ready with the pen. Thank you to VIP Killer Club member, Bonnie, for allowing me to bump him off as I saw fit. The list of suggested ex-husbands, boyfriends, and bosses from the VIP Killer Club has been a curious way to brainstorm and plot. I love it! Up next, the Cardboard Cottage friends travel to Ireland in book four, where they play *Killer Croquet on the Emerald Isle.* I hope you will join them for their second bucket list adventure. Many thanks to my editors, betta readers, proofreaders, and idea-givers who prove invaluable to this process. Much gratitude to my cover designer, Bailey McGinn, of Bailey Designs Books. And last but most importantly, thanks to all the readers who keep me pegging away because of your enthusiasm about the friends at the Cardboard Cottage. Without you, I have no story to share. Remember to leave a review and share a good read with a friend. Cheers!

About the Author

Jane Elzey is a mischief-maker, storyteller, and bender of the facts. A career journalist, she now writes modern-day, not-so-cozy mysteries with little regard for the truth. Born and raised on Florida's sandy beaches, Jane now lives in the Ozark Mountains of Arkansas with her family of felines. As an insatiable world traveler, she loves to turn her travels into backdrop settings for the Cardboard Cottage Mystery series, sharing destinations with armchair readers on the hunt for whodunnit. Jane Elzey writes about four friends who play to win . . . while the husbands die trying. (The husband always dies.) *Poison Parcheesi and Wine* is book three in the series. Be sure to catch up with *Dying for Dominoes* (book one), *Dice on a Deadly Sea* (book two), and stay tuned for *Killer Croquet on the Emerald Isle* (book four) slated for a 2023 release. To engage Jane for your book club, library, book signing, or to join the Very Important Players Club, visit JaneElzey.com. Be sure to sign up for the newsletter gossip!